PRAISE FOR

Serenade for Nadia

"Compelling...fearless and eloquent."

—*Wall Street Journal*

"[An] affecting novel about love, loss, and personal identity... Livaneli smoothly switches between 2001 and 1938–1942, offering insights into Turkey's rich cultural, political, ethnic, and religious divides. Livaneli's worthy portrait of a man coming to terms with his tragic past and a woman coming to terms with her Turkish heritage delivers a forceful plea for openness and tolerance."

—*Publishers Weekly*

"Heartbreakingly vivid...Livaneli's passion in exposing Turkey's and the West's culpability in real massacres is eloquent... [*Serenade for Nadia* is] hard to forget."

—*Kirkus Reviews*

"Writer. Musician. Philosopher. Zülfü Livaneli is one of my favorite authors. With *Serenade for Nadia*, he has written a masterpiece about love and music, connecting Turkey's complex and rich history to the present day. So happy that Livaneli's words can now inspire millions more with this new English translation, and that the world will get to know one of the true cultural treasures coming out of Turkey."

—Hamdi Ulukaya, CEO of Chobani

"This wonderfully evocative novel does far more than introduce one of Turkey's great creative artists to American audiences. It is also a fast-paced and intensely emotional account of modern history that leads us to reflect on the ways that people and nations confront their past."

—Stephen Kinzer, author of *Crescent and Star: Turkey Between Two Worlds*

Praise for *Disquiet*

"A tale of identities colliding from a writer who's held five passports... [*Disquiet*] unfolds in a border town caught between its ancient past and tumultuous present."

—NPR, *All Things Considered*

"A keenly wrought story... [whose] urgency comes through in its tight grasp on the problems of religious violence, misogyny, and the failures of compassion. The result is a memorable illumination of the Ezidi people's rich history." —*Publishers Weekly*

"A penetrating novel... indelible fiction based on real-life horror... [*Disquiet*] will demand attention, provoke outrage, perhaps even inspire lifesaving change."

—*Shelf Awareness*

"A moving novel set entirely in the modern-day Middle East."

—*PopSugar*, Best New Books of the Month

"Impactful... [a] fascinating novel about a man caught between cultures."

—*Foreword Reviews*

"In this soulful novel, Zülfü Livaneli presents a touching human story that unfolds alongside the real-life horrors of terrorist war. Set in and around the ancient crossroads city of Mardin—one of my favorite places in the world—it is both timeless and urgently contemporary. *Disquiet* is as rich in character and imagery as it is potent in moral clarity."

—Stephen Kinzer, author of *Crescent and Star: Turkey Between Two Worlds*

"This is a riveting story skillfully rendered. It is a gift to readers."

—Rafia Zakaria, author of *Against White Feminism*

"A journalist investigates his friend's murder and learns the truth about the brutality of war, religious intolerance, cultural chauvinism, hate, sacrifice, and love. Livaneli is a brilliant Turkish writer with a voice and a message that must be heard globally."

—Mahbod Seraji, author of *Rooftops of Tehran*

"On the surface, *Disquiet* is a quest narrative that follows a man searching for answers about a friend's horrific death, but beneath that framework pulse probing questions about the mortal cost of prejudice, the chasm between East and West, the mystery of obsession, and the necessity of recognizing our shared humanity. It is a slim dagger of a book that cuts deep."

—Keija Parssinen, author of *The Ruins of Us*

Praise for *The Last Island*

"This haunting fable of a President's war against seagulls feels all the more relevant to our times in its absurdity and heartbreak. Livaneli has written a lucid account of a community's shattering alongside natural devastation. A wise and piercing book."

—Ayşegül Savaş, author of *White on White* and *Walking on the Ceiling*

"In this beautifully written book, Livaneli poetically recounts the story of how societies get corrupted by self-serving autocratic leaders. Livaneli's riveting *The Last Island* provides a much-needed and uplifting read for all in need of resilience and hope."

—Soner Cagaptay, author of *A Sultan in Autumn: Erdogan Faces Turkey's Uncontainable Forces*

"Urgent and allegorical, Livaneli is masterful in his depiction of how authoritarian power destroys a community's people and environment. *The Last Island* is a stunning novel that will stay with me for a long time."

—Mina Seçkin, author of *The Four Humors*

Praise for *The Fisherman and His Son*

"This story of a couple who rescue a baby from a boat after their own son was lost at sea highlights environmental degradation, Mediterranean history, and the ongoing pain of refugees."

—*New York Times Book Review*

"Blends narrative seamlessly with reflections on political, social, and environmental issues as Livaneli deftly explores the hardships faced by refugees... powerful."

—*Reader's Digest*

"A fable-like tale with a strong moral message, tackling issues of immigration, climate change, and industrialization... never has a book been as relevant as it is today."

—*Litro*

"A novel in conversation with Hemingway, one that grounds Hemingway's seagoing theme of resilience with threads of pragmatism and an understanding of the larger consequences of conflict on individuals... [Freely] has translated the spirit of Livaneli's activism into a smooth prose unafraid of the complicated metaphors contained within the novel."

—*The Rumpus*

"At the center of this novel stands unfathomable tragedy. Gracefully, masterfully, Zülfü Livaneli does not force the reader into trying—and failing—to fathom the unfathomable. Instead, this novel, which is thrumming with Keatsian negative capability, intertwines human misery and nonhuman mystery—the contemporary refugee crisis; a small island crawling with snakes; invasive, poisonous puffer fish and encircling, crafty cats; national histories of population transfers and personal histories of rotten marriages and youthful romances; dreams of a shark-headed man; a baby delivered from the depths by a father dolphin; corporate rapaciousness and environmental degradation; jasmine flowers in evening bloom—and in so doing, creates a loose and intricate tapestry of sorrow and solace, one that invites the attentive reader to glimpse, if even for a moment, 'the size of the cloth,' as the poet Naomi Shihab Nye put it. Brendan Freely's translation is stark, elegant, and fluid; the story that unfolds is propulsive and dramatic, harrowing and multilayered. This is a wonderful book."

—Moriel Rothman-Zecher, author of
Before All the World and *Sadness Is a White Bird*

"In this tightly woven novel of the sea, Zülfü Livaneli writes of a deep sense of longing at the intersection of loss, environmental catastrophe, and the continuing tragedy of the Mediterranean refugee crisis. *The Fisherman and His Son* is a moving story that explores the ways in which everyday people navigate their lives in the shambles of the modern nation."

—Nishant Batsha,
author of *Mother Ocean Father Nation*

Praise for *On the Back of the Tiger*

"I loved this book. It reads with all the power and simplicity of a fable."

—Louis de Bernières, bestselling author of *Birds Without Wings* and *Corelli's Mandolin*

"A comprehensive... tale of Abdülhamid II (1842–1918), the deposed sultan of the crumbling Ottoman Empire... thrilling."

—*Publishers Weekly*

"A fascinating and charming account of the last days of the Ottomans as seen through the eyes of a deposed sultan and his skeptical doctor, as well as a thought-provoking study in political folly, personal responsibility, and hope."

—Jenny White, author of *The Sultan's Seal* and *The Abyssinian Proof*

"Through a fine narrative keyhole, Livaneli observes how isolation frees a toppled sultan to see the sweep of his dynasty's history, achievement, and error. Livaneli peers into closed quarters, where Abdülhamid II, aided by his physician's own humanity, locates new truth in his regrets and pride. Ultimately it is Livaneli's meticulous rendering and his own compassion and wit that allow us to be there as six centuries of Ottoman rule come to a close."

—Katherine Nouri Hughes, author of *The Mapmaker's Daughter*

Leyla's House

Also by Zülfü Livaneli

On the Back of the Tiger

The Fisherman and His Son

The Last Island

Disquiet

Serenade for Nadia

Bliss

Leyla's House

Zülfü Livaneli

Translated from the Turkish by
Brendan Freely and Yelda Türedi

Other Press
New York

Production editor: Yvonne E. Cárdenas
Text designer: Patrice Sheridan
This book was set in Times New Roman by
Alpha Design & Composition of Pittsfield, NH

1 3 5 7 9 10 8 6 4 2

Library of Congress Cataloging-in-Publication Data
Names: Livaneli, Zülfü, 1946- author | Freely, Brendan, 1959- translator |
Türedi, Yelda translator
Title: Leyla's house : a novel / Zülfü Livaneli ; translated from the Turkish
by Brendan Freely and Yelda Türedi.
Other titles: Leyla'nın Evi. English
Description: New York : Other Press, 2026.
Identifiers: LCCN 2025010744 (print) | LCCN 2025010745 (ebook) |
ISBN 9781635422061 paperback | ISBN 9781635422078 ebook
Subjects: LCGFT: Novels
Classification: LCC PL248.L58 L4913 2026 (print) |
LCC PL248.L58 (ebook) | DDC 894/.3533—dc23/eng/20250422
LC record available at https://lccn.loc.gov/2025010744
LC ebook record available at https://lccn.loc.gov/2025010745

Publisher's Note: This is a work of fiction. Names, characters, places, and incidents either are the product of the author's imagination or are used fictitiously, and any resemblance to actual persons, living or dead, events, or locales is entirely coincidental.

How Leyla, Roxy, and Ali Yekta Entered My Life

Most people like the Bosphorus in summer, but I so much prefer it in winter. When it snows I often sit and watch the currents turning aquamarine, the snow accumulating on the yellow, red, and blue rowboats that have been pulled ashore, and the seagulls searching for food.

As well as the launches that shuttle back and forth between the two shores.

One winter day when I had nothing to do I boarded one of these launches, crossed to the other side, and then came back.

That day, in the fog, Istanbul seemed wrapped in a mantle of fine, raw silk. The boats, barely visible, rocked like cradles on the choppy sea. I breathed in the smell of the rope, heavy with sea water, tied to the post on the pier, and listened to the creaking sound it made when the launch moved. When the rope grew taught, it sprayed out droplets of water.

Some of the passengers were buying the fish that were flapping about in the yellow, red, and green plastic tubs on the pier. They were grilling fish on one of the boats, and a man kept shouting, "Fish sandwiches, fish sandwiches!" Next to the fishermen's tubs there were flashes of green—romaine and curly lettuces and arugula—as well as lemons and radishes.

The weather was very cold and windy.

The passengers who'd arrived early had all found seats for themselves. A man with a mustache and sunken cheeks was smoking a cigarette, protecting it from the wind in his hand, as if he were hiding a sin. Squeezed in next to him was a worn-out looking woman with large black eyes—she'd clearly once been beautiful—who rested her head lightly in his shoulder. Even this little gesture summed up their whole story: a woman who needed to be protected from this harsh society and the man who protected her.

Three large young men stood whispering, huddled together against the cold. It was clear from their broad shoulders and from how tired they looked that they were manual laborers; the boys were from the East.

Suddenly, passengers started to crowd in. As the work-weary passengers propelled themselves down the pier to the launch, a steward stood by, moving his arms, ready to rescue anyone who might slip on the wet, wooden gangplank. The boatman shouted, "All aboard, all aboard!"

Suddenly the launch got underway. People in well-worn raincoats, overcoats, short-sleeved jackets closed their collars against the cold... blowing on their chapped hands to warm them.

Then the packed launch moved away from the pier in an arc and headed for Üsküdar, making its way deftly among the ferryboats, passenger launches, and fishing boats. The multitude of noisy passenger boats seemed to fly as if in a dream. Seagulls dove into the sea and emerged, appearing and disappearing behind the launch. In the darkness of evening their whiteness was more striking, and their cries became sharper.

If the boat captain weren't so skillful, they would surely have collided with the huge freighter that the terrified passengers saw only at the last moment. The huge ship passed before them like a slow-moving and unheeding giant. The passenger launch was tossed about a bit by the wake and then continued on its way.

Passengers held string bags full of fruits and vegetables. Hungry passengers began to nibble at the loaves of hot bread they'd been clutching.

Lights were burning on the Asian shore; from a minaret drifted an evening call to prayer that called forth a desire to weep. An eerie, haunting sound that echoed above the city...

The fish were still moving in the plastic bags, but the passengers were deep in conversation and didn't notice. The man with the sunken cheeks was saying something to the woman who rested her head on his shoulder.

From the shore came an appetizing smell of grilling fish.

The traffic on the suspension bridges was heavy, and thousands of cars were inching along. The darkness of evening was wrapping Istanbul like a heavy blanket.

I was watching all these people and thinking they were all migrants. Each of them was of a different type—some dark, some blond. If you didn't know, you wouldn't think they were all citizens of the same country.

Some from the Balkans, some from the Caucasus, some from Central Asia, some from the Middle East; they've fled from the Hijaz, Yemen, Jerusalem, Russia, Georgia, Bosnia, and Bulgaria and come here. This is a haven. They've left behind their homes and families, their gardens and fields, and even bitterly weeping cats and dogs. Those who arrived in this country settled in the houses of those who'd fled elsewhere.

The houses of the Greeks and the Armenians were given to these homeless people who had barely escaped death. They settled in these strangers' houses and began tending fields that belonged to people they didn't know.

The history of this part of the world is a history of people seizing each other's property. Competition for property is behind most of the wars and struggles. Houses emptied, houses inhabited anew, property disputes. Man's need for shelter, for a roof over his head, has led to many tragedies throughout history.

Just as in this novel.

The idea of writing *Leyla's House*, the story of a property tragedy that marked all our lives in some way, came to me that day on the passenger launch.

I looked across from me and saw an aristocratic Ottoman woman who had fallen on difficult times:

How elegant she looked!

Next to her sat a girl who had dyed part of her hair blue:

How rebellious she looked!

Next to me sat a well-dressed, elderly gentlemen whose tie was perfectly knotted and whose hair was slicked back with brilliantine:

How dignified he looked!

No one knew anyone else, and everyone was lost in their own inner world.

That was the day Leyla, Roxy, and Ali Yekta entered my life—never to leave it again.

Leyla's House

1

The old woman sat under the huge plane tree and didn't move for two days. She just waited there, perched on a hard, brown leather suitcase, under the giant, centuries-old tree. The suitcase, with the leather worn through in places, a thick band across the middle, and studs to protect the corners, was reminiscent of travelers of a long-past age.

The plane tree was on the narrow pavement at the foot of the wall of the waterfront mansion, on a narrow street where cars passed constantly. The nearby grocer, greengrocer, and coffee seller were all watching the woman. From time to time they sent her tea and water to drink and apples, roasted chickpeas, and cake to eat.

Later they went over from time to time to beg the woman: "Madam, please stop being so stubborn! We could be considered your children too. Come, come to our house!"

The old woman refused with a stubborn expression.

The greengrocer with the big mustache dried his hands on his blue apron and pleaded, "You've known me since I was a child; please, you know that my house is right over here; come on, come with me."

"Thank you, but I can't go with you."

"Madam, for the love of God, stop resisting. Why can't you come away?"

The butcher got involved: "You can't live in the street like this. You may have stood it for two days, but what will happen three or four days from now?"

Pointing to the waterfront mansion behind her, the old woman said, "I was born here, and I lived here all my life. I have no place else to go."

The tradesmen were moved, and one of them said, "We know, Madam. How could we not know? All of us grew up in your shadow. But these heartless people have bought the mansion; what can we do?"

"What recourse do we have?"

"This neighborhood has never seen such wicked people."

Wringing the cloths in their hands or agitatedly lighting cigarettes, they all cursed the new owners of the waterfront mansion in low voices.

The grocer's young daughter arrived with a bouquet of jasmine and gave it to the old woman. The woman took the flowers with a smile. The young girl said, "Aunt Leyla, do you remember how you used to give us jasmine from your garden every day?"

"Yes," said the old woman, smiling again. Her hazel-colored eyes lit up as she brought the flowers to her nose to smell them. Although she'd forbidden anyone to call her "Aunt" and insisted on being addressed as Leyla, she didn't say anything to the young girl.

Cars slowed down as they passed, some looking at this woman surrounded by people with surprise, some with pity, and some with anger. Who was this? Perhaps she was a madwoman who'd run away from home and got lost.

Those from the neighborhood who knew the woman said, "Look at the state the poor woman is in," and cursed the new owners of the mansion.

The place where Leyla had been sitting for two days was on the "shore road" of the Asian side of the Bosphorus. However, even though it was called the "shore road," it didn't actually run along the shore because the shore was occupied by waterfront mansions. It was only out of habit that the road behind these mansions' gardens was called this.

You couldn't see the shore itself because of the high back walls of these mansions. Indeed these mansions could only be seen from the sea. Only passengers on the white ferries that went up and down the Bosphorus, fishermen, and those on the excursion boats had the privilege of being able to see these elegant structures, with their boathouses beneath them, that leaned out over the blue water on cedar posts. As well, of course, as those on the ships that sail through the Bosphorus.

When the tradesmen realized that they would not succeed in convincing "the Great Lady," the women of the neighborhood got involved. Red-cheeked, fresh-faced brides came one after another and kissed her hand. "Madam, for the love of God, don't do this, come, I've made some fresh tea, I've prepared some food..."

"I was born in this mansion, I lived here all my life, and I'm going to die here. I won't go anywhere else."

The new brides looked at each other with pity in their eyes and started cursing the new owners.

"May they never have a day of peace in that house!"

"May God punish them for this!"

"How could they throw her out of her home after all these years? Have they no conscience?"

All the while, as they were saying these things, they could hear the sounds of work being done in the mansion and the shrill voice of a woman shouting at the designers and contractors.

"Design!" a woman was shouting in a bad accent, "All of this has to be done according to the design, not according to your own taste, do you understand? It's going to be done the way the American interior decorator says it should be done. The design is going to be followed exactly. Instead of standing there looking like an idiot, go in and take those ornaments off the ceiling."

Two days earlier, the new owners had come to the mansion with the contractors and the American interior decorator and had asked the old woman to move out of the house. On the edge of the mansion's large garden, at the foot of the back wall, there was a medium-sized, white, single-story house. The old woman had spent her life in that house. No one had ever thought of making her leave that house, but the new owners were evicting her anyway. "What right do you have to throw me out of my house?" objected the old woman, showing them the deed to this detached house, but to no avail. "There are laws in this country, there are rules," she said. "I don't understand how you can presume to evict someone from her own house."

Meanwhile, the new owners' two watchmen were filling the old woman's suitcase without giving her the chance to pack up her own things. Leyla lost her temper completely when they opened her closet and started gathering up the carefully ironed lace gloves, blouses, skirts, and, yes, even her undergarments with their rough hands. In what must have been forty years of privacy, no man's hairy hands would ever have been allowed to touch them. Meanwhile, in a voice that could be heard in the next neighborhood, the new lady of the house was shouting, "It's an annex! I'm going to turn it into a guesthouse, do you understand? I'm paying the interior decorator an arm and a leg to redo this little house. And why should I have a fossil living in my garden! I don't care where she goes."

The old woman heard these words and was more surprised at being evicted from a house that was legally hers than at being called a fossil. What disregard these newcomers had for the law! Even though the detached house was in the mansion's extensive garden, it was on a separate parcel of land and had a separate deed. The last time the house had been sold, the buyers had respected this deed and hadn't disturbed her. How could this woman who kept shouting about design throw her out of her own house?

But they did throw her out. Their servants took her by the arms and dragged her to the iron garden gate and deposited her and her suitcase outside. The tradesmen gathered and watched what was happening.

The Great Lady stood for a while, looking at the gate through which she'd just been ejected, and then grew tired and sat on her suitcase. Since then she hadn't really moved from this spot. From time to time, to answer the calls of nature, and taking care not to meet anyone face-to-face, she would go to the back of the grocery store, but then she would return and continue to sit in her place. Once or twice she got to her feet and started doing gymnastics. These movements didn't resemble any kind of gymnastics the tradesmen had ever seen. These were very slow, deliberate movements intended to strain the muscles. It was clear that, as with everything the Great Lady did, these gymnastics required a certain knowledge and training.

The Great Lady knew so many things like this. She helped the neighborhood children with their homework and talked to them from time to time; she gave them advice that no one else would ever give them and told them stories. The exotic flowers she grew in her garden weren't at all like the flowers the Roma people sold from colorful plastic buckets by the roadside. It was as if the Great Lady gave them a different fragrance, as if even their appearance changed when she touched them. There was no one in the neighborhood who hadn't received jasmine from the Great Lady.

The older people of the neighborhood had once called her "Little Lady," but the world had changed, and in time she became known as the Great Lady.

The sounds of hammering and sawing told of a great deal of work being done in the mansion. When the Great Lady heard these sounds she looked toward the mansion with curiosity and didn't try to hide the anxiety in her eyes. Whether it was a wall or a ceiling, something was being knocked down with a great deal of clatter.

The tradesmen, who had only ever entered the mansion on rare and special occasions, could never forget the magnificent ceiling moldings, the Ottoman ornaments on the walls, or the elegant portico. The new owners, who clearly didn't like these ornaments, were dumping these beautiful antiques in the garden. The trucks that were taking loads of rubble out of the mansion's gates were evidence of this. The trucks were taking the rubble, dumping it far away, and coming back for more.

When night fell, everyone dispersed; the Great Lady, who had ignored the entreaties of the tradesmen who wanted to take her to their homes, spent her first night in the Bosphorus damp sitting on her suitcase. In the morning, the grocer brought her tea and hot bread that had just come out of the oven. The Great Lady, who had grown quite pale, accepted them happily.

It was the kind of June morning on the Bosphorus that fills people with joy. From the woods that rose just behind the road came the beautiful chirping of birds and the smells of jasmine, laurel, and magnolia.

The Great Lady couldn't bring herself to believe that she'd been thrown out of the house she'd lived in for seventy-six years and had never left for even a single day. It had to be a mistake, so she sat there on her suitcase, waiting for this to be set right. Because this was not the jungle, but a nation that lived according to the rule of the law. No one could come and throw someone out of a house to which they had a deed. She resisted and wouldn't leave the front of the house because she was certain that this mistake would be rectified.

Meanwhile, the tradesmen and some of the others of the neighborhood thought about talking to the new owners of the mansion. Yes, the new owners were very rich and powerful; the man owned a large bank and had thousands of people working for him. Was throwing an old woman out of her own house going to make someone like that look good? Everyone embraced this idea enthusiastically. "It's not right! No one has the right to seize someone else's property." They were all the more agitated because of their deep attachment to their own property, but when it came to going and talking to the new owners they were less vociferous. And when a Mercedes with tinted windows arrived so pompously and drove into the mansion's garden they began to argue about whether they'd made the right decision.

"These people aren't children. They're bank owners. Who knows how many lawyers they have working for them. They wouldn't make a mistake like this."

"Let's try to listen to their side of the story; let's not rush into things."

"And we're going to have to look these people in the face tomorrow; we're going to make deliveries to them..."

The Great Lady didn't pay attention to any of this because the deed her grandfather the pasha had given her was in her pocket. After her grandfather's death, her grandmother had had to sell the mansion, and she had no rights left to that, she had no objections about that, but the little house at the foot of the garden wall belonged completely to her.

She'd known all the tradesmen gathered around her since they were little children. They felt for the Great Lady and didn't want to leave her side, but whenever the shiny car with tinted windows emerged they scattered immediately. They all acted as if they had something to do and went to their shops as if customers had arrived, and then later, when the danger had passed, they gathered around the Great Lady once again. The new owners could see them through the tinted glass and might even be noting who was there. When the car came out, the area was deserted.

"Please, don't insist, come with us. You'll get sick if you stay here."

"Who has the right to seize someone else's property? There are laws in this country."

"Is this the jungle?"

The Great Lady listened with a bitter smile playing about her lips to the people of the neighborhood who were insisting she come home with them, and shook her head with an expression that said she would not accept any of their suggestions.

Whether it came from a passing driver or a resident of the neighborhood, the news appeared in the papers that an old woman had been sitting under a plane tree on the Bosphorus road for two days. Was the woman crazy, or was she sitting there to protest something? Had her family thrown her out into the street? If that were true, it might be a good news item, a short piece that would arouse the readers' emotions. Human interest pieces were important.

For this reason, the *Today* newspaper's city editor didn't neglect to include the old woman in his notes for the daily meeting. In any event a reporter could wrap up the story within two hours. He mentioned the item when it came up on the agenda. For whatever reason, the words "crazy woman" escaped from his mouth.

"A crazy woman in front of the Bosnalılar Mansion..."

When Yusuf, who'd started at the newspaper six months earlier, heard this, he rose to his feet and asked, "Can I take this story?"

"Do you find it that interesting?" asked the city editor.

Yusuf said, "I know that woman. She's not at all crazy."

"All right, go look into it," said the editor, "But don't waste too much time on it because there are a lot of other things to cover."

"Don't forget to take a picture!" he called out after him.

"He thinks I'm still a rookie," Yusuf grumbled to himself.

2

As Yusuf drove out to the mansion across the Bosphorus bridge in a company car, he thought about the Great Lady. What had happened to make the poor woman spend the night outside? The Great Lady he knew wasn't someone who would just lose her mind.

He'd practically grown up at her side. His own grandparents had lived in the servants' quarters in the mansion's garden and had been the pasha's gardeners. Later, in his father's time, the family had moved to a shanty they'd built toward the top of the hill across the road. The apartment in which Yusuf first opened his eyes to the world was in a four-story building on the land on which the shanty had been built. It was not in the mansion garden but in the woods at the top of the hill, but unfortunately over time the trees thinned out more and more. After Yusuf's grandfather had built the first house, all their relatives and friends from Kastamonu had come and built houses nearby. There were now many houses on the hilltop that had once been so heavily forested. A grocery store, a greengrocer, and a butcher shop opened on the shore road as well. Yusuf's uncle and cousins ran the grocery store, and the greengrocer was run by the grandsons of the man who had once brought vegetables to the mansion.

Tourists insisted on describing Istanbul as being made up of both the European and Asian shores. Yusuf knew that the people of Istanbul crossed the Bosphorus bridge to the Anatolian side without ever thinking of it as Asia. Although he'd lived there until he went to university, he'd moved to Cihangir and had cut his ties with the neighborhood of old mansions. He visited his father's house once in a while, that's all. The last time he went he hadn't even stopped by to visit the Great Lady, even though when he was a child he had considered her his favorite adult. The Great Lady was the first person whose hand he would rush to kiss on holiday mornings. He felt at ease with her. The businessman Mr. Salih and his family, who had bought the mansion, were nice enough people, but somehow he felt shy with them.

That family treated him well, they stroked his head and gave him money, and when he started school they bought him a uniform and shoes and notebooks, but all this was a bit difficult for Yusuf. Because they didn't give him these gifts in the same spirit they gave gifts to their own grandchildren. Every time they spoke to him it was clear they were making an effort to be charitable and emphasized the fact that they were helping him. They would say, "Take it, my boy. Try this on, does it fit? Be a good boy. Here, take one of these chocolates. Don't be shy, don't be shy, take another one!" and pat him on the head. Yusuf would feel strange standing there, under the eyes of four generations of that family, with his mouth stuffed with chocolate.

However, the Great Lady never made him feel uncomfortable. She treated Yusuf just as she would treat anyone else. She would give him some of her famous jasmine and then casually say, "I'm going to eat some figs. You can join me if you like," and then without waiting for an answer would take out two small plates of the figs she'd picked from the garden that morning. When she gave gifts of money for the holidays they would always be accompanied either by a bouquet of jasmine or by a handkerchief embroidered with his full name in capital letters.

The Great Lady's house was like a seamstress's workshop. It was full of silk threads of all colors, spools, shiny and eye-catching cloths and laces. There were a lot of pictures on the walls. In the largest picture, her grandfather the pasha, looking very imposing in his uniform, seemed to be taking in his surroundings. Yusuf remembered his own father and grandfather often speaking highly of the pasha, saying, "May he rest in peace. He was very good to us."

The opinion he remembered having formed from bits and pieces of conversation he heard at home was that because the Great Lady was the granddaughter of a pasha, Mr. Salih's family, despite being such nice people, would not long be able to take the place of a true aristocrat.

Yusuf's grandfather's father had been wounded in the leg while serving under the pasha's command in some war he couldn't quite place (because there'd been so many wars, Yusuf couldn't possibly know which one) and had worked there for the rest of his life, with a limp, as the mansion gardener. He and the family he brought from Kastamonu had settled into a small house in the mansion's vast garden. According to what they say, the garden had been a paradise in those days: there were giant magnolias, fig and pomegranate trees, Judas trees, lemon and orange trees, the rarest roses, chrysanthemums, hydrangeas... The beautiful magnolia tree whose branches stretched over the house and almost completely hid the roof with its flowers, had been planted in Leyla's honor when she was born. It was such a magnificent and noble tree that everyone who saw the green brilliance of its leaves and smelled the fragrance of its large flowers was enchanted by it. At one time there had been a bubbling cascade in the corner. The colorfully designed paving stones, and the arbors, the magnolias, the Judas trees, and the ever-blooming roses were still there, but when part of the mansion was sold a wall had unfortunately been knocked down, and the harsh Bosphorus winds had killed the orange and lemon trees. The Armenian and Greek builders who built the old mansions used to take the winds and currents of the Bosphorus into account, but the builders today don't take that kind of care.

As Yusuf approached the mansion he saw the Great Lady sitting under the enormous plane tree talking to a policeman. When he bent down to kiss the Great Lady's hand he wasn't sure whether she was pleased to see him. Perhaps she didn't want little Yusuf to see her in that pitiful state. At least that's how he interpreted it.

The policeman said, "We can't allow you to sit here any longer, madam. We have a complaint from the owners of the mansion. They're being disturbed by this."

In a patient voice the Great Lady said. "Son, my grandfather built this mansion. My entire family lived here."

"Yes, but it's been sold; the property now belongs to . . . ," he looked at the paper he was holding and read from it, "Ömer Cevheroğlu."

"That applies to the mansion itself, but the little house I live in is on a separate parcel and has a separate deed. My grandfather left it to me. Look if you want."

In fact, on her identity card her grandfather the pasha was listed as her father, but, hoping the policeman wouldn't notice this detail, she didn't offer any explanations on the subject. Her being on record as her grandfather's daughter had to do with a great tragedy that had befallen the pasha's family. This tragedy had not only altered the family records, but changed the family itself radically.

The Great Lady took the carefully folded deed from her bag and showed it to the policeman. The policeman took the deed and peered at it and began reading aloud. Everything seemed to be in order. Now he had no idea what to do.

"You still have to leave this place," he said. "You may seek your rights, but I have definite orders from my superior. The new owners of the mansion have been disturbed. I've been ordered to escort you away from this place."

"Officer, please show this deed to your superior."

At this point the young policeman stopped being polite and respectful and said, "What are you talking about, lady? My superior has a superior. They got a call from the police chief. You can't go over these people's heads. The best thing for you is to get up and go. Otherwise I have to take you into the station, so you had better listen, lady."

"Leyla," said the woman.

"What?"

"Leyla, my name is Leyla."

"All right then, Miss Leyla," said the increasingly impatient policeman.

"No, just call me Leyla."

At this point Yusuf got involved. He wasn't surprised because he knew the Great Lady's temperament, but this policeman, who was meeting her for the first time, couldn't be expected to understand. This was a matter that had been very difficult for the people of the neighborhood. She's taught everyone since they were children to call her Leyla. Those who couldn't manage this called her "Great Lady."

To put an end to the argument Yusuf showed his card. "I'm a reporter, officer," he said. He didn't have his yellow press card yet, but he did have his newspaper's picture identification card. "No one has the right to throw this woman out of her house. She has a deed. There you see it."

The policeman took Yusuf a little off to one side. Lowering his voice, he said, "You know who the new owner of the mansion is, don't you? It's Ömer Cevheroğlu. The phone has been ringing since morning. Everyone but the interior minister has been called. Even the governor is involved. This woman sitting here is getting on Ömer's wife's nerves. The woman is a little strange too, isn't she?"

Meanwhile the grocer, the greengrocer, and their clerks had gathered around to listen.

Yusuf saw that this wasn't going to work and that the only thing to do was to go into the mansion and show the new owners the deed. He rang the bell on the garden gate. He waited a little while, and then the gate opened, and a large, mustachioed man asked him his business. Yusuf told the man he was a reporter and that he wanted to talk to Mr. Ömer about something. The man said, "Wait!" and then left. He came back a little later and brought Yusuf inside. It was strange for him to look like a stranger in the garden in which he'd spent his childhood. Yusuf knew every tree and stone in that garden.

Through the windows he saw that everything in the mansion had been torn out and that the walls and ceilings had been almost completely scraped.

The watchman brought Yusuf to the front terrace of the mansion. The waters of the Bosphorus were lapping the marble of the terrace and reflecting a blinding light. Yusuf couldn't see well in this bright light. That's why he preferred the dark coolness of the back garden. As always, his eyes watered. Then Mr. Ömer, who he'd seen so often on television and in the newspapers, was approaching him and asking what he wanted. He was a wiry and handsome man. He had short, regularly cut hair and wore red-framed glasses. He was wearing a very clean white shirt with the sleeves rolled up to the elbows.

Yusuf said, "There's an old woman sitting in front of the mansion. I wanted to ask you some questions about this."

In an understanding manner, Mr. Ömer said, "We gave the poor woman a lot of time. We'd been asking her to move out ever since the day we bought the mansion, but she wouldn't listen to us. In the end we had to move her out."

"But she claims that the house in the back garden belongs to her."

Mr. Ömer smiled and said, "The poor thing is lying."

"She has a deed in her possession."

A young woman, who Yusuf hadn't seen before because of the glare, started talking; she strode toward Yusuf and shouted, "Do you know who you're talking to?"

She was a thin, beautiful woman whose hair had been bleached blond. She was wearing sunglasses and short shorts. Mr. Ömer silenced her with a polite wave of his hand. The woman strode angrily into the house and continued giving directions to the contractors.

Mr. Ömer said, "Excuse me for a moment," and went into the mansion as well.

When Yusuf was left alone on the terrace, he looked at the front of the mansion. Here nothing had been changed yet. Indeed according to the building code no great changes were allowed. Yusuf knew that the mansion, which was set like a jewel on the Bosphorus, was supported on cedar columns.

Unlike the waterfront mansions built at the end of the nineteenth and beginning of the twentieth centuries, it did not evoke wealth and magnificence, but was a somewhat humble structure that evoked a quiet family life: it wasn't in the nineteenth century baroque Ottoman style, but was a wooden mansion that reflected Eastern sensibilities.

Today the sea was a color approaching lavender. For whatever reason, the Bosphorus was a different color every day, ranging from green to copper.

Yusuf's cell phone rang as he was watching a huge Russian tanker sailing up toward the Black Sea. He answered and found himself speaking to his editor. He was saying, "Come back at once," in a slightly worried voice.

"What?"

"Come back at once. The boss is very angry."

"But there's a woman here who's been evicted from a house she owns," said Yusuf.

"The woman is not sane."

"No, I've just seen her. She's quite sane."

"But," said the editor, "they have a doctor's report. The woman is not in her right mind. Because of this she was taken under guardianship, the court appointed a guardian, and the guardian sold her house to Mr. Ömer."

As soon as Yusuf heard this he understood the situation. It meant that, as had been the case with the elderly owners of a number of old mansions, Leyla had been declared incompetent.

He left the mansion under the mocking looks of the watchman. Mr. Ömer had come back out onto the terrace, but this time paid no attention to him.

When he left the mansion he found the policeman speaking into his radio, saying, "Yes, commander." When he'd finished talking he took Leyla roughly by the arm and tried to pull her to her feet. When the tradesmen started grumbling he said, "She doesn't listen to me, does she? I have very clear orders. If she doesn't leave of her own accord, I have to bring her into the station. I have to obey orders."

Yusuf asked the policeman and the people of the neighborhood to move away a little. They moved off a few yards. He leaned toward the Great Lady and said, "It seems we have no other choice. They have a doctor's report saying you're not in your right mind. They appointed a guardian. In this situation you have no rights to your deed."

The Great Lady opened her eyes wide in amazement. "But I didn't go to any doctor. How could they have a report like this."

"Ah," said Yusuf. "Do you think these people would have any trouble getting a false report?"

Then he told the Great Lady that she wouldn't be allowed to stay there. It would not be at all suitable for Bosnalı Abdullah Avni Pasha's granddaughter to be taken to the police station and thrown into the cells. So Yusuf was asking her to come to his own house in Cihangir. She could stay a day or two while they found a solution.

The Great Lady's elegant face darkened with sadness, as did her hazel-colored eyes. She remained this way for a time.

Yusuf was saying, "Leaving here doesn't mean that you're giving up on this matter. We'll do everything we can to have this false report canceled. But to do this you have to remain healthy. There's quite a struggle in store for you."

When these words had sunk in, the Great Lady said, "All right Yusuf, since there's no other choice, I might as well go with someone I've thought of as my grandson. Let's go to your house."

And so she got up from the suitcase on which she'd been sitting for two days. At first she swayed perilously, and then, with an effort that everyone noticed, she managed to stand straight. In a dignified manner she said to the tradesmen who had helped her, "I thank you, neighbors. May God bless you. Farewell."

She took one last look at the mansion before climbing into the little white car. Her lips were compressed, and a look of hatred had settled into her eyes.

She kept repeating to herself, "I'm leaving now, but I'll definitely be back. I swear I'll be back to wipe out this stain on the memory of my family."

3

As Yusuf drove back to the European shore he kept looking at the Great Lady sitting next to him and was amazed by her self-assurance. She'd seen a great many hardships in her life, and this was her temperament. She would not share her troubles with anyone, and they would not be reflected in her appearance or behavior. She'd lost her home, and perhaps for the first time in her life was going to stay in another person's house, but she didn't complain, and didn't even ask about where she was going. She'd sat on a suitcase for two days, but this showed only in the paleness of her skin and the shadows under her eyes.

The Great Lady didn't ask where she was going, but Yusuf was anxious throughout the drive. He'd been saddened by the situation he'd seen, and on a heroic impulse had invited the woman to his house, but who knew what the woman would think about the place they were going. Because the Cihangir neighborhood was unlike anything the Great Lady had ever seen in her life. What would she think when she saw the narrow streets, the dilapidated buildings, cross-dressers, gay people, long-haired rock musicians with earrings, hipsters in berets, prostitutes with long fingernails, and girls with multiple piercings? Of course these weren't the only types of people who lived in Cihangir. There were also intellectuals, reporters, academics, and foreign diplomats living in this lively neighborhood, but they weren't quite as noticeable as the others.

It would not be at all easy to introduce the Great Lady to Roxy. The more he thought about it the worse he felt. That was what he was like, he'd jump in without thinking, and get involved in something, and then have no idea of how to get out of it. That's how it had happened once again. Yusuf hated this part of his nature, but he didn't know how to get past it.

For five months he'd been living with Roxy, who was struggling to make her living as a hip-hop singer. They'd met so suddenly and unexpectedly, and recently his feelings for this girl he'd met at a popular hip-hop club in Beyoğlu and had taken a fancy to were growing increasingly deeper.

Her birth name was Rukiye. After a series of strange accidents during her adolescence that brought her from Duisburg to Istanbul, Rukiye found herself enchanted by this city's unusual energy, and changed her style and her clothes, and started living under the name Roxy, which she had adopted in Germany.

In recent years club after club had been opening in Beyoğlu, and all of them were always packed. What had been a chic Levantine neighborhood in Ottoman times, was now full of jazz clubs, rock music cafes, and hip-hop and folk music bars. The newspapers tirelessly referred to these clubs as "the pulse of Istanbul."

Yusuf had rented an apartment in Cihangir to be near this scene, and also so as not to break up with Roxy. And to tell the truth it was cheap around here. Because he made so little money at the newspaper, he'd borrowed several months' expenses from his cousin Hüseyin in Ankara. This little bit of money was enough for this neighborhood. He was still pleased that he'd been able to get out of his father's house on the Anatolian side and come here. Life had just begun for him.

The small domestic car that bumped among the potholes of Istanbul's streets eventually reached the labyrinthine streets of Cihangir and pulled up in front of an old, dilapidated five-story apartment building.

As he entered the building he saw that the trash containers next to the door were completely full and that two bold cats had scattered garbage in front of the entrance. He usually didn't notice these things, but now with the Great Lady at his side he was ashamed of how dirty the entryway was, of the smell of gas that assaulted the nose as soon as you entered, of the smell of damp and food, and of the peeling paint on the walls; if he could, he would have shielded the Great Lady's eyes from the filthy cats rummaging through the garbage and the mangy dogs roaming the streets looking for food. Because none of these things could be reconciled with the Great Lady, who always dressed in white, and who had given him jasmine throughout his childhood.

The Great Lady belonged to another world, belonged to the past; as for himself, he and Roxy lived in the present. Even if it was dirtier, and rougher, and more confusing, these were his own times. Times that set his blood racing and brought fire to his loins.

Yusuf practically had to drag the old woman, who was so tired she was on the point of collapse, up five flights of dim, dank, and filthy stairs.

He wasn't even sure if the Great Lady would be able to make it up the stairs. This woman had heart trouble, and if she died on the stairs his conscience would never be at ease.

Because Leyla didn't attach any importance to her heart trouble, the people of the neighborhood couldn't do much about it. When she didn't feel well she would just take one of the pills the neighborhood doctor had given her and lie down until she felt better. Yusuf had heard once from his father that everyone in the pasha's family had had heart trouble.

Even young people found themselves out of breath climbing these stairs and would start swearing about these Istanbul walk-ups. How was this ill and tired woman going to climb this tower, especially as she's spent two nights sitting on a suitcase. At least she could stop and rest a bit on the landings.

The exciting tumult of Beyoğlu and Cihangir had an indescribable attraction: the crowds of male and female students bumping into one another as they walked along the Avenue; the mix of ethnic music rising from the music shops on either side; the smells from the *köfte* and hamburger shops; the laughter of young girls; the movie posters, bright lights illuminating young faces; tourists looking around in bewilderment; rock, jazz, and hip-hop clubs; folk music bars; men with handlebar mustaches; cross-dressers; young men with long hair and earrings; worn-out, heavily made-up B-girls stumbling out of nightclubs; the orgy of eating and drinking in the Fish Market, fish glistening under naked bulbs, fruit and vegetables of all colors, cheeses, the smell of spices...

After his quiet childhood on the shores of the Bosphorus, all this made Yusuf feel as if the doors of life had been thrown open to him. If the traditions of the old way of life arose from tranquility, the new way of life was ruled by lust. It was as if the smell of blood, sweat, and lust that came from these crowds of people thrown together, the filth of the surroundings in which he lived, the packs of dogs who knocked over garbage cans at night, the piles of garbage in front of the restaurants, having to watch for puddles of drunken vomit as you walked, the puddles of urine at the foot of a wall, girls sweating under their arms at rock clubs were all essential elements of this lust. Lust was something inseparable from human sweat and blood.

But now he thought darkly about how he would show this new life to someone who had come from the past, or rather this beloved ghost he'd wanted to bring here, and he didn't know quite what to do.

He took the suitcase in one hand, took the Great Lady's arm in the other, and gently helped her climb the stairs.

4

In fact Yusuf was upset for nothing because the "beloved ghost from the past" was aware neither of the filth of her surroundings, nor of the dilapidated building, nor of the noise and smell.

She was overcome by the pain of having been evicted from her house and the shock of what had happened, contrary to how she'd seemed on the road. She couldn't think about anything else. It was as if she had been drugged. Perhaps she was also a bit frightened. She had been frightened ever since she'd gone outside the mansion walls that had formed a castle for her, and where she'd lived alone with her memories of her family. She didn't know these people, these buildings, these cars, these sounds, or these smells.

Her head spun as she climbed the stairs on Yusuf's arm, and in her clouded mind she could see the pale ghosts that remained in her memory from the black and white photographs, with their beveled corners, of her grandfather the pasha who had built the mansion, and of her grandmother and her mother and her uncle İzzet Kemal. As if it were they and not her house she'd left behind.

Indeed she hadn't lived in this world since the day her family was torn apart and she was left alone. She took shelter in the comfort of the hammock in which she'd been in the habit of lying and dreaming since she was a child. She wasn't interested in events that occurred outside of her, the passage of time and the changing world, but concerned herself with the Egyptian linen she'd bent over every day to embroider with silk thread, and the muslin cloth that seemed pale beside it.

"Grandmother," she said to herself, "you know that I didn't leave the house willingly. Otherwise I would never have left you behind."

Her grandfather's hazel eyes were smiling, looking as if he wanted to console her; behind him her grandmother's round, lovable face appeared. They seemed to say, "Don't worry. We know all." But silently, with their looks alone...

Her head was spinning as she leaned resting against a wall on the landing.

The waters of the Bosphorus splash against her face, because a large tanker is sailing past from the Black Sea to the Marmara. Waves from the tanker's wake are washing against the shore, and cool drops splash on the face of the girl leaning over the water. The smell of the fishing nets mixes with the rich smell of the cedar posts that have been under water for a hundred years. A flock of shearwaters passes, skimming the surface of the water. Where the little girl peers into the water the color is lighter, and further out it begins to darken, and where the ships pass it turns a deep blue. The smell of jasmine wafts from the back garden. The jasmine trees are right next to the magnolia tree her grandfather planted in honor of her birth: white Cyprus jasmine. Her grandfather planted a lot of jasmine. It was his favorite fragrance because it seemed to wrap the heart in velvet.

As she thought of jasmine, she suddenly remembered Yusuf next to her. The gardener's grandson, that polite, well-behaved boy. But she forgot immediately because she didn't want to tear herself away from the smell of jasmine and from her grandfather's hazel eyes.

Her grandfather is not speaking, he's not saying anything, but there's nothing unusual about this. Because she'd never heard her grandfather the pasha speak. He's been unable to speak since the day his son İzzet Kemal was martyred. Leyla remembered her grandfather as an old man who looked at her with moist hazel eyes. On summer days he would be brought out into the back garden with his tattered wicker chair, and he would sit there silently all day, watching his grandchild's games, and the beautiful magnolias, and the jasmine, and Judas trees, and the laurel bushes, and the hydrangeas and the violets.

Little Leyla would climb onto his lap, and play with his beard, and pull his nose, and feel the love in his hazel eyes. But one day she saw two streams of tears falling from those hazel eyes, and she didn't understand why her grandfather was crying like a child. The pasha was weeping, but his expression didn't change. The tears wet his wrinkled cheeks and flowed as far as his mustache. The surprised Leyla called her grandmother, who wiped away the tears with the silk handkerchief she always kept in her sleeve. When she thought of this incident years later, Leyla remembered the music that completed the picture. The Balkan folk tune from the radio in the salon reached the garden. A thin and emotional woman's voice was singing: "I'll get up and go to Urumeli / I'll give a petition to the governor." When Leyla grew up, she thought of her grandfather's tears every time he heard this song. The song that had made the paralyzed Bosnalı Abdullah Avni Pasha weep always swelled her heart and brought tears to her eyes.

Leyla never knew whether he wept out of longing for his native Balkan lands, or from the pain of those lands having been lost in war. The loss of the Empire's beloved European lands hung like the shadow of death over this family, and they never ceased to mourn for it. Even when Leyla was a child she knew that this was a wound that had never and would never be healed.

She had learned that her grandfather Bosnalı Abdullah Avni Pasha, who fought on horseback, was one of the officers who had done his utmost to defend the Balkan lands. But these struggles were to no avail, and the Balkan lands where her grandfather was born were gradually lost.

The tribulations of the hundreds of thousands who were displaced by the defeat in the Balkans were always spoken of tearfully at home. People who had fled, leaving their pots on the stove when they heard the cry "The enemy is coming!," the suffering along the road, princes who begged for bread from merciful Roma, mothers who were forced to abandon their babies by the roadside, brothers who lost each other—these were stories that were told daily.

The pasha's relatives had shared the same fate, and one day had had to leave Nevrokop. There was a trek of hundreds of kilometers ahead of them. Mothers who had just given birth thought strapping their babies on their backs was the best way to make this long trip. Some of the women who didn't do this were left helpless by the side of the road with their babies; when you carry a baby for hours it becomes very heavy. Helpless mothers had been seen abandoning their babies by the roadside.

When the pasha's relatives fled Nevrokop they were carrying a two-year-old boy whose mother and father had been killed. Before the Bulgarian bandits raided, his father had hidden him in the closet. It was thought that the child fell asleep in the dark of the closet, and then, when he woke, and when no one came to open the door despite his crying at the top of his lungs, he managed to push it open. Because the door was open, and the child could not have remained alive unless he'd been hidden. They would have killed him with his parents just as they had killed thousands of other children. With difficulty, the child managed to reach the living room. His mother and father were lying on the floor. His mother was naked, and her breasts were exposed. The child crawled to her side and waited for her to give him milk, but she didn't move. Then the baby took his mother's bloody breast in his mouth and began to suck. His relatives found him in this state, and they had difficulty pulling him from his mother's breast. The child's lips were covered with blood. This child whose parents were killed by Bulgarian bandits was Bosnalı Abdullah Avni Pasha's nephew. He was Leyla's great uncle's son. These refugees from the Balkan War, forced to flee on foot, tied this unfortunate baby to their backs and managed to bring him as far as Istanbul.

The family walked for days with the thousands of other refugees, and when they ran out of the provisions they had consumed so sparingly, they began to go hungry. Just at that point, they received help from the self-sacrificing Roma of Nevrokop. In the old days, on Fridays, bread used to be given as charity to the Roma, who would fill their blackened bags with it. Now, when it was needed most, they took out those bags and returned the charity to those had been charitable to them.

They were to receive help from unexpected quarters once again on this eventful journey, and this time the family was saved from certain death. After walking for weeks, their lacerated feet finally brought them to Kavala harbor; from there they were to board a ship for Izmir, and safety. But in those days, crowded Kavala was under the control of Bulgarian bandits. These bandits were massacring the refugees mercilessly. If they were caught, the pasha's relatives would undoubtedly be killed. As the family was struggling to get onto the ship they fell into the hands of the bandits. As they were on the point of lining them up to shoot them, a respected leader of the bandits stepped forward. He ordered that these people be released. According to the story, this bandit's name was Lademir.

Among the good deeds that the elders of the family had performed was to bring Christian children into their home and raise them and see to their education. Lademir was one of the children who had grown up in that house. Unable to bear seeing the family wiped out, he gave them permission to board the boat.

As the boat rocked like a cradle on the sea, they gathered gratefully on the deck and said a prayer for Lademir.

This story was told by the refugee family who came to the mansion, and was passed on to Leyla by her grandmother. And one day while she was thinking about this bitter story, her thoughts turned to Lademir. What had his fate been? Did he fall victim to a bullet in one of Macedonia's deadly traps, or was he one of the Vladimirs who went down in history for their role in the foundation of Bulgaria? Who knew? Leyla guessed that Vlademir was the real name of the Lademir to whom her family referred so often.

After the defeat in the 1912 Balkan War, the pasha's family, like all the people of Istanbul, tried to help these poor people who had escaped death by walking for days. There was no place in Istanbul to shelter, clothe, and tend to the wounds of the hundreds of thousands of Balkan Turks. So they took shelter in the courtyards of mosques, hospital gardens, government buildings, and the homes of charitable people. A cry was rising up from every corner of Istanbul: the heartrending cry of those who had lost their loved ones on the road, who had lost their homes and hearths and fields, of these hungry, sick, wounded, and pale people.

Abdullah Avni Pasha did not stop at bringing relatives into the mansion, he brought as many as a hundred compatriots to the mansion garden, and set up tents and cooking cauldrons, and like many other Istanbul families he did his best to ease their pain. Men and women were housed separately in two large tents. After filling their stomachs for a few days, the children who slept with the women set out to explore the secluded corners of the garden and amused the family with their various antics.

Istanbul was weeping blood, but at the same time life went on. The pasha was a very compassionate person, and he watched children with great tenderness from beneath his thick eyebrows. Leyla's mother, Handan, took the children under her wing and tried to give them everything they wanted. From the days of strict separation of the sexes, there was a rotating cupboard between *harem* and the *selamlik* to facilitate the serving of food. The food that was cooked in the *harem* would be put in this cupboard that was no longer used, and then by turning the cupboard the food could be passed into the *selamlik*. This device had been used especially when there were guests invited to the *selamlik*, but the refugee children discovered this exciting toy within two days. They would squeeze into the cupboard on one side and emerge on the other. It was a very enjoyable game, and it continued only until the cupboard was broken, and it was only after this that Leyla's grandmother Üftade learned of the game. Handan felt sorry for the children and hid the fact of their having broken this cupboard from her mother. They were in such desperate need of tenderness and of games…

Sometime later the government gave the refugees from the Balkans houses and land in Adapazarı, Bergama, Istanbul, and Bursa, and helped them settle there and begin their lives anew. But with the loss of the Balkans and the victorious Ottoman army suffering one defeat after another, such as the one at Çatalca just outside Istanbul which seemed an omen of the end of the pitiful Empire, the school day would begin with tearful laments for the Balkans.

Leyla was told all of this. She knew by heart all that had happened in the mansion before she was born. She had written down what her grandmother had told her in a notebook and had saved the faded family photographs. Indeed there was no one else except her grandmother to tell her about these events. She hadn't grown up during the time when her grandfather the pasha still spoke, and she knew him only as a silent old man. And her mother had died giving birth to her. Her uncle İzzet Kemal was martyred by the English during the occupation of Istanbul. She knew this handsome uncle with the wavy, sandy hair only from photographs. So there was no one else except her grandmother Üftade, with whom she was alone in the mansion, to tell her the family history. Perhaps this is why Leyla accepted what her grandmother told her as a sacred trust and never forgot it. As if, should she forget even one of these events, or remember it incorrectly, or if one day it would pass out of her mind, the family would disappear. The glorious past of Bosnalı Abdullah Avni Pasha's family lived on only in Leyla's memory. The day she no longer thought about this family, they would finally be dead.

Even though the mansion was sold and passed out of their hands after her grandfather the pasha died, to be able to see the house, and touch the trees, and smell the jasmine enriched these memories with details and brought the past to life.

When those rough, dirty hands rummaged through her lavender-scented linen, they were throwing not only her but her whole family out into the street.

Leyla was frightened.

This was why, now, as she climbed the steep stairs of the building in Cihangir, out of breath and with her head spinning, she thought so anxiously about her family.

As Yusuf carried the hard, heavy, genuine leather suitcase, he was worried about the woman who was climbing the stairs, short of breath, with her head spinning, and feeling a tightness in her chest, trying to gather her strength between floors.

When they reached the fifth floor the Great Lady could hardly move; her chest was tight, and her head was spinning. Yusuf stopped in front of the door and put the suitcase down on the dirty marble floor. Leyla saw that the marble was as old and worn out as she was. Then they went inside.

Leyla, who was a little pale, tore herself away from her memories, and looked around at the place she'd just entered. What she saw in the dim apartment was a terrible, untidy mess. Her eyes were struck by the dusty, faded-brown velvet sofa, a small Formica table covered with dirty dishes, worn-out chairs, and the books on the bookshelf. There was a motley carpet on the floor. Her heart sank as she became aware of her surroundings. Leyla hadn't seen a place like this for many years; perhaps she hadn't even seen something like this in the past, perhaps she'd never seen anything like it. Having grown up in a house where even the old Philips radio in its walnut cabinet was covered with spotless lace doilies, she tried not to touch anything as she entered. The walls were so damp and stained that one had to look carefully to see that at one time they had been painted a dark yellow. Her attention was drawn to the small electric piano in the corner and the red electric guitar. These musical instruments weren't familiar to her either.

Yusuf was aware of the situation as he sat her on the velvet sofa and carefully put her suitcase behind the sofa.

He murmured something like, "I'm afraid it may not be so comfortable, but...," but what he said wasn't quite audible. Yusuf had always felt awkward in front of Leyla. And in a situation like this...

Yusuf rushed to the kitchen, and Leyla heard clattering sounds. A little later he came in with two cups of tea and offered one to Leyla. Just at that moment, the call to prayer could be heard from nearby mosque. With the loudspeakers on at top volume, it was as if the *muezzin* was in the house with them. The man didn't know how to recite the call properly, the way it used to be done, and was simply shouting.

Yusuf saw that Leyla's hand was trembling slightly as she held the teacup and thought: even this iron constitution is finally succumbing to tiredness. His heart went out to this pale-faced, thin, tired old woman who had purple rings under her eyes.

He helped her gently to her feet and brought her to a room. It was a small room, and there was no furniture except for a single bed in the corner. Yusuf showed Leyla the bed and insisted she lie down for a while. He brought her suitcase and left saying he would see her in the evening…

Leyla was grateful; she was in great need of a place to lie down, but she couldn't help noticing the dusty blanket and the discolored pillow. She opened her suitcase, took out a cream-colored slip, and spread it over the pillow. Only then could she rest her head on the pillow. The silk carried the damp of the Bosphorus; it was cool and clean and smelled of lavender.

Before falling asleep, she could smell the smell of the laundry bubbling in the cauldrons in the mansion garden. Four cauldrons had been set up at the edge of the garden, and fires had been built under them, and the laundry was stirred around in the boiling water with wooden paddles. Steam rose up to the sky. Later this laundry would sit in water to which indigo had been added, then it would be dried in the sun, ironed with a coal iron, and be put away in the closet carrying the scent of Bosphorus breezes. In time, the lavender in the closet and the mansion's own particular moist smell would seep into them, and when you smelled it, it was like being drawn into the Bosphorus.

5

After Leyla left, Ömer Cevheroğlu, the new owner of the waterfront mansion, received a visit from his father Ali Yekta. Ali Yekta was a large, clean-shaven man whose white hair was slicked with brilliantine and carefully combed back, who wore glasses with thick tortoiseshell frames and a beige suit with a carefully knotted paisley tie and a starched shirt. That is, he was dressed just the way a mansion owner of old would have been expected to dress. He had a handsome, fine-boned face.

He was wearing two-toned white and brown shoes of a kind that are rarely encountered today, and that drew attention.

The tradesmen and the people of the neighborhood who were watching everything with curiosity began to speculate about who this ostentatious gentleman might be.

Cemal the greengrocer said, “This man looks as if he could be the president!”

Hasan the grocer said pretentiously, "He's exactly the type they call an Istanbul gentleman." He actually considered himself to be from Istanbul.

However, there was a strange detail about this respectable gentleman's arrival at the mansion that aroused their curiosity; somehow, they just couldn't figure it out.

The gentleman didn't arrive at the mansion in a showy car, but on one of the red city buses on which one rarely meets men so ostentatiously dressed. They continued watching the mansion, hoping somehow that they would be enlightened.

When the watchman opened the gate, Ali Yekta said, "My boy, is the gentleman at home?" in an authoritative voice, then strode into the garden without waiting for an answer. The large and well-tended garden had taken on the appearance of a construction site. He noticed the old marble basins, the faucets, old toilets, cedar side tables, grills, pieces of wall and ceiling ornaments, decorative glass lanterns and lamps, piled up here and there. There were several rolled-up carpets lying on the ground.

When his son came out to greet him respectfully, he asked, "What's all this?" His voice was deep but soft.

Ömer said, "Just some odds and ends from the mansion. Worn-out things. Necla doesn't want them. That's why we're having trucks come and take them away."

"You mean you're throwing it all out?"

"I have no idea where they bring it. It's probably all sold at some flea market. None of these things have any value as antiques."

After thinking it over for a while Ali Yekta said,

"Look, son, don't send this stuff away by truck. Give it to the mountain people."

"The mountain people?"

"Yes, because you're moving here, or rather we're moving here. It's very important to be gracious to these mountain people, the former servants and so forth, to show them who the new master is. You gain feudal authority by being generous. If you give these odds and ends to the mountain people, they'll be grateful and faithful for the rest of your life."

"I would never have even thought of that."

"As I always tell you: Money is important but it isn't everything. You have to use the money properly, like a gentleman, and you have to be respectful and dignified wherever you go."

In response to his father's commanding words, Ömer said, "All right, father, I'll call them in and give it to them."

After this talk, father and son walked around the mansion to look at the work that was being done. Necla was not around, and her voice couldn't be heard.

No one knows when the owners of the waterfront mansions began using the phrase "the mountain people." Perhaps it came from the time when the owners of the waterfront mansions could no longer feed and house all their staff, and these people started settling in the hills behind.

The asphalt road that now runs behind the waterfront mansions was once a dirt path only wide enough for a single carriage, and the wooded hills rose directly behind it. These hills belonged to the owners of the waterfront mansions. On these hills with their walnut trees and giant plane trees, where springs rose and where in spring people are intoxicated by the Judas trees, there were small structures such as barns, warehouses, and laundry houses that were lost in the wilderness. In later years the people who worked at the mansions sought permission to build small houses. These houses grew larger in time, and with the arrival of relatives from Anatolia, these collections of houses became neighborhoods, and the number of shops began to increase. Then the people in the mansions began to call this new population "the mountain people."

The mountain people Ali Yekta spoke of to his son were the people of the neighborhood.

Toward evening the mountain people started entering the mansion shyly in groups of two or three. They felt like strangers in this garden they knew so well because they were frightened of the new owners. They were very surprised when one of the watchmen came and said they could take away the "antiques" from the mansion. What generous people these new owners were. How could they give them these things that had once belonged to a pasha.

Those who went into the garden soon lost their shyness and threw themselves on the piles of old furniture. Some were trying to carry away rolled up carpets under their arms, and others were trying to lift marble basins without considering that they might injure their backs. The large carpets were being carried by two people at a time. Everyone was in a rush to find the most valuable pieces and take them home. It wasn't easy to take possession of these things that had passed from generation to generation in Abdullah Avni Pasha's family, to carry the marble toilet and install it in one's own home, or the coffee brazier that would sit in the center of the living room.

A short while later the women arrived in the garden, pushing and shoving at each other silently, and began gathering up the things. Soon, there wasn't even any rubble left.

Ali Yekta, watching through the window with his son, said, "You see how it is Ömer? You have to know the soul of the servant class. One of the greatest arenas of competition for the wealthy, as important as property, is the respect of those who serve them. Of course these people aren't your servants; they're the children and grandchildren of mansion retainers, but they still have the habit of servitude. Even if one day they should become wealthier than you, they'll never overcome this."

Ömer, who had heard this lecture countless times in his life, said, in an impatient tone, "Yes, father. I'll do what has to be done. Don't worry."

"You'll be stern, you'll never let go of your authority, but you will not be cruel. You'll never be unjust. Then the servant will be bound to the master and will remain obedient for the rest of his life."

Ömer wanted to say, "So how did you escape it then?" but of course he couldn't say anything. He loved his father, but he'd heard this talk so many times, and he was fed up with hearing about the master–servant relationship. There was nothing else that Ali Yekta wanted to talk about, nothing else that interested him.

"Where's Necla?" he heard his father ask petulantly.

"She had a headache, father," he said. "You know she has migraines. She apologizes for not seeing you. She's hidden herself away in a quiet corner."

Ali Yekta said, "I've never known that woman not to have a headache. Whenever I come she has a headache." He spoke through his teeth, with hatred and resentment.

When he fell silent, Ömer felt the need to break the silence, to say something: "No, father!" he said, "You're mistaken, Necla would never be disrespectful to you, but she really does have a headache."

A little earlier, though, as soon as she heard the man had arrived, Necla had disappeared, saying, "I really can't take this! I'm going to go somewhere. Please, get rid of the man as quickly as you can." Necla almost never saw her father-in-law.

Ali Yekta sighed and said, "Whatever!"

Then the father and son climbed to the top floor of the mansion.

After Ömer and Necla had talked to the American architect at length about the need to finish the work in a hurry, he'd seen that it was not necessary to knock down any of the interior walls or change the shapes of the rooms. The mansion was already very well laid out, and the rooms, the living room, the kitchen, and the servants' quarters were perfectly arranged. So they hadn't made any structural changes and had left the lower floor as it was. On the upper floor, the wall decorations that had been stained and darkened by the Bosphorus damp were removed, and the walls were scraped and made ready to be covered with imported wallpaper. Indeed the largest room in the mansion, the room that had once been used by Avni Pasha and his wife, Üftade, was already being covered with paper brought from England that looked like silk. Üftade had given birth to her children in this room, which was as big as the salon and whose windows looked directly onto the sea. Leyla's mother, Handan, and her uncle İzzet Kemal had come into the world in this room.

Ali Yekta inspected the room carefully and said, "It would be better if you put the bed over here. That way you can look at the sea and the passing ships." When he said this, it touched a sore spot for Ömer.

Ömer knew that his father wanted to move in with them and to have this room. But Necla had already picked this room out for themselves and had given the architect instructions to this end. She'd had to run around London for days to find the right wallpaper. He was sure that the war between his father and Necla would break out into the open over this room and that there was nothing he could do to prevent the tension and fighting that would ensue.

Indeed Necla didn't even accept the idea of Ali Yekta moving in at all, let alone having that room, and every time the subject came up she had a fit.

"Let him stay where he is!" she would say. "What sense does it make for him to leave the Kadizade Mansion and come live with us after all these years?"

But Necla was not aware of the passion, which Ömer was so familiar with, that had been burning within Ali Yekta for so many years. She had no idea what the largest room in the mansion meant to him. If she had known, she would have behaved more cautiously toward him and would have been careful not to anger him.

Necla was the daughter of a mid-level civil servant who had moved to Istanbul after retiring and had bought a little apartment in Bahçelievler to settle down in. She was ambitious and had her eye on the main chance. Necla, who'd spent her girlhood in Anatolian cities such as Malatya, Manisa, and Uşak where her father was stationed and, having moved to Istanbul after he retired, had had her life altered by meeting Ömer, saw her father-in-law as pitiful and somewhat deranged. The idea of his moving in with them, which kept coming up, was enough to drive her crazy.

When Ömer brought the subject up she would say, "I understand, darling. He's your father and I can't say anything, but after all, he is a servant. He spent his life as a servant. How could he have the best room in your new mansion? And how are you going to introduce your father to guests? Are you going to say that he used to be a servant and now he's the boss? You already have a lot of enemies. If they find out who your father is and what he did for a living, the newspapers will embarrass you to no end."

"My love," Ömer would say, "I can't say no to my own father. What can I do?"

Then Necla suggested an easy solution: "Let me speak to him. I'll say, sir, it's more suitable for you to live where you've lived until now. He's already living in a mansion as it is, and one he was born in too, even if it was on the lower floor."

"It's not the same thing; he wants to move here, into the pasha's room, that's his dream, his passion. Living in the servants' quarters on the lower floor isn't living at all."

Of course Ali Yekta didn't know about these arguments. He detested this "common girl," who he didn't think was worthy of his son, and had done everything he could to obstruct their marriage. And he would never have guessed that she would behave so insolently toward him. Because his son came between them. His son who had never been disrespectful to him, the apple of his eye, his reason for living, his everything…

He was going to move to the new mansion, into the pasha's room on the top floor, and there he would live like a pasha. On holidays his grandchildren would come to kiss his hand and wait expectantly for the gifts he had bought them. The servants would bring him tea and coffee, knock gently on the door before entering, and tiptoe out without turning their backs. And, like the pashas of old, he would say, "Thank you my son." They would take his clothes out of the mahogany closet to air them; they would shine his shoes. He would ring the bell whenever he needed them. These were modern times, after all, so perhaps he would have an electric bell installed. The servants would feel a mixture of respect and fear; they wouldn't be able to raise their eyes to look in his face but would await his orders with bowed heads.

Ali Yekta knew only too well how servants should behave because he'd been a servant all his life. He had brushed the clothes, shined the shoes, served food to, and held towels for pashas and governors and their sons and grandsons. He had tended to them when they were ill and had prepared home remedies for them.

Not only he himself, but his father and even his grandfather had been servants to pashas and governors. According to family legend, his grandfather Halepli Cevher Ağa had been a butler at the famous Dürrizade Palace and had once even had the honor of serving Sultan Mahmut in person. His father used to tirelessly tell him and his brothers this story with great pride and would talk about what a great man Halepli Cevher Ağa was.

Sultan Mahmut had heard about the richness of the Dürrizade Palace at Paşakapısı, and of its owner's elegant pleasures, and suddenly decided one day in the month of Ramadan to perform his prayers at Yeni Cami in Üsküdar. The sultan, with his retinue of at least a hundred and fifty men, including grand viziers, viziers, and pashas, crossed to Üsküdar in the imperial caique, and reached the mosque half an hour before the cannon that marked the end of fasting was to be fired. "Here," the sultan said, "go inform them that I am going to break my fast at Dürrizade." They went at once. The Dürrizade immediately called Ali Yekta's grandfather Halepli Cevher Ağa and explained the situation to him. After the Ağa said, "Have no fear, master," orders were given to the *harem* to bring food to the *selamlik*, and for them to make a separate meal for themselves, and then he rushed to the mosque, kissed the sultan's hand and hem, and performed his prayers with him.

After prayers, the sultan mounted his horse and, followed by his retinue, proceeded to the palace. The sultan was invited into a room that had been lined in silk. Then a hundred and fifty people were seated at separate tables. The double doors of the room where the sultan was welcomed were opened, and servants in silk caftans entered. They placed a small table covered in velvet and studded with silver in front of the sultan. He was given a napkin embroidered with gold on which to wipe his blessed hands. Then three or four servants brought a huge silver tray and placed it on this table. The tray held golden plates of every kind of food, from jams and cheeses to sausages and fish eggs. Golden goblets contained water from the holy well of Zamzam. Those who saw them were amazed by the dessert spoons with ivory handles inlaid with turquoise, ruby, and emerald; soup spoons with coral handles; the paper-thin ebony pilaf spoons with mother-of-pearl handles; and the little stewed-fruit spoons enameled in gold and inlaid with pearls. Then delicious soup, meat, chicken, sweets, pastry, and pilaf were served. Then stewed sour cherries were brought out in a large bowl that looked as if it was made of crystal. Sultan Mahmut took a spoonful and said, "How cold it is!" and Dürrizade said, "My Powerful Ruler, the bowl is made of ice."

Every day, Halepli Cevher Ağa had water from Çamlıca frozen in a mold the shape of a bowl, filled it with compote, and served it to his master this way.

This story had been told in the mansion hundreds of times since Ali Yekta was a child, to let the guests know what noble lineage the servants came from. Indeed, when this story was told to foreign envoys who were guests at the mansion, they were told politely that the sorbet that was so fashionable in Europe had its origins in the *şerbet* prepared by the Ağa. Later Ali Yekta read this story in a book by Musahipzade Celal about life in old Istanbul. Even though his grandfather's name wasn't mentioned in the book, he had no doubt that his father's stories were true, and he passed this family legend on to his children just as it had been told to him.

The children, that is Ece, Melike, and Ömer: two girls and a boy. He never discriminated among his children, but he was perhaps a bit fonder of his son. In any event, his daughters would get married and leave, but the youngest, Ömer, was the source of all his dreams, plans, and hopes for the future, his most important passion, and just about his only reason for living. When his wife left him and went to Germany, he didn't object when she took Ece and Melike, but he refused to allow her to take Ömer.

Ali Yekta took the greatest care of this lovable and beautiful child, defending him even against his own mother, never laid a hand on him, sent him to the best schools, provided him with private tutoring, and raised him as if he were a prince.

Ali Yekta had worked all his life at the Kadizade Mansion. His father had been butler in the magnificent, seventeen-room mansion. He himself was born in the mansion, and when the time came he took his father's place as butler. The things he had lived in that place, the things he had seen.

The large room on the top floor where the kadi once lived was passed in time to the son, and for this reason it became known as the "gentleman's room."

For years he served the gentleman, brushing his clothes, shining his shoes, and with age taking responsibility for directing the many other servants, and doing what he could to see that when guests came the service was perfect.

So many people had sat at that table…In the Republican period, famous poets, authors, diplomats, and businessmen had eaten and raised their glasses in this dining room that reflected the magnificence of Ottoman times. Ali Yekta's esteemed father Suleiman, the Kadizade's chief butler, had heard authors such as Yahya Kemal, Cenap Şahabettin, İbnülemin Mahmut Kemal, and Abdülhak Hamit argue, make puns, and satirize each other at that famous table. Hamit, who was close to the state and had served as ambassador, was one of those who used to criticize the other authors and poets with an air of nobility. He had heard the famous arguments between Hamit and Muallim Naci with his own ears.

During one of these arguments the crystal chandelier hanging over the table fell and smashed to pieces! Fortunately no one was hurt, and, once they got over their initial surprise, the authors continued arguing with pieces of glass glittering on their heads.

When lightning struck nearby as the sultan was having Nefi's *Siham-i kazası* read to him, he had the poet executed, and the date of his death was remembered as "the day a poem about Siham-i kazası and its poet came down from the sky." When an inexperienced poet who knew this story referred to that evening as "the night the chandelier came down from the sky onto his head," an older poet said, "We have heard the appalling voice of a clumsy oaf!" and thus showed his skill.

In the life of the mansions jokes and witticisms such as this were repeated for as long as they were remembered and were passed down from generation to generation. Being the owner of a waterfront mansion meant not only being rich, but also having good manners and knowledge, and being close to poets and authors. Just like the newly wealthy bourgeois of nineteenth century Europe, the owners of waterfront mansions in Istanbul would have literary evenings, and have their children take piano lessons, and learn foreign languages, and be taken care of by foreign governesses. For the past two centuries these mansions had embraced European fashions. Because France was at the forefront of cultural and political events, they imported their styles of life and education from France.

Ali Yekta was proud that his family had been in Istanbul for four generations. How many of the aristocracy could say this? Some had come from Anatolia, some from the Balkans, and some from Arabia. His own grandfather's grandfather had come from Aleppo, but at least they'd been in Istanbul for four generations, and in waterfront mansions and palaces at that. As the poets said, "Paris is a lovely salon, London is a beautiful park, Berlin is a good barracks, but Istanbul is a beautiful city." For four generations the Cevheroğlu family had looked out on the splendid domes and elegant minarets of this golden city and had shared an unparalleled life in these mansions set like jewels amidst the legendary beauty of the Bosphorus. According to Yahya Kemal, these waterfront mansions, which were not found in Byzantine times, had a wholly Turkish way of life, and, despite the European education that was given to the children, their style reflected Turkish culture.

The most glorious day in the history of the mansion occurred during his own childhood. Gazi Mustafa Kemal visited the mansion and ate there with his entourage and, because of his father's intelligent and capable preparations, was very pleased with the meal. Ali Yekta watched from a side door and, with his heart pounding, melted with pride as he saw the Gazi's blond head. Everyone listened carefully to what this great man had to say as he sat at the table talking and drinking *rakı*. Meanwhile the people of the neighborhood had gathered in the back garden and had waited for hours in the hope of catching a glimpse of him as he left.

While they had cigarettes and coffee in the salon after diner, musicians began to play folk music. The exuberant sounds of a tambourine, a zither, an oud, a fiddle, and a clarinet spread through the mansion, now playing Balkan airs that brought tears to the Gazi's blue eyes, and now playing lively dance tunes. Even the liveliest dance tune that set everyone's blood racing was not enough to get people moving. Because they were in the presence of the Gazi. In the end even the Gazi himself couldn't stand it anymore and got to his feet and, after taking off his jacket, did justice to the music with an energetic dance. In order not to miss this historic event, Ali Yekta watched everything through a door that had been left ajar. Because seeing the Gazi dance wasn't something that happened every day. When the dance was over, the Gazi sat down, out of breath, his white shirt drenched with sweat. At just that moment Ali Yekta's father Suleiman entered the room with a very clean, carefully ironed, starched shirt, and bent to whisper something into the host's ear. The host then got up, brought the shirt over to the Gazi, and saying, "You've perspired, perhaps in order not to catch cold you might wish to change your shirt...," arranged for him to change his shirt behind a screen. Such were the manners and upbringing of Halepli Cevher Ağa and his sons and grandsons. These qualities emerged when they were most needed and showed his master in a very favorable light. The shirt the Gazi had taken off and hung on a corner of the screen was taken by one of his retinue, and the wet shirt was passed from hand to hand. Ministers and aides competed with one another to smell the Gazi's blessed sweat. There were people who kissed the shirt, and smelled it, and tried to pull it away from each other, but fortunately Mustafa Kemal Pasha didn't see, because this kind of thing made him very angry.

Ali Yekta may have been proud of the tradition of service that had been passed down to him by his great-grandfather, but he did not raise his son Ömer to follow in his footsteps. Because he wished the family's profession, and by this means its fate, to change with Ömer. After Ömer, the Cevheroğlu family would no longer be servants, they would be a family of gentlemen who owned a waterfront mansion. He had raised his son so that with his education, fortune, and knowledge he would be the most dazzling gentleman in Istanbul. There was no desire for revenge in this passion, nor any feeling of ill will toward his masters. He loved them very much, felt as tied to his master as he did to his own family, and served him wholeheartedly. They had been very good to him. But he wanted to live his old age as a mansion owner, and to be respected.

To this end, he spent no money on his own pleasure, and made no investments, but put everything into raising his son. When the other mansion servants were occupying land on the hilltops and building houses illegally, Ali Yekta wasn't interested. He spent his small inheritance, and the money he had saved, on Ömer. In any event, the owners of the mansion treated this likable and clever boy as their own, and he was inseparable from their children. So Ömer took French and English lessons with the other children at the mansion, learned to play tennis and ride a horse, went to the best schools, and graduated with honors in economics. After that his father sent him to Brown University to do his master's degree. The little money he had saved was being used up quickly, but Ali Yekta had no complaints about this. Because his son was doing his master's degree at an important university. The inheritance and the future now belonged to Ömer. His one and only son, the apple of his eye, who would bring renown to the Cevheroğlu name and give him dutiful grandchildren. When he looked at his son and saw how handsome, well-educated, and knowledgeable he was, he swelled with pride at this wonderful boy.

6

Leyla generally slept very lightly, but now, exhausted from the past few days, she drifted off into the deepest sleep. She slept dreamlessly, without moving, until evening. But when darkness fell she could hear people speaking in the mansion garden. It began as whispering but rose steadily. She tried to understand what was being said. A woman's voice was shouting, "I don't want this!" Perhaps this argument in the garden was about the refugees from the Balkan War. Some wanted these people to be put up in the mansion, and some were against it. "I don't want someone like that in my house," said an annoyed woman's voice.

Just then she woke. There was a strange taste in her mouth. She looked around in surprise, trying to figure out where she was; then she realized that the arguing voices were on the other side of the door, in the living room.

She heard Yusuf's voice; he was pleading, arguing with a harsh-voiced woman. The more he begged, the more annoyed she became. "I don't have to put up with this!" she shouted.

"Be quiet, speak softly, she'll hear us," Yusuf was saying.

"Let her hear. If that fossil has ears to hear. I don't fall for any of this family loyalty business. I don't have time for people from that kind of family. They're all the same. I'm telling you, Yusuf, get that fossil out of this house at once! Do you hear me?"

"Do you want me to leave her in the street?"

"Leave! Aren't there a lot of women on the street or in shelters? Is she any better than they are, that we have to take her in like a stray cat? No, no! I won't let these two-faced people who think they're better than me run my life anymore. I'm not going to live through that again now because of your stupid sentimentality. *Scheisse, scheisse!*"

These words stung Leyla when she heard them. Never in her life had she heard herself spoken of in this way, never had she heard such insults. Now she was hearing them from a girl who had never even seen her face. These poisonous words hurt her so much that she was on the point of tears. She wanted to get out of there at once and go back to the wall outside the mansion, but she was afraid to come face-to-face with this girl. She wondered how the girl would look at her and whether she'd be at all ashamed of herself. Feeling threatened, she stayed in bed a little longer, but when she realized she had no other recourse and that the argument wasn't going to subside, she got up and opened the door.

In the living room, Yusuf was standing, and a dark girl was sitting cross-legged on the old sofa. Immediately Leyla saw the girl's black hair, with its streaks of blue, her black leather pants, her boots, and her large earrings. The girl looked at her angrily.

In a panic, Yusuf said, "Are you up? Look, this is my friend."

It seemed very strange to introduce the girl to the Great Lady as Roxy, so he said "Rukiye," and immediately regretted it. Because Roxy looked at him as if she wanted to kill him.

Leyla walked unsteadily into the living room and sat in the old armchair that Yusuf showed her. Roxy pretended to be looking at her broken fingernail and didn't even look at the woman. A little later she stretched her legs out on the sofa.

Leyla noticed that Yusuf was afraid of this girl.

Meanwhile Yusuf was asking how she was, and bowing and scraping, and wanting to bring her tea, and do anything he could to put her at ease. Fortunately Roxy had shut up when she'd seen her and hadn't repeated her words to her face.

Leyla was trying to decide whether to let on that she had heard everything. She knew that she shouldn't stay there after being insulted in this way, but it was evening, and she didn't know what she would do in this strange and unfamiliar neighborhood. Perhaps the best thing to do was to pretend she hadn't heard and act as if nothing had happened. That would make things easier for everyone and would put Yusuf at ease. It was a mature and necessary solution.

Leyla said, "I'm sorry to put the two of you out." When Roxy heard the woman's tone of voice and her regular accent she couldn't help looking up, but then she went back to her broken fingernail. She was putting on black nail polish and inspecting her nails carefully. She turned her hand this way and that, looking with endless curiosity at the black polish on her fingernails.

Leyla, not heeding Yusuf's rush to apologize, said, "Sometimes a person can't help ending up in an undesirable situation. One finds oneself in the midst of events one would never have even imagined. This is what has happened to me, and suddenly I'm in the position of someone who is interfering with your private life. Otherwise, how different everything was even this morning..."

As Leyla was speaking, Roxy got up and went to the kitchen. She was acting as if the woman wasn't there, as if she couldn't hear her words. She behaved in an offended and slightly threatening manner—a rebellious, intractable manner.

When the girl had gone out Leyla asked Yusuf, "Is this girl your fiancée?"

Yusuf, who seemed as if he wanted to sink through the floor, answered, "No!"

"Your girlfriend?"

"Yes, you could say that."

"Where is she from?"

"Her family lives in Germany, but..."

"What does she do?"

"She does hip-hop."

"What?"

"Hip-hop?"

"What's hip-hop?"

"How can I explain, it's a new thing..."

"Is it something like acrobatics?"

"No, it's a kind of music. They sing songs as if they're talking. And Roxy..."

"Who's Roxy?"

"Well, Rukiye actually."

"Is the girl's name Roxy or Rukiye?"

"Her real name is Rukiye, but she doesn't like it, so she uses her stage name, which is Roxy. It makes her angry to be called Rukiye."

"Then she was very angry at you a little while ago."

"Why?"

"Because you introduced her to me as Rukiye."

"Yes, she must hate me for that. But that's not the only reason she's angry."

"There's also my situation, isn't that so?"

"No. No, please don't misunderstand. It has nothing to do with you."

"Yusuf, is this your house or is it Roxy's?"

"I pay most of the rent, but everyone helps me out as much as they can."

"Who's everyone?"

"The musicians in Roxy's band. They come here to eat. Everyone brings something. Then they practice here. They're good kids. They grew up in Germany too."

The old woman and the gardener's grandson sat in that dilapidated, run-down apartment in the darkness of evening, talking softly as if they were partners in crime. Leyla, who still couldn't believe the situation she'd fallen into so suddenly and was trying to deal with this change by hanging on to the details of her daily life, took a strange, almost pathological pleasure in this.

In spite of her peevishness, she found that irritable creature Rukiye–Roxy quite interesting. She wasn't at all like any of the women she'd ever met in her life. The delicate ladies of the subdued world of the Bosphorus never raised their voices, faced whatever befell them with resignation and patience, and, when the pain and reproach in their eyes grew to the point where they could no longer stand it, they would attempt suicide by drinking mercuric chloride. The face powder that came from Europe and was widely used at that time contained mercuric chloride; when the women who applied this to their faces to make them white like Noh masks discovered that it was poisonous, it was put to a new use.

Leyla was looking around for clues about life in this house, commenting to herself as she did so.

She felt that Yusuf's good intentions were understandable; indeed she didn't see anything extraordinary about it. He was a polite and thoughtful boy, that's all. Leyla loved him. But Rukiye–Roxy was a type of person she had never seen or met, or indeed even imagined until today.

Just then they heard the girl's voice; she was calling Yusuf to the kitchen.

Leyla remained alone in the living room. She could hear that another argument had broken out in the kitchen, but this time, because the tap was running and the girl was speaking softly, she couldn't make out the words. Again, she could hear in the girl's voice that there was a great and boundless anger she was trying to suppress.

Suddenly she felt very tired. This was all too much for her. After all that had happened, she couldn't bear having to stay in a house where she wasn't wanted. On the other hand, she was terrified by the thought of taking her suitcase and descending those stairs. She remembered the filthy streets she'd glimpsed on the way, the crowds, dogs knocking over garbage cans, the sounds of shouting, the sirens, all the different kinds of music the mingled together in a hellish cacophony, the drunks... No, she couldn't go out there at night; it wasn't possible.

If Leyla had been a little bit weaker she would have wept then. She wanted to cry, and there was a lump in her throat, but she knew how to keep herself under control at all times. She wasn't one of those delicate flowers of the Bosphorus; she was a logical person. She had been taught not to show her feelings, and even when there were storms raging within her, no trace of it would show on her face, and her hazel eyes would look straight at whoever she was talking to.

In this distressing situation she was trying to look at things objectively and see them from a different perspective: there were some courses of action she could definitely rule out. First, going outside at that hour. Because she couldn't do that, she had no choice but to stay the night in that house. She was unwanted, just like the Balkan refugees who had taken shelter in their garden, and on top of this she was helpless.

Second, she couldn't stay another day in that house. She would have to find a place for herself, and since she didn't have any relatives it would have to be a cheap hotel. She'd never stayed in a hotel in her life, but she'd read so many English, French, and German novels that took place in hotels that she didn't think she would feel out of place. She'd even be willing to go to a sanatorium like in *Der Zauberberg*. Yusuf was a journalist, so he must know about places like that. But she wouldn't mention Thomas Mann's novel to him, she'd put it in a way he could understand. The biggest problem with this plan was money. How much money did hotels cost?

Just as she was thinking these things she heard the sound of a key in the door. The door opened, and three thin, young men came in.

7

It was as if this bitter smoke, this bitter smell had been with Rukiye since childhood and just wouldn't go away. On those dreadful, endless Sundays of her painful adolescence, when the closed shops of Duisburg made the deserted avenues even lonelier, she was never sure which was more deadly, the poisonous yellow smoke or the looks people gave her.

The thick smoke that rose from the smokestacks of the Krupp and Thyssen factories . . . it felt as if everything under the leaden sky could be rolled into a ball and get stuck in your throat, suffocating, ready to explode at any moment.

Rukiye, Rukiye, Rukiye . . . she hated this name, as if it was a symbol of her own worthlessness, of having to live in the world as a good-for-nothing Turkish girl; Rukiye put on water for tea, Rukiye set the table, Rukiye close your collar, Rukiye don't talk to the German boys,

Rukiye don't stand up to your father; Rukiye, Rukiye, Rukiye...

As if the name's fate had been decided before she was born, as if the baby born that day in Duisburg had been deemed different from the other babies and was given a lower place in the order of things—indeed was placed at the very bottom.

Rukiye knew how to live in a world that she hated. The worst thing about it was that she knew that life wasn't hell for everyone, and that happier lives existed.

This was a hell of idiots who constantly called her Rukiye. Those who didn't yearn for a better life, and perhaps the comfortable deafness and oblivious blindness of those who didn't know.

Rukiye knew this, but the knowledge didn't help, and no matter how she tried she couldn't change these conditions. That's why some people said she was crazy. She said this to herself: "I'm crazy! I'm crazy!"

There was no other explanation for the way she behaved when her first boyfriend Joachim kissed for the first time. She'd pushed him, shouted, "*Ich bin verrückt!* I'm crazy!" and then started crying and ran away.

It was as if she took a secret pride in calling herself crazy: when she behaved that way she could feel a kind of peace spread through her. And this was her only shield against her family: the sense of freedom behind the judgment that "this girl is crazy."

My Family and Other Animals: simply because of its title, this book was very important to her. She guessed that Gerald Durell had suffered at the hands of his family as she had and that he was too sensitive to express this in any other way. She'd found a German translation of the book at the local library and had brought it home, and, despite all the warning letters she got, she never returned it. Because every time she saw the book on the side table it calmed her down: My family and other animals, she would repeat to herself, my family and other reptiles, my family and other bats, my family and other pigs...

If her father had known what she was thinking, and particularly if he'd known she'd compared him to a pig, he probably would have beaten her. He was suspicious of all the food that came into the house; he was imprisoned by thoughts that the lamb had been cut with a knife that had previously used on a pig and drove himself crazy wondering whether his children were committing the sin of eating pork.

For that matter, like any healthy child in Germany, Rukiye loved to eat bratwurst smeared with sweet ketchup and mustard. In fact she even licked her fingers when she was finished.

This idea was as nonsensical as all her father's ideas. Because on the days when he still had hope of being able to educate her, he told her about the Islamic prohibition against pork. "Pork is abominable."

"Then," said Rukiye, "pigs should like Muslims more than anyone."

Her father became quiet and hung his face.

"Isn't that so, father? If the whole world was Muslim, no one would slaughter pigs, and they could live in peace.

If I had been born a pig, I would want everyone in the world to be Muslim."

This conversation always ended in her getting two slaps in the face and a spanking.

But Rukiye still thought that what she said was logical.

One day one of the German teachers addressed her as Roxy in class. She felt as if a light had shone within her. Roxy, Roxy, Roxy. What a nice name. She was surprised she hadn't thought of something like that before. From that day on, she insisted everyone call her Roxy. She even managed to convince her father. She lied and said the school insisted she change her name, and so she became Roxy. Crazy Roxy, Roxy who would either run away or bite her boyfriends' tongues when she kissed them, Roxy who was as quick as a squirrel, Roxy who hated her family and other animals...

Did I have to be born into a family like that, she wondered. They were both empty-headed and presumptuous. Forty years ago these people were stupid enough to leave their villages because they heard that workers were needed in Germany. Idiots, because as her toothless grandfather said, they'd believed that "the Germans will make soap out of you." All of them had come to Germany despite believing that they'd be used to make soap: uncles, aunts, in-laws, cousins...a family of animals. *Scheisse, scheisse!* Some of them worked at an *Imbiss*, some, like her father, at blast furnaces, some were cleaners, some worked at shops that sold electrical appliances...Some of these stupid animals, like her uncle, fell victim to their own ignorance and were killed when they were banged on the head with a winch. The compensation payments they got didn't help. They spent the money building an ugly, four-story concrete building in the mind-numbing Anatolian village they called home: a stupid building with unpainted bricks and sagging balconies that didn't look anything like the other houses in the village. Roxy knew that her father had only built that building to make the villagers who hadn't gone to Germany feel bad and to show them what an important and wealthy man he had become.

This is what Roxy's family and other animals were like.

The men were bad, and the women were worse. Roxy believed that people were poisonous, and that females were more poisonous. The women told Rukiye poisonous lies as if they were giving her friendly advice: Don't touch yourself there or you'll get worms. If you become close to the Germans in school you'll burn in hell.

Even from the first time they said these things she was curious and asked herself, "What's so special about it that makes it so important?" That's why when she was a child she locked the bathroom door and examined herself between the legs with a small mirror, though this inspection didn't enlighten her in any way. Why does everyone talk about this, why are they so uptight about this? It was impossible to get answers to these questions. Later they taught everything in sex education class at school, but by that time there was no need left for this. Her friends' porn magazines showed her the way and were like a manual for her.

As Rukiye grew up and developed more relationships outside the house, pressure from her family increased. She wanted very much to go to the disco where boys and girls danced together on Saturday nights, but her father wouldn't let her. "Only sluts go there," he said. She didn't know what kind of reception she'd get at the disco, whether they'd make fun of her, whether they'd even let her in; she didn't know, but her father was the first obstacle to the fulfillment of this desire that set her heart trembling.

Roxy wanted her father to die; at night she prayed for this to a god of whose existence she wasn't certain. She prayed so much that her wish was granted, only with a slight misunderstanding: her mother died instead of her father. The woman who was already sickly, who'd lost the luster in her eyes, who went around from morning to night with a cloth tied around her forehead, groaning, expecting to die at any moment, had died. They put her body in a coffin and placed it in the baggage hold of the Turkish Airlines flight. Because the funeral in the village was being held by rich people who worked in Germany, it became a race to get hold of money. The religious teachers tried to drown each other out as they recited the Quran in louder and louder voices.

Roxy thought to herself that if they were going to have to go through all this distress, they might as well have gone through it on account of her father rather than her mother. But no such luck. Despite working for years without a rest, he was as healthy as a pig, standing there with his black mustache. If only she could say this to him: like a pig, like a pig. Her father ate like a pig, snored like a pig, and rutted like a pig all night with the German woman he'd married three months after her mother died.

Roxy's life became more difficult now. To her the German woman looked like a turkey that had been plucked and smoked. What was she expecting, she thought, that an animal like her father would go out with Claudia Schiffer? Who else but a turkey who had no other hope of finding a husband would come to a vomit-like house such as this. Her white skin was just like a plucked turkey, scaly and bumpy. She looked naive, but she wasn't at all naive; she was a provincial widow who could even be said to be crafty. They became enemies on the first day. Ute tried to rein her in and impose her authority, so Roxy shouted, "I'm crazy!" at the top of her voice. "I'm crazy. *Ich bin verrückt!* Do you understand?"

The woman was frightened. So she started to behave in an underhanded manner. Once at dinner she pointed out to her father how her breasts were growing, and said it was time he made his daughter wear something more modest. The man looked at his daughter's breasts bulging out of her sweater. They weren't large, but they seemed firm enough to pierce the thin sweater. The father shouted at his daughter: "Do you want to be a slut, do you want to be a slut?" He shouted that she could no longer wear such revealing clothes.

That weekend it was "long Saturday." He and his wife went to Hertie to buy his adolescent daughter stiff, rough bras reminiscent of gas masks left over from the war, and thick, vomit-colored sweaters. These were perhaps the worst things in the discount store. Roxy wept when she put them on, but she knew that there were worse things. Because some of her girlfriends' fathers wanted them to cover their heads. At least her father didn't have rules like that, at least for the moment.

She could end up like the two twin sisters who couldn't stand the pressure being put on them, and attempted suicide, and failed, and remained suspended between life and death.

But amid all this distress and humiliation and sadness there was a surprise waiting for her. The German boys at school were crazy about Roxy. She knew this from the way they looked at her. She met their glances when she walked down the street with her friends, and when she bought soft Italian ice cream from the *Eiscafé* on the corner by the school. There was a fear deep within. Later she got used to it and felt more at ease. She examined her reflection in the dark glass of the stores. She had a thin, small body and black hair down to her shoulders... Roxy didn't quite understand what it was about her that they liked. Because the German girls who walked down the avenues were tall and blond; they had clear skin and cheeks like peaches. Her lips weren't as red as theirs. She couldn't compete with those girls, she wouldn't think of it, but apparently she had something that attracted the German boys. She didn't know quite what it was, but she could feel it.

It didn't take long for her to understand. Joachim, who she'd liked at first, but who she'd run away from when he kissed her and who she'd avoided ever since, was replaced by a German boy with curly, red hair who attached himself to her. He was sharp; he wouldn't tell Roxy that he liked her. But he said such nice things to her and gave her such loving and desperate looks that, without thinking about it, without really making a decision, Roxy started going out with him. They met secretly to hug and kiss, and he would say sweet things to her. "*Mein schatz, meine hübsche* Roxy, my beautiful darling."

Then, unavoidably, they were kissing in Mauritz's room at home and started moving toward the bed. But by that time Roxy had long since made up her mind. She wanted to be free of her virginity as soon as possible. Her virginity seemed to symbolize everything that suffocated her and tied her down.

She didn't really understand what was happening. She only saw Mauritz's excitement and his convulsions. She doesn't feel a thing. The greatest change of her life lasted only a minute or two, and when Roxy went home that evening she didn't feel guilty, just a little disappointed. She smelled Mauritz's sour smell on her skin. And felt a bit worn out. "*Ich bin verrückt!* I'm crazy," she repeated to herself, "I'm crazy." As if she derived strength from saying this.

She met Mauritz a few more times, but she didn't feel anything at all for him. Neither excitement nor titillation nor warmth. Meanwhile Joachim was going out with one of the big girls in the class. Roxy saw them kissing a few times, but she didn't feel a thing. She didn't understand anything about this exalted thing they called love. She thought that there was something missing in her, that it was because she was crazy that she couldn't feel love, but when she looked at the girls and boys around her she decided that they were the same. They kissed each other, they slept together, they exchanged bodily fluids, but none of them were on fire for each other. Anyway, they changed partners quite often. A girl slept with a boy for a week, then the next week went up to her former lover with her arm around another boy's waist. They laughed. Is this love? thought Roxy. This must have been it because she didn't see anything else... That meant the people who talked so much about love were lying.

A while later her relationship with Mauritz came to an end of its own accord, without talking, without even mentioning the possibility of breaking up. They met less and less often, and then suddenly Mauritz was just another one of her school friends. It was as if nothing had ever happened between them. Everything was so ordinary, so normal! Boringly natural.

Her family and other animals had no idea what was going on. She was just tired of Ute's hateful looks, and the way she seemed almost jealous of her. She was always putting the girl down to her father. Everything she did was wrong. The man shouted at her every evening, and swore, and threatened. Roxy couldn't stand it and thought: I'd like to burn this house down so you all die; but she wasn't quite crazy enough to do that.

Instead she did another crazy thing. One day she played hooky from school with Naciye, who was two years older than her and was a distant cousin. When she was fourteen Naciye was married to a boy who had been brought from their village, and had stayed with him for a year, and then, for whatever reason, got divorced. The boy went back to the village. Roxy didn't know the details but knew that later they'd sent her to school to get a grant from the government.

Naciye was showing her the tram line that passed near the school, "We just hop on, and we'll be in Düsseldorf in five or ten minutes." She was talking about Königsalle, the famous boulevard, and the fashionable stores, and women who looked as if they'd stepped out of the pages of a magazine. Roxy said, "I'm crazy anyway, let's go."

They got on the tram and Naciye bought the tickets. Naciye also bought the ice cream they ate later in a cafe by the river. A lovely place, shaded by white umbrellas. The waiters were all young and handsome German boys, thin, with bangs hanging in front of their eyes. Women in tailored suits and wide-brimmed hats sat at the tables. Next to them were little white dogs and bags from nearby luxury shops. It was clear they knew the waiters well because they spent a lot of time chatting. These elegant women exchanged jokes with the waiters who came to take their orders. They exchanged a few words.

Roxy was surprised to see that Naciye had money, that she was taking wads of money out of her pocket. She asked how she got so much money because she was in desperate need of money. Naciye laughed, and didn't say anything for a while; then she said she had something to show her and got up from the table. They walked together. Naciye was taller and fuller than Roxy. She brought Roxy to the front of a shop. It was one of those shops with pictures of naked women and sex toys and things in the window. There were red neon XXX's blinking on and off. Even if she'd never been to one of these shops she'd known about them since she was a child, but she didn't understand why Naciye had brought her there. "What are we doing here?" she asked. With a knowing air Naciye said, "Come, let's go inside." They entered a dimly lit shop that had never seen sunlight and smelled of plastic. There were several men in front of the counter, and there were films on the screens. Again Roxy asked, "What are we doing here?" Naciye said, "This is where I make my money. If you tell anyone I'll kill you. No one knows about it, but I come here two afternoons a week; you're the only person I've confided in, and if you tell anyone I swear I'll kill you."

Roxy, completely astounded, asked, "Do you mean you're working as a whore here?"

"No, no," insisted Naciye. "I'm not working as a whore. I don't touch any men. I just go behind a window, and strip, and touch myself here and there, and they give me a lot of money. There are men watching but I don't even see them. What's wrong with that?"

"Let's get out of here," said Roxy. "It smells disgusting."

Naciye said, "I can't go, in a little while I have to go in behind the window and strip. Ten minutes later I'll come out, wait a while, then do the same thing once or twice more. Two hours altogether. If you don't want to stay here, wait for me outside, at the cafe we saw on the way here for instance. I'll come and get you later and we can go back together." Just then a male voice began making an announcement, "Come watch the exotic Turkish Ayşe." A few men started making their way toward the back.

Roxy left and went to the cafe by the riverbank, this time sitting in the shade of a wonderful chestnut tree rather than under the white umbrellas. A different waiter came up to her, and she asked for water. A little later there was a bottle of Apollinaris in front of her. As she drank the ice-cold water she thought of Naciye, trying to picture what she was doing at that moment, wondering just how much she exposed herself. Did she show *that* too?

If Naciye's family knew about this they'd kill her; but she was a brave girl, considering what she was doing. It wasn't easy stripping in front of men in Düsseldorf. She wondered why Naciye had brought her to Düsseldorf, whether it was because she couldn't bear keeping this secret alone and needed a confidante, or whether it was because she wanted to drag her into this work too. To tell the truth, this had occurred to her. Perhaps the owners had said, bring some Turkish girls like yourself and we'll give you money. Why not? German men want to see these covered, religious Turkish girls expose themselves.

Then she decided she definitely wouldn't do this kind of work. I may be crazy, but I won't do that, she said to herself.

Two hours later Naciye came along all happy and smiling. "There's nothing to it, I just got undressed as if I was going to take a bath, what did I lose? No one touched me, and I didn't touch anyone. I didn't even see their faces. I just undressed by myself, as if I was going to take a bath. What did I lose?"

Roxy said, "Yes, what did you lose? You undress as if you're going to take a bath and you get a lot of money."

They were getting on the tram and going back to Duisburg. That night in bed Roxy thought about Naciye and wondered if she might be right. What did she lose? With Mauritz she lost something, but no one even touched Naciye. Later she thought: I'll never do anything like that, but if I did, would they like me, would they want me? Naciye had big breasts and full buttocks. I don't have anything like that. Small breasts and slim hips, even a little boyish. I wonder if they'd like me, if they'd pay to see me strip.

The next day she and Naciye went to school together, and talked about this and that, and didn't even mention Düsseldorf, but the day after that Naciye wasn't at school again. In class Roxy thought about her: Is she stripping right now? Is she showing everything? As if she were taking a bath.

Roxy had nothing to do when she wasn't at school. She wandered the streets and sat in the park. She didn't have a boyfriend. She didn't really have any friends except Naciye. And after the Düsseldorf adventure they didn't see each other quite as often as they used to. That's why she was always alone. Loneliness was getting her down. She didn't want to go home because the house was poisonous. She didn't have enough money to go to the movies. The little bit of money her father begrudged her wasn't enough for anything. That's why she wandered the streets penniless.

At night in bed she thought about Naciye. How much money did she make? Enough to put some aside? Where did she hide her money? After a while someone would notice she wasn't in school two days a week, then what would she do? Her older brothers would beat her until her bones broke.

The house was still like hell. Ute wanted her to come home early and look after her younger siblings. Three little children, busy making a mess of the house. Two of them were her siblings, and one was Ute's child. She didn't have the strength to go home; she couldn't stand to breathe that poisonous air. She walked until her feet began to swell. Taking care not to step in dog shit, she wandered the deserted avenues, passing streets she'd passed a hundred times, looking into shop windows she'd looked into a hundred times.

One day she sat on a park bench and thought about committing suicide. She couldn't think of a good way to kill herself. Indeed even when she thought about suicide she knew she wouldn't; she couldn't, she couldn't, it wasn't possible. But it helped her to think as if she was going to commit suicide, to think about the details.

There were the millions of other people living on earth, and then there was Rukiye. Everyone was right, and she was wrong. Everyone was intelligent, she was stupid. That's why she always lost. No one suffered the way she did, which meant that there must be something wrong with her.

Around Rukiye's lips there were lines of unhappiness you wouldn't expect in someone so young. Her face forgot to smile. She was always blaming herself, putting herself down, thinking she was the only person in the world who was worthless.

It was toward the end of this period of self-denigration that she asked Naciye to bring her to that place. Her sense of self-worth was so low that it didn't matter to her whether anyone saw her naked!

It isn't easy to get to this point; not thinking about what you have to do first, but just dreaming about the things you can do with the money. Money meant escape, it meant being able to get out of that house. She didn't give a thought to what she had to do. She wasn't going to do it anyway, so what was wrong with fantasizing about it? It's like planning suicide, something you'll never go through with, but which it helps to think about. But in time she got used to the idea. Naciye is right, she thought. What do I lose by showing myself?

In fact a lot of Turkish girls did this kind of work, and some of them did even worse. The evening newspapers were full of little ads by Turkish girls looking for customers. There were girls who were in porno films. They were always talking about that in school; the boys loved these films. Roxy had never been to one of those evenings, but they said that sometimes girls and boys watched porno films together and laughed.

Roxy would have liked a Walkman, and perhaps one of those disc players that were becoming so popular at school. Then she wouldn't be so bored, she could listen to music as she walked; she could sit in the park for hours listening to Eminem and Usher.

English, German, Turkish—whatever language it was in, hip-hop music set Roxy's blood racing. She identified with the rebellious lyrics and the defiant manner. But whenever she watched this on television at home, the channel was changed to some Turkish series or some wailing singer. Ute watched German programs during the day. In the evening no one could get the remote control out of her father's hands.

Roxy went to the music shops and listened for hours on headphones: Eminem and Usher were her favorites. She liked all the Turkish groups.

One day, she discovered that she could write hip-hop songs too. Without having made any decision, without having planned it at all, the lyrics for a song came to her:

If the world would suddenly stop
And start to move backward
If animals became people
And people became animals
If the rich were poor
And the poor rich
If mice killed cats
And sheep killed wolves
If we dealt the cards again
If the world was turned upside down
If we chewed beneath our feet
These louts they call fathers
Then I'll laugh

Then I'll laugh again
At you, the shitty world.

She realized that she could sing these lyrics in both German and in Turkish. She sang them above the drumbeat she could hear in her head. The association was so strong that she could rap for hours without preparing beforehand or writing down any words. The words flowed like a river. She moved her hands the way rappers on television do.

The day she discovered this she felt more refreshed than she had for years. Now she definitely needed to buy some hip-hop discs and a disc player.

Indeed this is how she spent the first money she earned from the sex shop. She went straight to an electronic goods shop in Düsseldorf and bought a Sony disc player. She liked touching its shiny gray surface. It made her so happy that she forgot what she'd lived through in that sleazy sex shop.

In fact everything was exactly as Naciye had described it. She went through a door and lifted a red velvet curtain; then she lay on a revolving bed and started taking off her clothes. As if she was by herself. Indeed it was so dark in there that she doubted if anyone could see anything by the dim red light. The bed beneath her rotated and made her private parts visible to the customers watching on the other side of the glass. There was even something almost funny about it. To tell the truth it was hard to believe that men would pay money to go and look between Roxy's legs in that dim light. Why would anyone want to do that?

It didn't make any sense. Naciye didn't understand this either, but it must mean that this is just the way men are.

When she returned to Duisburg Roxy felt satisfied that at least she'd taken a step. When she got home she had to find a way to hide the disc player and the money. Perhaps she could say she had borrowed it from a friend. That night she dreamt she was behind the glass again, singing hip-hop in the nude. She was keeping time by slapping her naked legs.

Within a couple of weeks she was making good money because the men who came to the sex shop liked the girl who called herself "Tamara" and couldn't get enough of her. "*Die exotische Schönheit, die blutjunge Tamara aus der Türkei!* The exotic beauty, the young virgin from Turkey!" These announcements could be heard in the sex shop. She cut school two days a week and went to Düsseldorf to lie naked on the revolving bed.

On one of these trips she saw a poster. On Sunday there would be a hip-hop festival in a place called Grugahalle in the city of Essen. A number of German groups were going to appear. As Roxy looked down the long list, she encountered the name of a Turkish group. She was excited. Essen was nearby like Düsseldorf. Now that she had the money to do it, she was definitely going to go. And she went.

Grugahalle was a huge concert hall where thousands of people stood on their feet drinking beer and listening to music. She wandered through the crowds, drank beer from a plastic cup, and even had a bratwurst with lots of ketchup. The sound of the drums was deafeningly loud.

Everyone was swaying to the beat. She started to sway as well. She loved this. One group after another came to the stage and shook the world with their rebellious lyrics.

As she wandered around she heard people speaking in Turkish. Three scrawny boys were drinking beer and shouting to be heard over the deafening music. She went and said hello to them. She asked them if they knew the Turkish group that was going to appear. They laughed and said, "Yes." They were the group. They'd come from Cologne. Roxy was pleased and told them that she was interested in singing hip-hop too. As an amateur, of course, she didn't neglect to say. The boys were happy to hear this. In the evening, when their turn came, they went up on stage. Roxy didn't like them too much because they sounded soft and weak after the hard, stormy sound of the German groups. They didn't get the crowd moving. And the singer didn't have a clear voice. They were even weaker when they switched from Turkish to German; his German wasn't that good, and you couldn't understand the lyrics. The audience lost interest, and people started talking among themselves. A little later a man walked out onto the stage and said something into the singer's ear. The boy nodded his head, and they finished the piece and left the stage to tepid applause.

After they'd packed up their instruments they didn't seem happy. Roxy told them they were good, but this didn't appease them. That evening in the pizza garden they explained that they didn't really have a singer, they played instruments but none of them could really sing. One played drums, one played keyboard, and the other played bass. As they parted that night they promised to meet in Cologne. They were going to have a practice session there next Sunday. This interesting rebellious girl, whose German and whose knowledge of rap they admired, was going to join them. They had to share the table, and she talked so fluently to those drunken Germans. Her accent was perfect. She ordered the pizza and the beer too.

That week Roxy went two more times to lie on the revolving bed in Düsseldorf. As time passed she became more accustomed to this work, and her movements on the bed became more seductive. As she lay there naked, turning left and right, she was thinking about rap lyrics. She got so involved in one song that she didn't notice the time passing. She didn't forget these lyrics afterward either.

In Cologne, the day they had agreed to meet, she sang "The World in Reverse" with the group when they practiced in the empty hall of a Turkish association. She gave the rhythm, told the drummer what to do, and started singing. As she sang they experimented with the keyboard and bass to best accompany her.

The boys were thrilled because Roxy sang wonderfully; "The World in Reverse" was a great song too. She sang with a strong, harpoon-like voice, moving as if she had been dancing hip-hop for forty years, stepping hard and using her fingers. She even had that defiant expression; it was unbelievable. That day they decided to work together. Roxy was going to write a lot of songs, in German and in Turkish. But they had to find a good name for the group. The name the boys had picked, Kölün

Rangers, didn't work. Besides, no one knew that *Kölün* was the way some Turks pronounced Cologne, so no one understood.

And so Rukiye, who was known as Roxy at school and as Tamara at the sex shop in Düsseldorf, started her life in music as Roxy. The group became known as Roxy and Other Animals. They shortened it to ROA. The letters ROA embroidered in bright red on a green background. Later on they would sell T-shirts with this design at concerts. They could no longer rein in their fantasies.

For whatever reason, the boys found the name Roxy and Other Animals very amusing and weren't bothered by it at all.

8

The mountain people gathered up the things that had been piled in the garden and started to carry them to the houses they'd built toward the top of the hill. They were reminiscent of a colony of ants tirelessly carrying food back to their nest. One person carried an ornamental sink, another the head of a faucet, and another a prayer rug.

Broken appliances, night lamps, coffee pots, wooden bath slippers inlaid with mother-of-pearl, photographs of ancestors, photograph albums with copper corners, embroidered curtains, glittering plasterwork, marble basins, engraved banisters, book rests, and hundreds of other items were being carried in quiet haste up the hill.

They didn't know quite what they were going to do with these things, but it seemed a good idea to bring them home. This was the furniture from the mansion in which they'd been servants for so many years; could it be a bad thing?

In the old days the pasha had been a benefactor to the neighborhood; the disasters that befell this unlucky family had affected them too. Salih, who bought the mansion, was a gentleman, but he wasn't a nobleman like the pasha. He was a businessman. He was just a little man, but he had shops on Yüksek Kaldirim and warehouses in Sirkeci. He was the first Muslim to open a shop on Yüksek Kaldirim, which had previously been controlled by Greeks, Jews, and Levantines. There were two other Turkish shop owners on that street besides himself. Kelkitli İrfani Bey and Erzurumlu Fevzi Bey. But as the years passed there were fewer non-Muslims on the street, and it quickly became more Turkish.

While Salih was a good man, he lacked personality, and so did his wife and children. The family was from Bitlis and treated the mountain people well. They were very respectful to Leyla, the last of the pasha's family, who lived in the little house in the garden, and invited her to dinner, and sent their children to kiss her hand on holiday mornings. The mountain people got used to the new family quite easily; they were self-effacing people who never caused problems for their workers. But after Salih died of a heart attack, the family put the mansion up for sale, and this is how Ömer came into the picture.

The first thing the young couple did was to evict the Great Lady, and the second was to strip the mansion bare in a couple of days. The things they thought valuable remained in the house, and the things they thought worthless were thrown out.

For the first few days the mountain people complained about these uncordial new owners, but one gets used to things. It was clear that they were very rich; they were going to have huge parties in the garden, they were going to buy meat from the butcher and vegetables from the greengrocer. Perhaps some of the young people of the neighborhood would be hired as drivers or as waiters.

They felt for the Great Lady and were very upset about her being evicted from her own house, but it was clear that there was a new order around here.

Indeed things changed drastically the moment they heard that they were being given the antiques. The new owners had now established order.

The grocer's wife Cemile got two faucets, an old panel with writing on it, and a dusty old photograph album. The faucets would be installed in her house, and the panel would be hung on the living room wall. Perhaps the writing on the panel was a prayer that would bring blessings to the house.

Doing things that rich people did always brought good results.

The panel Cemile had brought home to hang on the wall read *This too shall pass*. Cemile didn't know this—it was written in the old Arabic script—and thought it was a verse from the Quran intended to bring work to the unemployed, husbands to unmarried girls, and healing to the sick. Eighty years ago everyone in Istanbul would have known that phrase. Because during the years Istanbul was occupied, panels with this phrase were hung everywhere. When the people of Istanbul saw this panel hung in public places, they would grit their teeth and look forward to the day of liberation. It became a secret symbol of resistance. The English officers saw this panel everywhere, but because they were in a Muslim country, they didn't want to interfere with religious beliefs and didn't even wonder what it meant. The panel Cemile had hung on a nail on the pink wall of her living room had once been seen on the mansion wall by English officers who didn't do anything about it.

Among the visitors to the mansion by members of the occupation forces was the famous Captain Bennett. There was another English officer there—Lieutenant Robert Whitaker—who was to play a very important role in the fate of both the mansion and of Bosnalı Abdullah Avni Pasha's family. When Cemile was going through the photograph album she'd picked up in the garden she found a picture of this tall, thin-faced officer. This picture interested Cemile a great deal because the English officer in the picture was seen with the pasha's family. In another picture, there was a young girl standing next to him who was clearly Turkish.

But what interested Cemile the most was how much the Great Lady resembled the officer in the picture. Their faces were shaped the same, they had the same nose and the same eyes, and the same erect and self-assured posture.

After dinner, Cemile, who had only moved to the neighborhood after she married, showed her husband the photograph and asked him who the officer was.

Hasan the grocer didn't know these people himself, but as far as he'd heard from older people, this English officer must be the Great Lady's father. He didn't know whether it was true or false, but there were rumors to that effect. He took the picture and looked at it carefully. The Great Lady did indeed bear a great resemblance to the officer.

Cemile was very confused by this, and asked, "Do you mean the Great Lady's father was English?"

"That's what they used to say," said her husband. "It used to be said that during the occupation an English officer seduced the pasha's daughter, and that Leyla was the result of this union. Indeed there were those who said that this was why the pasha declined the way he did, and couldn't pull himself together, and left the world. I don't know whether it's true or false, but there are those who believe that the Great Lady's father is that English officer."

He looked even more closely at the picture. The young girl next to the English officer must be the pasha's daughter who died in childbirth; she was the Great Lady's unlucky mother.

Hasan had heard this story since he was a child, but it didn't really mean anything to him until he saw the picture. Like everyone else who had played in the garden as a child and who had received gifts from her, he was very fond of the Great Lady. But now, for the first time, he wondered what religion the Great Lady belonged to. If her father was English, did that mean she was Christian? Had she taken her father's religion or her mother's religion? But how could the pasha's granddaughter be Christian!

At this point his eyes wandered to the pink wall and the carpet with the deer hunting scene on it, then he saw the panel that read *This too shall pass*. "What's this?" he asked his wife.

Cemile said, "It's a prayer. Perhaps it will bring blessings to our house."

Hasan had hung a prayer in his shop to bring blessings, but he'd never seen one like this. He looked carefully at the panel with its yellowing edges and its old frame. "Perhaps it's valuable. Perhaps we should sell it to an antique dealer."

The woman was against this idea. "If we keep it hanging here in the house it will bring in a lot more money. It stayed in that pasha's house all those years; let it bring us some benefit for a while."

"It's not quite like that," said Hasan. "Look at how there's no one left alive in the pasha's family, and in the end they threw out the Great Lady. Whatever this is, it didn't bring them much good luck."

Cemile thought about this for a while. She didn't know how she was going to find an excuse to redeem this panel.

Later she said, "It was the English officer who brought them bad luck. If you bring a foreign officer into the pasha's family, it's not the prayer's fault."

Hasan said, "That's true." He decided to give the prayer a chance.

When Cemile came from Kastamonu as a bride, she was very taken by the beauty of the Bosphorus and thought herself in an enchanted place. She was still very young, not much more than a child. As time passed and she became accustomed, she wanted a place in this world for herself and her children and wanted to drive along the Bosphorus in a nice car.

When she came from her village to the big city, she didn't have much interest in religion. Like other village girls, she lived her life without giving this too much thought. Islam was a part of life: like funeral prayers, the elderly going to the mosque, everyone meeting for holiday prayers, and distributing candies on holidays. The way she was raised, there wasn't much difference between cooking *tarhana* soup and reciting a prayer. They were both things that had been done since the dawn of time, and that she had been taught to do.

But after she came to Istanbul there was Sister Hoceste, who enlightened all the neighborhood women about religious matters, showed them they were all on the wrong road, and got after all of them to come with her to the Naqshbandi Sheik in Beykoz. This devout woman in her fifties taught them about religious devotion and practice; she informed them that being attached to a sheik and declaring allegiance to him could protect themselves, their marriages, and their children from all kinds of accidents and troubles.

One day she brought Cemile and the other women to the sheik's house in Beykoz so that they could see his blessed face. Since that day Cemile had thought more about her religion, and did her best to be a good Muslim, and not to stray from the sheik's dictates.

For this reason the picture in the album was like a slap in the face, and she felt herself almost cooling toward the polite Great Lady. Is the Great Lady an unbeliever? she kept thinking to herself, and she couldn't get over it. How could this beautiful, elegant, and compassionate woman be an unbeliever? Was such a thing possible?

On the other hand, the picture showed everything. The Great Lady looked exactly like the English officer. The young officer couldn't have resembled the Great Lady any more if he was her son. But he wasn't her son, he was her father.

Her husband's nephew Yusuf said bad things about the sheik in Beykoz and warned the women of the neighborhood not to go to him, but after all, he was a journalist. Journalists were not to be trusted at all.

Hasan, and subsequently Cemile, were very proud that Yusuf was a journalist and to see his byline in the newspaper. It made Cemile very happy that Yusuf was doing such important work, but it seemed as if he had changed. After moving to the fleshpots of Beyoğlu he seldom visited his old neighborhood, and when he did he said strange things. Most of the things he talked about were against religion and the state.

Another of her husband's nephews, Hüseyin, was a source of greater pride for the family. Because two years earlier he had been elected to parliament and gone to Ankara. Throughout the election campaign, all the people from Kastamonu had worked for him, and the women had gone to Beykoz to distribute pamphlets from door to door. Because he was twelfth on the list of candidates, no one thought he had a chance of getting elected, but the party was more successful than anyone expected, and even candidates who had only been put on the list for form's sake ended up going to parliament.

Because Hüseyin was intelligent, he rose quickly in politics. In parliament, he'd become the something or other of some commission; Cemile couldn't keep the facts straight in her mind, but she knew that because of his position, Hüseyin went around in an official car with a driver. He'd become a big man, as was clear from the crowds that came out to greet him every time he came to visit the neighborhood.

She looked again at the prayer on the wall.

"Ha!" said Cemile, "So this means the Great Lady is an unbeliever."

She was impatient to share this secret that she was still shocked to have just learned. She fed her husband, covered her head, and rushed out to tell her friends.

Just two days earlier she had felt sorry for the Great Lady and had been insisting she come home with them, but now she was feeling increasingly cooler toward her. It's a good thing we didn't bring her home, she thought; she might have upset the order of the house.

She realized that she had never seen the Great Lady pray. Did she attend church secretly? If she had deceived them like that, then they shouldn't be angry with the new owners of the mansion for what they'd done. What could they do? They couldn't allow an unbeliever to live in their garden. And they seemed like such generous people.

9

The tension they'd experienced over Leyla did not prevent Yusuf and Roxy from making love that night, but as they entwined with each other in the bedroom they had to be careful not to make noise. Because they were not alone, and Leyla was in the next room, they had to stifle their cries and make sure the bed didn't creak or bang against the wall.

For Roxy, this in and of itself constituted torture.

"Let's just say it's uncomfortable," said Yusuf.

"What?"

"It's not torture, dear. That seems an extreme thing to say. It's just a temporary irritation."

"How temporary?"

"I don't know, but obviously we can't continue like this. We'll find a solution."

"I don't understand you at all Yusuf. What kind of obligation do you feel to this old woman that you have to bring her home?"

"It's not an obligation; you just don't know Leyla. I've never met as good or as interesting a person as her. She was so good to me when I was a child that I was almost closer to her than I was to my own grandmother."

"Please," said Roxy, "grandparents just make things too crowded."

"I know you can't stand extended families, but Leyla isn't like that at all. If you just made a little effort to get to know her..."

"What will happen, will I suddenly want to hug her?"

Yusuf started to laugh, and, saying, "There's no telling what you might do," embraced her naked body and started kissing her breasts.

Roxy believed there was a chemical bond between her and Yusuf. Because until now, no man's skin had appealed to her as much as his. For this reason she wanted to attach herself to that body like a suction cup every night. She forbade Yusuf to use shaving lotion because she loved the smell of his body. It was a smell that calmed and relaxed her and that, as time passed, she found she could not do without. She'd read an article in a German magazine about neurological memory. For instance the hand was able to remember skin it had stroked years earlier. And the body could also remember a hand. Her body had now become accustomed to Yusuf's body, and to embrace him naked had become a kind of calming therapy for her. In addition their sexual compatibility had another important aspect to it. That was the respect that Yusuf showed her and her body while they were making love. This was the first time this had happened, the first time she'd seen a man respect a woman's body. The German and Turkish men she'd slept with until now had treated her roughly, or had watched her, and had treated her almost as if she were an inflatable doll. Because now young men didn't learn about lovemaking in the traditional way, from experienced women, but from the porn films that you could find everywhere. Roxy had seen the same thing in Düsseldorf, and in the porn films her school friends had watched. Porn distorted the relationship between men and women and was a terribly cruel arena. These films, aimed at a male audience, treated the female body as worthless, something to be belittled and defiled, and brought it down to the level of a piece of meat at the service of men. This was a terrible violence. But young men thought this was normal and brought what they had seen in these porn films into their own beds. Roxy was not one to bow down to violence and humiliation. For this reason she became irritable in bed, and didn't do what men wanted, and tried to maintain her self-respect. Her body was not an experimental laboratory or a firing range. It was a human body.

From the first night, Yusuf approached her with great respect. What could be called an old-style intimacy, whispers of love, soft caresses, and above all respect, respect, respect. As a woman she felt sublimated both before and after making love.

All this bound her to Yusuf with a deep love and caused her to feel a kind of admiration for him. Because he was different from any of the men she'd ever met. At first she thought he was putting it on and thought: no way, nobody could be that nice. But later she was surprised to see that he really was nice, a nicer person than could possibly be real.

The harsh and intractably rebellious side of her nature stayed with her, and by day she continued to give Yusuf a hard time, but at night she turned into a calm and compliant girl.

That night, after they made love silently, she asked Yusuf, "Does this woman have a husband?"

"No!"

"Did he die?"

"No, she never had a husband."

Roxy asked for confirmation.

"You mean this woman never married?"

"No, she never married. She never had a boyfriend, and indeed you could say she never even had a girlfriend either. She has no family either. She's lived alone since she was a young girl. No mother, no father, no relatives, no husband, no child. She's all alone in the world."

Then Roxy began to feel a deep interest in this woman. What did it mean to not be dependent on anyone, to not carry the weight of a family, to defy the world? Hadn't she thought this very thing in Duisburg at the end of every bad relationship and whenever she rushed out into the streets to escape the hell at home? Since people inevitably caused each other pain, the best thing was to defy life and chose complete loneliness. Human relationships were inadequate and lacking. There must be something about this that everyone but Roxy knew. She didn't have many complaints about loneliness. When she was alone at home or in the street she felt good, but it seemed that to do anything you had to be dependent on other people. Being a good hip-hop singer meant managers, concerts, tours, musicians, record companies, and a group that you lived with constantly. This part of it was very difficult for Roxy. Thankfully the boys in the group were quiet and calm and comfortable with themselves and didn't bother Roxy at all.

Meanwhile, arriving in Istanbul with such high hopes only to be met with denigration and to be stamped as *Almancı*, a Turk from Germany, turned out to be even harder than her life in Germany.

Yusuf was the only evidence she had that there were good people in this cold, alienating world.

10

After Ömer had said goodbye to his father at the mansion gate, his feeling of being suffocated grew stronger, as if an invisible hand was squeezing him by the throat. As always, the man hadn't taken a car and had insisted on going to the bus stop. Because Ali Yekta believed that great men must be "men of principal," and that they must have their own individual particularities. For instance, the famous journalist Lastik Sait, who was the lead writer for the *Vakit* newspaper, wore rubber boots winter and summer, and therefore had earned the nickname "Lastik," and Meserret was famous for the alarm clock he put on the table in the coffee house every day when he was writing his daily column. He lived like this until Abdülhamit exiled him to Sana Castle in Yemen for writing a poem in praise of Sultan Reşat's horses. The angst-ridden sultan couldn't stand even Sultan Reşat's horses, but of course this is another story.

Yahya Kemal lived for years at the Park Hotel, Abdülhak Hamit never took off the clothes that in those times were called "bonjour," Sakalli Celal insisted on going around with his chest exposed, Refi Cevat insisted on riding a donkey, and Neyzen Tevfik was never without his cane.

The great men for whom Ali Yekta had been servant had all had their habits. They drank their coffee at a certain hour, they did certain things on certain days of the week, and they clung to these habits even when those around them began to think them eccentric. For this reason Ali Yekta also had two habits that he clung to: one was the revolver he always kept tucked in his waist, and which he cleaned every week, and the other was that he went everywhere by bus.

The revolver was a keepsake from his father and represented the traditions to which he was bound. As for the city buses, that was another matter altogether. Even though Ali Yekta's son, Ömer, was a big businessman who owned a bank and a holding company, and had a fleet of Mercedes at his disposal, he saw his habit of going everywhere by bus as a sign of nobility and decisiveness.

He imagined he could hear what was being said behind his back.

"That's the way Ali Yekta is; he goes everywhere by bus."

"If you see a gray-haired gentleman on a city bus, you can be sure it's Ali Yekta."

"He wouldn't ride in a private car if his life depended on it."

So, despite his son's insistence, he waited at the bus stop with perfect seriousness and climbed onto the red city bus in clothes that would inspire respect.

Ömer could see that things were coming to a head. His father was preparing to realize his lifelong dream and thought that the pasha's room on the upper floor had been reserved for him, but his wife wasn't willing to even talk about such a possibility. She wouldn't even countenance the idea of his moving into the mansion at all, let alone his living in the pasha's room. "He's a butler," she would say. "He's a butler, what else could he be? Are you going to share this mansion with a butler?"

Ömer objected to this, and tried to defend his father, but his words weren't even heard over the woman's irritable shouting.

Ömer who was famous in his working life for his pitilessness, his agile mind, and his lack of moral scruples, was defenseless against this woman. When they argued, he always tried to be gentle with her.

Ömer stood by the mansion gate, watching sadly as the bus moved away. "Ah, father," he said with a sigh, "I just don't understand why you're doing these things."

To be rich, to live a better life, to be respected in society: these were all nice things, everyone wants to have these things, but with one caution, this is a passion that is particularly for the young. There was something unhealthy and wrong for an elderly man to have such social ambitions. In the old days, his father himself would have criticized such ambition in someone of his age.

Throughout his childhood, Ömer had been frightened of Ali Yekta. He'd been instilled with a fear of the man's passion and his authoritarian manner.

Everyone could see how passionately he wanted to raise his son well, but no one said anything. Indeed the owners of the Kadizade Mansion could never have imagined the extent of his ambition.

One day when they'd all gone to Büyükada as a family, he sat the thirteen-year-old Ömer at the table, in the master's chair, and served him food.

This meal was one of the unforgettable nightmares of Ömer's life. It was like a pitiless ritual.

That day, Ali Yekta made Ömer wear the dark, double-breasted suit he'd had made for him at the tailor Sitki's shop in Beyoğlu. He'd been cautioned to wear his gray tie and to comb his hair nicely. He himself wore the elegant uniform he wore when guests came.

A thirteen-year-old boy in a suit sat at the head of an antique table that sits twelve, while his aging father served him respectfully. When his father stood behind him to his left with the serving plate, he became so uncomfortable that he turned his head to look. When he did this, Ali Yekta shouted at the child, "What did I say to you? I told you: You never look at the waiter. Let him wait. If you're talking, you won't stop. The more you make him wait the better. Don't turn around and look. Never look! Act as if he's not there."

Then the child turned red, and stared ahead, and made his father wait. It wasn't easy to ignore the commanding and frightening man he felt breathing down his neck, and Ömer couldn't do it, and sat there with his shoulders hunched in fear, as if he were waiting for a slap on the back of his neck.

Later his father poured him water from a crystal pitcher and then moved across from him to watch him eat. These were some of the worst hours of Ömer's life.

After dinner, the competent butler brought his son to the room where the gentlemen drank coffee and smoked cigarettes, and showed him how to cut a Cohiba cigar, and which glasses were used for brandy, though fortunately he didn't want him to try these things.

Ömer had to know everything there was to know about the rich. And with time he became more and more like them. He always wore clothes made from English cloth, he flew first class whenever he went abroad, he knew which champagne was good and how to judge the quality of caviar, and slowly he turned into a strange creature.

Ali Yekta neglected nothing in making sure his son received an education fit for a prince, except for one single point.

The boy didn't know anything about his sexuality. The conservative Ali Yekta could not have prepared his son for this, and indeed father and son never even mentioned this subject.

For this reason, Ömer Cevheroğlu's relationships with women were the weak point in an otherwise well-fortified castle. Because of his strange upbringing, he wasn't able to behave normally, and he was unable to form natural relationships with girls the way his school friends were.

Ömer's youth passed without his so much as touching a girl. He was too haughty and strange to form a relationship with any of the girls in his circle, and too honorable to go to the brothels the way some of his friends did. He had relations neither with prostitutes nor with other women.

He had to be content with the strip clubs he went to when he was a student in America.

When he started his first finance company in Istanbul and stated his rise, he didn't know what to say or how to behave to the women who worked for him. He didn't know what degree of closeness to establish, or where to stand, or whether to address them formally or informally.

Necla, who discovered this weakness and, one evening when they were working late, planted her lips on him and gave him the gift of his first kiss, turned Ömer's life upside down and pushed him into a deep passion from which he would never be free. Two weeks later, during another late-night working session, this beautiful woman from the personnel department took Ömer's virginity, and gave him her own, on the Chesterfield sofa in the newly furnished office. From that moment on Ömer began to live the intoxication of a happiness he had never tasted. He didn't see Necla as a woman, but as a superhuman being, as something like a miracle. He was prepared to do anything for or give anything to this woman who had introduced him to the hitherto unknown delights of the world of sex. He felt as if he would be indebted to her for the rest of his life.

After they married the passion didn't diminish, and indeed grew stronger. For Ömer there was only one woman in the world; the name of this woman who embodied every feminine quality was Necla.

He couldn't get enough of making love to her and felt each time as if he were being brought to the very gates of paradise. In his working life he was everyone's boss, but in this paradise he was a willing slave and took great pleasure in being this way.

Naturally Ali Yekta opposed their marriage, saying this civil servant's daughter was not suitable, and insisted he marry one of the daughters of the mansion owners. This was the most certain route to gain possession of this mansion that was a symbol of the wealth, power, elegance, and nobility of the Bosphorus. This marriage would solve everything and would make Ömer a mansion owner in an instant. But his son was blinded to reality. For the first time, a will stronger than his father's was pulling him toward Necla. His father was now of secondary importance. He tried not to hurt the old man's feelings, and even tried to fulfill his wishes from time to time, but when, in the dimness of the elegant bedroom, Necla said, "My man!" he forgot all about his father and the rest of the world.

Necla, who was aware of this power, first began to put Ali Yekta down to Ömer in small ways, and then later spoke against him more openly. Istanbul's most attractive, successful, and wealthy couple were not going to bow down before a butler. Necla saw that he couldn't stand up to his father, so she made it her business to make sure he was strong enough to do so. A little later she began to prevent them from seeing each other and wanted to erase forever the stamp of "servant's dynasty" that hung over Ömer like a stain.

With his cunning mercilessness, his financial education in the world's best schools, and his knowledge of the system's weak points, Ömer Cevheroğlu had a style that no one in Istanbul was accustomed to, and on the one hand by maintaining good relations with the government and on the other by using his business connections, he soon became the owner of a bank and a holding company. He made money in his sleep; and it was a lot of money.

Necla could not countenance losing this empire on account of an ambitious old man.

It would take time to realize this goal. Because Ömer had been under his father's influence since he was a child. He hadn't been able to grow out from under this influence and still felt he was in his father's debt. Perhaps he was even afraid. He was incapable of standing up to his father. But recently his objections were becoming weaker, and he didn't react as much to Necla's harsh words about his father. Necla took care to bring this subject up in bed, after they'd made love.

She'd gone as far as to have a wide bed put in the room Ali Yekta wanted so that they could rest from time to time. Once everyone had gone, she lay on the salty sheets and drove her man crazy by wrapping her thin legs around him. Already she had turned that room into a temple of lovemaking.

Ömer had long been willing to lose his mind for this hormonal harmony that occurs so seldom in this world. He had so little experience with these hormones and was easily enthralled by them. There was something in his wife's smell, her skin, her voice, and her sweat that drove him crazy. These, together with the cool breezes, dampness, and intoxicating smells of the Bosphorus, made for a completely different synthesis. The cries on reaching orgasm mingled with the foghorns of passing freighters, and the cedar posts, walnut furniture, and mahogany closets all trembled.

Necla called it "our sin room." "Isn't that so, my love? It's our sin room. Have you ever in your life had as much pleasure as you've had here? Because I haven't. There are things that draw us here, things that belong to us. Let's make love in this room every night, my darling, my powerful man, and when we wake in the morning we'll make love again."

At moments like these, Ömer Cevheroğlu felt himself to be endlessly powerful, powerful enough to do whatever he wanted in the world.

Necla wasn't someone to be content with simply being happy. Rather, her nature only allowed her to recognize her own happiness when she saw the unhappiness of others. This was the measure of life. That others around her be beneath her, and fear her, and be oppressed by her. It was only at such moments that she could feel happiness deep within her, and apart from that, neither nature nor family nor friendship gave her any peace. She saw all of these as weaknesses.

She had discovered that when she raised her voice, other people cowered. As long as people around her saw her as a problem there was no trouble, because they were gentle with her, and tried not to make her angry, and did everything they could to solve the "problem." These small people's sense of shame was the source of the panic they felt when confronted by the powerful. When Necla became irritable and shouted at people who did not respond in kind, they cowered even more, and became even more embarrassed, as if they were responsible for the situation. Even as she put them down, she demanded more of them. At times like these her little nose wrinkled, and a cruel look settled into her eyes, and she looked like an angry lynx.

Because she had planned and prepared so well for the restoration of the mansion, work was proceeding quickly, and the look of the house was changing every day as the imported materials were put in place. The bathrooms were being covered with Italian tiles that had been given antique designs and made to look old, rare English wallpaper was being put on the walls, and porcelain doorknobs bearing the designer's signature were being put on the doors. The architect wanted the high-quality walnut floorboards to stay in place.

Soon the mansion had changed so much that Necla convinced Ömer to stay at home and appreciate the fragrant, starry nights. They sat on the quay in front of the mansion, drinking whisky, listening to the sound of the waves, and taking in the smell of the sea that washed their feet. Later, Ömer would wrap the thin Necla in arms that had been developed by fencing and carry her to their room for a long night of pleasure.

However, these nights were invaded by a strange sense of worry and fear. Because the calm of the Bosphorus, when nothing was heard but the waves washing against the shore, was being broken by a hellish noise. On summer nights a terrible sound of music came from the clubs on the European shore—drums that made the heart leap, and that sounded as if they were being played in the garden. Some of these clubs, the violence of whose music increased steadily until four in the morning, were directly across from them. If this weren't enough, the party boats that sailed up and down the Bosphorus passed right in front of them. Some of them played disco music, some traditional music, and some arabesque. Hundreds of noisy boats passed in front of them, so close they could almost reach out and touch them, and as they enjoyed themselves the passengers stared at the inhabitants of the mansion. The air was so filled with the smell of anise from the huge amounts of *rakı* being drunk on these boats and in the restaurants that lined the shores of the Bosphorus that one could become drunk without drinking.

The crazy energy fueled by Istanbul's steadily increasing population had of course affected the Bosphorus as much as it had every other district of the city. Where once there had passed the occasional ship, and the oar-powered imperial caiques, hundreds of large ships now sailed down the Bosphorus every day. Huge freighters, oil tankers, and giant cruise ships competed with one another to make the dangerous passage through the currents of the Bosphorus. It was considered normal for these ships to crash into the mansions or to run aground once in a while.

Once, a large ship carrying animals to a zoo in Russia sank, and the poor animals drowned in the Bosphorus.

For days after this terrible accident, dead animals occasionally rose to the surface, giving the mansion owners an unpleasant time.

This situation became a scandal at a party at a waterfront mansion given by one of the wealthiest people of Istanbul. Because that evening, the owner of the mansion had gathered everyone of importance on the quay in front of the mansion. Ömer and Necla were there too. In a corner, an orchestra in evening dress was playing Viennese waltzes, and the well-heeled and elegantly dressed guests were sipping whisky and chatting. As smells of grilling meat drifted across the garden and guests began to line up at the buffet to sample the hundreds of delicious dishes from the Middle East, the Caucasus, and the Balkans, a woman's scream was heard, and everyone looked at the water. The swollen carcass of a giraffe was bumping against the quay. It seemed even bigger lying on its side. Its elegant neck was being washed this way and that by the current, and its head was hitting against the quay. A little later two tigers rose to the surface. The waves were rocking the swollen tigers like a cradle. The panic-stricken guests began to catch the smell from the tigers' wet red and brown fur. Later they saw a large bear rise to the surface of the water. Suddenly, the front of the mansion was strewn with dead animals. They bobbed on the waves and remained clustered together as if they were performing some kind of strange death scene for the circus. Guests fainted and vomited. No one felt like eating any more, and the party was soon over.

That summer the Bosphorus smelled of dead animals for days. Some of these rare circus animals were carried by the currents as far as the Sea of Marmara.

But people soon forgot this disaster and continued to enjoy themselves on the Bosphorus, on boat trips, at mansion parties, at fish restaurants, and festivals that lasted until morning, under deafening fireworks that painted the sky red.

In spite of the noise, Necla and Ömer were delighted with the enchanting atmosphere of the Bosphorus, and, with the benevolence of couples in love, felt that no harm could come from people enjoying themselves. In any event, the American architect had installed strong, triple-paned windows that didn't let in any sound. It wasn't worth getting upset about.

Two night watchmen stayed in the little house at the back of the garden that had once belonged to Leyla. They, too, enjoyed the summer evenings, sitting on stools in front of the house, talking and drinking tea amidst the fragrance of the jasmine. They didn't hear the screams of passion from the mansion, but they did hear the cacophony of the Bosphorus, and from time to time they lifted their heads to watch the fireworks from some rich person's party. Then one of them would lie on Leyla's bed, and the other on the red sofa, and they would drift off into a deep sleep. The little house was no longer as clean and well looked after as it had once been. There was less furniture too; because the mountain people had been in there to take the Great Lady's cushions, the paintings on her walls, and her bed covers. They would never have done this if the Great Lady had been there, but as things were, none of it was doing her any good. It was better for them to use these things in their own homes than for them to just lie around.

The little house got more sunlight now than it used to because, in order to enlarge the house, Necla had cut down the giant magnolia tree whose branches had sheltered it. Everyone who saw it was saddened to see this beautiful tree, that Leyla's grandfather had planted in honor of her birth, cut down with power saws. Because they'd never seen a tree so healthy, dense, green, and full of life. When the great tree fell to the ground like a person, the air was filled with the smell of the sap that seeped from its trunk. It was as if the place where it had been cut was alive.

11

Evening fell in Cihangir. The dim lights in the apartment on the fifth floor were not sufficient to illuminate it and reminded Leyla of some strange ritual. In this strange house, the two lamps on the table had been covered with shawls so that they gave out less light. There were also three candles burning on top of a stand from which the varnish had been stripped.

While Leyla watched the young people, she thought about the Cihangir neighborhood's strange fate, and the poor, sick, fearful hunchbacked prince from which it had taken its name: Hürrem's youngest son, the apple of her eye, who she did everything in her power to make sultan. Everything she did to get the poor prince onto the throne backfired, and her struggles ended in great tragedy. Life was like that, and didn't proceed according to plan. If it did, it would surely have followed the plans of someone as intelligent and ambitious as Hürrem. It was a turning point for both Hürrem and for the Empire when she had Suleiman the Magnificent kill his oldest son, Mustafa. This was a tragedy Leyla had read about many times, and she was always moved by it. When he was strangled by seven mutes in a tent that had been covered with seven layers of leather to muffle the sound, he'd shouted, "Father, help me!" but Suleiman, who was sitting in a corner watching the execution, didn't lift a finger to help him. All of this had been done so that Cihangir could become sultan, but when he learned what had happened to his beloved stepbrother, he took to his bed in anguish and soon died in fear. It must have been terribly bitter to see this boy who had been raised to rule die this way just when he was on the point of reaching his goal.

Of course the young people who were playing music in this apartment in Cihangir didn't know about this. She didn't think they even had any idea what the name Cihangir meant.

Leyla watched them without quite letting on that she was doing so. Although she was only watching from the corner of her eye, she didn't miss a thing. Meeting these three young men after Roxy was quite an adventure for someone who had led as secluded a life as she had. She'd never seen anyone like them in her long life. Even though she hadn't met many people, there had always been people coming and going during her childhood, the German piano teacher, the people who worked in the mansion garden, the mountain people and their children, refugees from the Balkans and Anatolia, the family who bought the mansion later on, and so she'd seen many different kinds of people. But these young people were completely different. There was an indescribable aimlessness and indifference about their movements. Leyla would have called this "nonchalance." To be nonchalant was to seem indifferent to one's surroundings, to act as if one felt neither sadness nor delight, to not be able to carry on a real conversation, uttering random words, or simply making sounds . . . Leyla had never heard them talk in a manner that showed consistency or the ability to follow an idea through.

She noticed how they kept calling each other "old man." At first she thought this was a crude joke referring to her, but then she realized that for these young people it was a normal form of address.

"How's it going old man?"

"Not bad old man!"

"Can you toss me that pick old man?"

They also said "son" and "brother."

Everyone including Rukiye–Roxy was addressed as either old man or son or brother.

They used a lot of German words too; for instance they said stop, pronouncing the "s" as "sh."

Leyla observed all of this with a strange feeling, taking pleasure in discovering a side of life she hadn't known. She'd been through a great deal in the past few days, but she wasn't the kind of woman to let anything like this get her down. This was not how she was raised, and she had weathered many storms in her long life.

When they came in, the young men were very surprised to see an old woman sitting on the sofa, but after some whispering in the kitchen they managed to ignore her. Even when they each took a plate and started eating noisily, they managed not to look at her or to ask any questions.

The Great Lady could sense that Yusuf was terribly distressed by this. The boy was trying to combine worlds that were not at all compatible, and he was having no success.

The young men also looked so strange. Three of them were wearing skullcaps, and all of them wore trousers that seemed to have been deliberately ripped at the knees. Like Roxy, something seemed to be hanging from every part of them. The gnarled hair under their skullcaps reached their shoulders.

Leyla also found their accent in Turkish strange. They didn't stress their words properly, and it was as if they were speaking a completely different language. Leyla even had difficulty understanding what they were saying at times.

One of them started playing the electric keyboard in the corner, and from the first note he played, Leyla decided that he was not a good pianist. He didn't have the touch. He couldn't even get the simplest chords right. This meant he hadn't had a good education. As soon as she remembered Fräulein Anneliese, who had tortured her for hours at a time, she couldn't help but remember the exercises her bony fingers had done for thousands of hours on the keyboard, and without realizing it she found herself taking the proper position.

The fräulein, who always wore her hair in a tight bun, with never a single strand out of place, had been created to serve as an example to others, not just in art but in all aspects of life. Leyla thought that no one could wear a white shirt the way the fräulein did, and no one's starched collars had ever been so straight. Even after lessons that lasted for hours, Fräulein Anneliese's hair would look as if she had just stepped out of the hairdresser's. Her straight shoulders and transparent skin were of great help to her in this regard.

"*Ach, ich glaube, du bist mude heute mein Fräulein Leyla!* You're playing lifelessly. You're tired."

As soon as she heard the fräulein speak in this tone of rebuke, her fingers would grow heavy, and the Schumann lieder she was playing would start sounding like a funeral march.

As she clenched her fingers, Leyla felt she didn't belong in that house and was seized with shame. She tried to resist this feeling but then gave up. Because she suddenly felt very tired. Her head dropped forward, as if something had hit her. No one could help but look at the woman. Yusuf realized she was exhausted from all she'd been through and rushed to her side. He took her arm and led her slowly to the other room and to the bed.

Leyla was on the point of collapse. As he put her to bed, Yusuf noticed that she had a fever. The woman's aged body was no longer obeying her.

The Great Lady drifted feverishly off to sleep and into a nightmare. She thought she was in her bed at the mansion, but she didn't understand why the blanket was so heavy and stiff, and she heard music, but thought it must be coming from a passing ship. The music coming from the warships of the English occupation forces anchored in the Sea of Marmara reminded her of the song "Üsküdar."

The last image Leyla saw before she drifted into deep sleep was a black-eyed Turkish woman dancing with a tall English lieutenant on the deck of a warship to the music of an orchestra.

12

According to some, the most beautiful buildings on the Anatolian shore are the Kuleli Military Academy and the Selimiye Barracks. If it were not for the rats that fled one of the Egyptian ships anchored in front of this magnificent barracks, the story of Bosnalı Abdullah Avni Pasha's family would have developed very differently. It was just after the armistice. The people of Istanbul woke one foggy, rainy November morning to see English and French warships. The city was under occupation. This wasn't the first arrival of the English. The last time, during the Crimean War, they had come as allies, and they hadn't stayed in Istanbul long. Indeed there were some bridge players who insisted that the game had been invented by bored English officers to pass the time while they were stuck in Istanbul. According to them the name "bridge" came from the Galata bridge. Later, someone else found out that bridge was actually invented on Finnish ships, but it was a nice story.

The ships that had brought grain to Istanbul from Alexandria to prevent famine also brought unwanted passengers. When the rats on the ships anchored in front of Galata and the Selimiye Barracks reached land, they started spreading the plague. The source of the plague was not known for a long time. Sometime later, the rowboats going between the ships and land came to mind. Because the plague had broken out at the bakery next to the Selimiye Barracks too. One of the Turkish health officers suspected that the virus might be coming from the rats on the ships, and to prove this he embarked on systematic research in the enormous Selimiye Barracks. He searched everywhere in the barracks for proof of his theory. The only proof might have been the dead rats. This intelligent health officer was named Hüseyin Ferit, and he was the son of Bosnalı Abdullah Avni Pasha's brother Ali Rıza Pasha. Like many male members of the family, Ali Rıza Pasha had served the Empire by fighting on many fronts and, again in accordance with family tradition, fell in the Balkan War.

Hüseyin Ferit was not slow to find the proof he was seeking. He found the stiff carcasses of rats in the basement of the barracks, and he put them in bags and sent them to the laboratory. He was so sure of himself that he didn't even wait for the results from the laboratory and immediately took steps to save Istanbul from the Black Death. He mixed gasoline and carbolic in equal amounts in large vats and gave orders that every corner of the barracks be cleaned with this mixture. However, because it was met with strong opposition, this task was ended on the evening of the day it was begun. Like many other important places in Istanbul, the Selimiye Barracks were under the command of an English officer. This captain, whose name was Throllope, was against the washing of the barracks, and because he thought it was nonsense he put a stop to it. According to him, this idea had no scientific basis. Hüseyin Ferit was certain he was doing the right thing, and he wanted to stop the disease before it spread. So he went to his uncle Avni Pasha, told him the situation, and asked for his help.

Leyla's grandfather Abdullah Avni Pasha had many reasons to get involved: The first was that he loved his little brother Ali Rıza Pasha very much and still felt pangs of grief when he thought of his death. He could not refuse to help his nephew.

Second, he was enough of a patriot that he could not countenance the obstruction of a plan that might save the people of Istanbul from the plague.

Third, the city was under occupation, and he was very angry at these supercilious English officers.

This was why he no longer went to the Cercle d'Orient, where he used to love to play bridge with his friends, and he barely ever even left the house so as not to encounter the arrogant and insulting behavior of the officers of the occupation forces.

But he left his house to help his nephew, and, putting on his embroidered pasha's uniform, climbed into his coupe carriage, and went straight to the Harbiye Command Headquarters.

It opened a deep and unhealable wound and caused an offended look to settle forever into his hazel eyes. Had it been up to him he would never have left the mansion garden, let alone go to the Harbiye Command Headquarters, but he had no choice.

He explained the situation to the commanding officer, who welcomed him politely. He told of the rats who were spreading the plague virus among the already traumatized population of Istanbul and asked for assistance for his nephew.

The commanding officer moved impatiently from his seat. He knew how difficult it was to deal with the occupation authorities, and he didn't want to get involved, but this illustrious veteran of the Balkan Wars had influence. Besides, he was also afraid of the plague.

The commanding officer promised he would do everything he could.

The following afternoon, a launch belonging to the occupation forces pulled up along the mussel-encrusted quay of the mansion, and a young English lieutenant leapt energetically from the boat and entered the fate of Abdulla Avni Pasha's family.

The lieutenant, whose name was Robert Whitaker, had arrived with a translator, under orders from headquarters to investigate the matter of the plague.

The pasha called his nephew Hüseyin Ferit to explain the situation. Robert Whitaker was invited into the mansion. After coffee was served, Hüseyin Ferit eagerly explained his theory about the plague and how he believed it was being spread by the rats from Alexandria. But at this point something strange caught their attention. The Turkish translator who was translating what they said into English was speaking in a mocking tone and occasionally laughed openly. Hüseyin Ferit became irritated by this, stopped explaining, and asked the translator who he was. Was he from Istanbul? What kind of work did he do? What family was he from? The translator explained who he was: He was the son of a Bulgarian family that had settled in Istanbul. His name was Boris Palenko.

At this point the pasha, who had fought Bulgarian irregulars for years, reacted: he didn't want this man in his house, and couldn't tolerate his presence for another moment, and if he didn't do his job properly he would be thrown out at once.

Hüseyin Ferit shouted that the man was not translating accurately, and that while this Bulgarian was mocking them and laughing at them, who knew how many more people in Istanbul were being infected with the plague.

After this argument, Lieutenant Robert Whitaker had no choice but to send the translator away. He tried to apologize to the owners of the house, but because he didn't know Turkish, he could only repeat the words "*merci, merci*," which he knew were understood here.

The lieutenant was clean-shaven, with light-colored eyes and a dreamy look.

Because the pasha couldn't understand the lieutenant, he had no recourse but to call his daughter, Handan. The best way to be sure of an accurate translation was to use Handan, who had learned English, French, and German from foreign governesses.

A little later Handan arrived. She was wearing a loose silk scarf that didn't completely cover her hair. When she entered and the lieutenant saw her large, surprised-looking eyes, he rose and greeted her with a reverent bow.

Handan spoke fluent English, and she translated Hüseyin Ferit's words convincingly. As she spoke, she looked directly into the lieutenant's eyes. The lieutenant was so unsettled he didn't know what to do with himself. For years the idea of the "Oriental woman" had taken a thousand and one mysterious forms in his mind, and it intoxicated him to look closely into her eyes. This intoxication was enhanced by the mysterious beauty of the Bosphorus; the smells of jasmine, magnolia, and linden that wafted from the garden; the taste of the coffee that had been made on the coals of a brazier; and the charm he felt coming in waves from the girl.

The lieutenant left that mansion that day in a state of intoxication. When he leapt back onto the launch that had come to get him, it was with less energy and self-assurance than when he had leapt off. As the launch moved away he stood looking back at the mansion. He wanted to have one last sight of the girl in the windows that were lit by light reflected from the surface of the water. He didn't see her because at that moment Handan was hiding behind a curtain, looking at this handsome young officer whose eyes reminded her of clouds in the sky.

When he got back to headquarters the lieutenant gave his report. He said that what the Turkish health officer had told him was completely correct and that he should be given permission to take the precautions he felt were necessary. Meanwhile, he would take a personal interest in the matter and would keep track of what the Turkish officer was doing.

He considered meeting Hüseyin Ferit every day, but because he felt this wouldn't be proper, he decided to go either to the Selimiye Barracks or to the mansion every other day.

In any event, whether it was at the mansion or at the barracks, it was Handan who would be doing the translation.

Once he'd got the necessary permission, Lieutenant Whitaker could hardly contain himself.

Had it been possible he would have got into the launch and gone to the mansion that evening when the waters of the Bosphorus were turning lavender. But he contained himself and put his visit off until the next day. As he did every day, he began writing in his morocco-bound diary.

For the first few days, Robert didn't know how he had ended up in this interesting and fabled Eastern city. He'd wanted to see the world as a sailor, had joined the British army to fight in France, and had suddenly found himself here. In truth it suited his adventurous soul, but if a fortune-teller had predicted this when he was a student he would not have believed it.

This part of the world was very different from the green hills and dewy meadows of his native Hampshire. On the other side of the South Downs there was a channel that separated the British Isles from Europe.

Because his seafaring family was prosperous enough, Robert was sent to the High Field Preparatory School.

The school was famous not only for its large and magnificent building, but also for rugby, hockey, and cricket.

During his first week at school, he was frightened of the teachers, who dressed in black, with wide-brimmed black hats, and wandered the corridors of the eight dormitories that were named according to their direction on the compass, but none of them frightened him as much as Miss Hodgstone. Miss Hodgstone, who, with her two assistants, took charge of the boys after dinner and lined the boys up before breakfast to inspect their ears and noses, became his childhood nightmare.

The thing he remembered most from his five years at High Field was the cold. Because according to British tradition, the school had to be harsh, serious, and cold. Robert remembered that on many nights he tried getting into bed with all his clothes on, but the difficult part was getting undressed during the pillow fight that started before Miss Hodgstone came to inspect the dormitory.

After getting high marks in history and geography at school, Robert Whitaker was sent to school in the port city of Southampton, from where ships set sail to five continents. After finishing school he wanted to become a sailor so he could see all the seas of the world, and all the most interesting cities, but the winds of war brought him to Istanbul as a soldier.

Now he felt as if this city was changing his fate, and he was shaken by the looks of the young girl he had learned was named Handan. Just as he would never have imagined he would end up in this city, so it had never occurred to him that he would fall in love with a Muslim girl, and the daughter of a pasha at that.

Lieutenant Robert Whitaker saw Handan two more times that week. The attraction bctwccn thcm had rcachcd the point that they could hardly look at each other, and from the look on their faces it was clear they were in another world. One day he dragged his best friend Captain Bennett to the mansion because he wanted him to see Handan. They had a photograph taken with the pasha's family under the magnolia tree. At this point they started passing notes to each other. First a few poems, from Wordsworth and Nigar Hatun, then the day and the time when they would meet.

One night, with the recklessness of someone in love, Robert climbed the back wall and met Handan in the little building at the back of the garden. This meeting had been arranged when they were having the photograph taken, and he managed to squeeze a note into her hand. The note said, "Tomorrow night at twelve, at the foot of the garden wall." But one of Istanbul's famous rains began that night. Sometimes on the Bosphorus it rains furiously, and you can hardly see a thing. Even though he was soaked to the skin, Robert saw this as a blessing because it was less likely that anyone would see him, and, besides, everyone was inside. He didn't know how Handan would react to his message, or whether she would come, but during their last meeting it had become clear that a powerful bond had formed between them, and they would not be able to ignore this. Robert knew that Handan was as attracted to him as he was to her because she couldn't speak to him without blushing, and without her voice trembling. In spite of this, he wasn't sure he could take such a risk. Because it simply wasn't proper for an officer of the occupying forces to sneak into a pasha's garden and meet his daughter secretly. But with his blood racing the way it was, he would have gone into the garden even if it meant risking the death penalty.

Before Robert even saw Handan, he felt her hand take his and lead him into the little house. Without speaking, without saying a word, they began kissing. Nothing could be heard except their breathing. Within a few minutes Robert found himself melting inside his lover's warm body. As he lost himself in the girl's smell and female warmth, he felt himself brimming over with the ecstasy of their union. He didn't think anything as Handan trembled with little moans, because the desires of their bodies were uniting too quickly for the mind to grasp. This night of pleasure lasted until the early hours of the morning. They made love three more times. They didn't speak about anything. When they weren't making love, they embraced each other's bodies. When dawn broke and a pale light illuminated their bodies, they realized it was time to part, but they parted as if they were going to their deaths.

In the following days, they missed each other constantly and yearned for each other with all of their being. Handan wandered around the house in a daze. Twice her mother found her sobbing in her room, but no matter how much she pressed her she couldn't get a word out of her.

Handan just stared at the walls and didn't hear a word that was said to her.

They met two more times before Handan's pregnancy started to show, and by some miracle they weren't caught. One day, just as they were beginning to believe that there was a god who protected lovers, Handan turned white and began to vomit, and so Üftade succeeded in learning her shameful secret. She had noticed something strange about her daughter for some time and was trying not to put a bad interpretation to it. When everything came out into the open one day, so much pressure was put on Handan that she had to tell her mother whose child it was. She couldn't stand the pressure being put on her by İzzet Kemal, and so she gave Robert's name. İzzet Kemal, who worked for the National Defense Organization, now had only one goal: to kill this occupying officer who had seduced his sister and so remove the stain on the family's honor. It wasn't enough that they had defiled their sacred city, now they'd also insulted his family.

İzzet Kemal told his friends in the Sariyer branch of the organization to follow Robert Whitaker. He didn't give any details, but there was no need to do this. After following him for a while, they understood that he met his closest friend, the famous Captain Bennett, every day. They were very close friends. Captain Bennett was an intelligence officer bent on uprooting the resistance. This officer, who cut a dashing figure with his patent leather boots and his riding crop, was staying at the Novotni Hotel in Pera and was using the hotel basement as a center to interrogate suspected members of the resistance. No one who entered left without being beaten for days.

It was decided to get rid of both officers at the same time. They watched them for days and discovered that the place the two friends went most often was Pandeli's in Büyükdere. This place was very popular among the non-Muslims of Istanbul and offered live music as well as delicious Bosphorus fish and ice-cold *rakı*. The Armenian Madame Elmasyan of Büyükdere, who informed on the nationalists and collaborated with the occupation forces, went there two or three nights a week. She was also on the death list, but her execution was carried out long after that of the two officers, and she was to be found strangled one night in her luxurious villa.

That night İzzet Kemal and his most trusted men cut down a tree on the deserted Maslak road that led through the woods to Büyükdere. They tied thick ropes to the tree and pulled it to the side of the road. They waited silently until a little past midnight. A little later the sound of a motor was heard. The noise approached steadily. When they saw the headlights, they realized this was the car they were waiting for.

Captain Bennett and Lieutenant Whitaker, groggy from the *rakı* they'd drunk, closed their eyes as they rode through the dark back to their hotel in Pera. A soldier was driving, and another guard was sitting in front.

All night Robert had been talking about his undying love and his unborn child, while Bennett told him he'd made the biggest mistake of his life, that it would end in his death, and that it would create an incident between two countries that nothing could offset.

From time to time, Bennett couldn't help teasing his friend: "You know that if you agree to convert to Islam to marry this girl, you're going to have to get circumcised."

Robert grimaced at this bad joke, but his friend had no intention of letting this go: "Yes," he would say. "Perhaps it's a small price to pay for all the pleasure you'll get later. A small and worthless piece of skin. Nothing in life is free."

"You're drunk, don't say any more," Robert warned him.

When the car was just about to pass them, one of the resisters cut the rope and blocked the road. The car came to a halt with a screech of its brakes, and shooting started from both sides of the road. The officers and the soldiers were taken unawares. All of them were hit several times before they could even get their hands on their guns. İzzet Kemal went up to the car and angrily emptied his gun into Robert. When the attackers fled, the only one still alive was Captain Bennett. He was on the point of death from loss of blood, but a car reached him in time and brought him to the La Paix Hospital. After a long course of treatment, the captain had recovered enough to leave the hospital.

As for Lieutenant Robert Whitaker, he drew his last breath in that car. When they found him he was clutching a bag tightly to his chest. Inside, there was a morocco-bound diary. He had added that day's thoughts to the diary in which he had recorded the memories of his childhood and youth.

After her father died, this diary was sent to the lieutenant's family in England, where Leyla would never be able to see it.

Years later, after her grandmother's death, when she was sitting along one evening in the mansion garden, Robert's nephew Geoffrey was to give the diary to Leyla and say, "If I don't give this to you now, you'll never be able to read your father's true memories. There's also a letter in it addressed to you."

As soon as she saw this Englishman Leyla felt as if she knew him because he looked like her. Their eyes, their height, and their stance were the same.

As evening fell in the garden, Geoffrey and Leyla sat on stools and talked for hours. It seemed strange to Leyla that this man she'd never seen was a relative.

Of Robert, Geoffrey said, "According to what the family said, he was a well-brought-up young man who had great hopes. But this unexpected end devastated the family for years."

"Did they blame the Turks?"

"Not quite, and besides, we were the ones occupying this city. But they found it very tragic that it was his love for a girl that led him to his death. And when you think that it was the girl's brother who killed him out of revenge..."

"Is this spoken of often in your family?"

"No! This was the biggest family secret. No one talked about it, and my generation had to piece it together from things that were said and from letters. When we were curious and asked about the story, the older generation denied it and closed the subject."

"Did they know that his daughter was living in Istanbul?"

"Some people knew, but they said that this was a story made up by a Muslim family who wanted to get a share of the Whitaker inheritance. I'm sorry, I didn't mean to upset you, I didn't choose my words well."

The man was saying that Lieutenant Whitaker was a source of both pride and shame for the family. Because the elders of the family believed that the Muslim girl with whom Robert had a relationship was a fortune hunter, they didn't approve of it, and even the possibility that Robert had a child was kept secret. This young man who had come to Istanbul so many years later to see Leyla had been curious about this matter and had squeezed the story out of the older members of the family. Later he would talk about how he almost fainted when he entered the garden and saw Leyla. Because Leyla was a female version of the Robert he knew only from photographs.

Leyla was so unsettled by this incident that for a long time she didn't look at the diary in the old leather bag.

She thought that Lieutenant Robert Whitaker, who she had never seen, was responsible for her mother's death and for the disasters that befell her family, and she didn't feel any closeness to him.

She would only understand the young lieutenant's true feelings when she read the diary, and then she would feel slightly ashamed of her previous prejudices. As she read the diary, this person who had seemed abstract to her slowly became a real person with real sorrows.

Leyla, who was left completely alone after her grandmother's death, sat under the ancient trees in the mansion garden and thought about the past until evening.

Now, after so many deaths, the Bosnalı Mansion was like a cemetery.

Of her now extinct family, she had seen only her grandparents. She only knew her uncle, İzzet Kemal, who was killed by the occupation forces shortly after he led the attack on the officers, from faded photographs in the family album. He was a young man with a thin face, a long chin, and messy hair who wore suspenders and round glasses.

On the day he learned his son had been killed, her grandfather collapsed, and he was so grief-stricken that he never spoke again.

Somehow, she couldn't quite conceive of the beautiful, mysterious woman in the pictures as her mother. Even in these faded old black and white pictures you could see the silkiness of her wavy hair and the beauty of her eyes. Leyla knew that this beautiful young woman died after giving birth to her. Her grandmother didn't hide this from her, because every child has a mother and father. There had to be an explanation for Leyla being all alone with her grandmother in this huge mansion.

The family had reached the end of what had seemed from the outside to be a life of splendor, and indeed was collapsing from within. The land, houses, and shops in Bosnia from which they had received their income had been lost, and no investments had been made here to replace what they had lost. Recently, the Ottoman State, which had not even been able to pay its civil servants, had collapsed, and the Republic had been established amid deep poverty. The pasha had practically no income left. So he began to make secret visits to Mihran at the Grand Bazaar to sell off all the family jewelry, apart from a few pieces he'd given the children, and to go heavily into debt. The pasha's family became indebted to loan sharks who charged outrageous interest. When her grandfather died her grandmother survived for a while by selling off her dowry, but in the end she was so burdened by debts that she had to turn the mansion over to the loan sharks. The loan sharks sold the mansion to Salih, one of the merchants whose fortunes had begun to rise with the establishment of the Republic.

Her troubled grandmother complained constantly about the family's fate, and wept bitterly, but at the same time she did everything she could to see to the upbringing of the last surviving grandchild, and spent whatever money she could scrape together.

After thinking for years about the bits and pieces she'd heard from her grandmother and from other women in the neighborhood she came to the following conclusion: the truth was that her mother, Handan, had decided to die after giving birth to her.

To bring a child into the world and then die is a strange wish, but Handan had no other recourse and no other escape. The child's father had died because of this love, killed by her brother, who himself was later killed, and these blows had been too much for her father to bear, and he had a stroke. Practically all of Istanbul was talking about what had happened. The pasha simply couldn't take this. Was it the pain of losing a son or the staining of the name of such an old family? During every moment of her pregnancy in that little house, Handan suffered a great deal. Every time she looked out the window and saw the motionless, silent figure of her father, her heart broke. She would rather have died the most horrible death than to hurt this man, but she had hurt him more than anyone ever had or would. There was no way to make up for this. They would never come face-to-face and speak to each other again. She could no longer live. Because no person was created to bear so much pain. She didn't know which loss to mourn. Giving birth to this baby would be her last duty on earth.

She had thought about this so much that she came to believe it, and after finally bringing the baby easily into the world, she buried herself in the white sheets and waited for death. She saw the baby once, and took it in her arms, said, "Give her the name Leyla. My grandmother's name," and then cut her ties with the world. No one knows whether choosing this name was an effort to mollify her father at least a little. She didn't eat or drink and tried to stop her wounded heart. Not very much effort was needed for her to do this. When her heart, no longer able to bear this suffering, finally stopped, Handan looked like a pale angel among those white sheets.

Handan was buried in the family cemetery, next to her brother, İzzet Kemal. After the funeral her grandmother took Leyla in her arms and said, "My poor, motherless Leyla," and as she looked at her, she was like a living corpse. As for her grandfather, his motionless face was wet with tears. He hadn't been speaking to his daughter, but after she died he wept for days. It disturbed everyone to see this unmoving and expressionless face streaming with tears.

For years her grandmother had only one purpose in life: to raise Leyla. After she died the girl would be completely alone in the world. So she had to be raised well and taught to look after herself. She wore herself out for years. When she sold the mansion no money came to her, there was only enough to cover the debts. She had to sell the jewelry that had been given to her at her wedding, as well as the medals her husband had received from the sultan, and so managed to get by without having to become dependent on anyone. She didn't take out any more loans.

In this life of poverty, having left the mansion and squeezed into the outbuilding, the thing she cared most about was the girl's education. So she contacted Handan's teachers and made special arrangements with them, so that they would give lessons cheaply, or even for free. At least the family name had its influence.

Leyla couldn't go to school. Because the adventure between Robert and Handan had become exaggerated as it was repeated, and as people often do when there is blame to be assigned, they blamed Leyla. She was an unlucky girl, and her arrival in the world spelled the end of the pasha's family. Above all she was an English officer's bastard. After the war of independence and the enthusiasm for the new Republic, a person like this was not accepted in society. People were against both those who had become wealthy during Ottoman times and those who had occupied the country. Leyla was a product of both.

The new Republic established its capital in Ankara, and Istanbul was left alone with the criminals, the collaborationists, the war profiteers, and those who had served the occupying forces.

The new generation was being taught the Latin alphabet in the new schools and were learning every day about the treachery of the Ottomans. The Ottomans and the occupying forces were considered the enemy. In this atmosphere there was no possibility for Leyla to go to school or to move openly in society. Indeed there was a big probability that she would never be able to marry.

Her long-suffering grandmother knew about this atmosphere, so she raised her in the house in the corner of the garden, out of sight. When the grandmother and daughter did go out hand in hand, it was to the family cemetery plot, with its tall, dark cypress trees, where Handan and İzzet Kemal were buried, or to the pawn shop.

So Leyla, growing up alone and out of sight, memorized every stone, every flower, every bug in that garden, when each tree flowered and how each plant smelled. As if real life and dreams had changed places. At night she listened to the heavy propellers of the huge ships passing in the deep waters in front of their house, saw herself being chased by Hera across these same waters, and lived adventures that were difficult even to imagine. One day a young man was going to get off one of those ships and come and take her hand: "You don't know," he would say, "but I'm your father. I had to travel to far away seas. I traveled around the world twice, but in the end I came back to you."

She even knew each of the birds that landed on the quay and in the garden. Every day the shearwaters that flew over the blue waters of the Bosphorus would carry her to the far shore and bring her back.

Leyla's grandmother told her the truth little by little, so that she could digest it. When she reached the age of fourteen, she knew the history of the family, and her cold-blooded and strong personality accepted it all maturely. The walls had been hung with oil paintings of members of this family that had left the world while they were still angry with each other. Oil paintings of Abdullah Avni Pasha, Handan, İzzet Kemal, her grandmother, and herself hung side by side, together, as they had been on happier days. There was one picture missing, that of Lieutenant Robert. Üftade could not bear to see that man.

One day that picture fell out of the diary Geoffrey had brought her, and since her grandmother was dead, it took its place with the pictures of the rest of the family. The picture had been taken on a beautiful summer day in the mansion garden. The whole family was there, as well as the two English officers. Leyla saw that she bore a marked resemblance to one of them. The other English officer must have been Captain Bennett.

Leyla had never seen this picture before, and she guessed that they had hidden it from her.

The cornerstone of Leyla's education was Fräulein Anneliese, the German governess and piano teacher who had raised her mother. Miss Crane came for English lessons and to teach her literature and general culture.

When Leyla became a young lady, she knew a great deal about things that many people don't know. It was not just the family history; her general level of education was definitely higher than that of most children. As always happens in this kind of situation, her knowledge and breeding were to push Leyla into lifelong loneliness.

Her grandmother would sit in the chair from which at one time her grandfather had never risen, and would talk for a long time, not hiding her anxieties about Leyla's future, and trying to prepare her for a life of loneliness.

The new owners of the mansion, Salih and his wife and three children, led a quiet life, and were faultlessly respectful to Üftade and her granddaughter, who had moved to the outbuilding.

When Leyla was nineteen she realized that her grandmother wanted to die. Like her daughter, she could no longer bear the weight of the world, and having fulfilled her duties, wanted to join her loved ones. Her legs ached from a life in the damp of the Bosphorus, and she couldn't walk comfortably because of the swelling of her knees. She was often out of breath, and she spent her nights moaning.

One day she collapsed when she was gathering the sheets that were hanging to dry in the garden. Leyla heard her fall and ran to her side and saw an expression of peace on her face. Like her daughter, she had willed her heart to stop and had embraced death.

After the funeral, Leyla sat under the magnolia tree that had sheltered first her grandfather and then her grandmother, and suddenly burst into tears, crying until she had neither the strength nor the tears to cry any more. She wept all her tears that day. She shed a lifetime's worth of tears, sobbing her heart out, pulling the leaves off the lower branches of the magnolia tree, trampling the flower beds, ripping up the jasmine and kicking the cats that wandered beneath her feet.

She remained completely alone. This crisis was her first and last. Leyla, who had been a cold-blooded girl since childhood, would never shed another tear in her life. Only once did her grief for her lost family, for her grandfather the pasha, and her grandmother, and her mother, come out into the open, and this became a rule she would keep for the rest of her life.

She never even thought of the English Lieutenant Robert Whitaker. Her curiosity about him developed years later, after Geoffrey came and brought the diary, when she decided to read the diary in the blood-stained leather bag. She didn't think that at this point she would be shaken emotionally. As she read the diary, she felt as if she was watching a stranger's life. She didn't know the man who had written the diary, and she didn't know anything about his life. Because this subject was taboo in the pasha's family. It was never spoken about. All families have their secrets, but the secrets of mansion families were more deeply hidden and closed within.

According to the diary, the Englishman had fallen terribly in love with Leyla's mother, and this passion had led him to behave recklessly. It described how he entered the mansion garden one rainy night and made passionate love to Handan. Leyla couldn't believe this when she read it.

How could a lieutenant of the occupying forces dare to sneak into the garden of an Ottoman pasha? And what about her mother? How could she have put herself in such danger?

It was the story of a great love, the likes of which she had never experienced. It was a love that accepted the risk of death and, more importantly, even of humiliation.

When it came out that Handan was pregnant by the lieutenant, all hell broke loose. İzzet Kemal, who already hated the English out of nationalist sentiment, strode about the house swearing to kill this dishonorable enemy. Her grandfather the pasha flew into a rage. What tremendous shame!

The occupation forces humiliated the Turks at every opportunity. Ships sailing down the Bosphorus were forced to salute the English warships, and Turkish aristocrats were turned away from the doors of Istanbul's most prestigious club, the Cercle d'Orient. No one forgot the Turkish soldiers who were killed when the English opened fire on the police station on March 16th, nor the members of parliament who were arrested. Like other Turks, the pasha looked at the panel that read *This too shall pass* and bade himself to be patient and to wait for the day when this humiliation would end. In a situation like this, how could his daughter, Handan, give birth to an English officer's child. His mind could not grasp this.

After everything came out, Handan was closed into the little house, where she sank into a deathlike silence, and was treated as if she had been quarantined with a contagious disease. No one spoke to her, and the servants wouldn't even look at this "dishonorable girl." Her grandfather the pasha, driven half-mad, paced up and down all day saying, "I don't believe it, I don't believe it, my mind just doesn't grasp it."

At this time the lieutenant wrote in his diary that, "I was even willing to accept death. Because I couldn't live without her. I couldn't breathe. I had two options left. Either to commit suicide or to be willing to accept any humiliation in order to be reunited with Handan. I chose the latter."

Leyla didn't understand this love, but she felt that the young lieutenant named Robert had suffered deeply. He wrote of the pressure put on him by his best friend the intelligence officer Captain Bennett to give up this insanity, and of how he resisted this pressure. To tell the truth, it wasn't easy.

Leyla tried to get a sense of her mother from this diary, but somehow this love-sick man's words don't bring this elegant, beautiful woman to life for her.

The pasha could not countenance the presence of a girl pregnant with an English child in his house, so he banished her to the little building in the back of the garden. This single-story house was wide and well lit. The walls were painted white. Leyla was born in this house.

But her birth is not mentioned in the diary. Because Robert had already been killed, he didn't know that the woman he loved had died after giving birth to his child, and so he didn't write about it in his diary.

As Leyla read the diary, she could understand how her birth had been a great disgrace for the family. For a long time the pasha's family hung their heads in shame, while gossip about them spread through Istanbul. After he killed Robert, her uncle İzzet Kemal fell into an ambush set by the occupying forces and was killed.

After these disasters and deaths, people started to say that the Bosnalı Mansion was an unlucky place, like all the waterfront mansions on the Bosphorus. These waterfront mansions did not bring people happiness. Some lost their fortunes, some committed suicide, and some covered their walls in black cloth and buried themselves in grief when a young daughter died.

Perhaps rumors like this were medicine for people who could see the beauty of the waterfront mansions of the Bosphorus but could not even dream about a life like that, and eased hearts that were filled with envy. They could tell themselves that, even though they couldn't live in these waterfront mansions, at least they didn't have to experience the disasters that seemed to come with that life.

The strangest thing, though, was that the residents of these mansions were constantly repeating these stories to each other.

For instance, the story of the black mansion was told for years, and on long lazy afternoons, as they talked and did their embroidery, it would bring tears to the eyes of women who were already on the point of crying. They talked about the mansion owner who couldn't accept his daughter's death and painted his mansion black. On the blue waters of the Bosphorus, where ferryboats and rowboats pass to and fro, a black wooden building was now seen where a brick-red mansion had once stood. The chimneys, the roof tiles, the window frames... everything was completely black. Inside the house there was nothing that wasn't covered in black cloth. The magnolia trees in the garden had been cut down, and the jasmine, laurel, wallflowers, and whatever else was growing had been uprooted. The poor man wore black himself, and for the rest of his life he never left this black mansion.

The disasters that occurred at the Bosnalı Mansion, once a seat of power, splendor, and wealth, were an unlucky sign.

What other explanation could there be for the family to be reduced to a grandmother and her illegitimate granddaughter, and for the mansion to pass out of their hands because they'd become so poor?

On the last page of the diary, Leyla found the unfinished letter addressed to her that Geoffrey had mentioned. The letter began, "My dear child," and not "son" or "daughter." Because the English Lieutenant Robert Whitaker didn't know whether the child would be a girl or a boy.

> My dear child,
> About six months before your blessed birth, as I sit watching the sunset on the shores of the Bosphorus, I wanted to write you a letter. At the

moment I am in Pandeli's restaurant, in the Greek neighborhood of Therapia, on the Bosphorus, near the Black Sea. At the moment I'm watching the light of the setting sun reflected on the water. There are Turks, Greeks, Armenians, English, French, and Jews sitting at the table. Several languages are being spoken. In a little while my friend Captain Bennett will arrive, and as we talk about your mother we will have an interesting evening in this interesting country. I don't know whether you will be a girl or a boy, and I may not be able to give you the surname of Whitaker, but I want you to know that I already love you very much and that I long to see your face.

But I don't know whether I ever will be able to see your face, nor do I know if I'll be able to see your mother again. Because standing between me and Handan, who I love enough to sacrifice everything in my life, there are separate religions, separate nationalities, and war. This situation did not prevent us from loving each other, but it does prevent us from being together socially.

For this reason, they may not even mention me to you. They won't tell you that I'm your father, to try to escape the shame of your being the illegitimate daughter of an officer of the occupying forces.

But I know that one day this letter will reach you, and that you will forgive me. Because even though I'm still quite young, I've lived enough to be able to know the human heart.

If it turns out that you resemble your mother, the most beautiful woman in the world, I would like you to have been named Io. I'm looking at the waters of the Bosphorus now and am thinking of the goddess Io from which it took its name. At boarding school in Southampton, studying Greek mythology, I had to write a paper on the story of Zeus and his lover Io, never imagining that one day I would see the Bosphorus. In a fit of jealousy, Zeus's wife Hera changed Io into a cow. She fled here from Ionia, and then swam across the Bosphorus, and this is how the straits got their name. Do you know why I wanted to give you this name?…

The letter ends there. His friend Captain Bennett must have arrived then.

On that page of the diary, the date 24 September 1922 was written. Leyla remembered that her father had been killed by her uncle on that date. Which meant that this letter was written only a few hours before he died.

When this young man arrived here, he could not have thought that he would be returning to England in a coffin. Had he liked this country? This wasn't clear to Leyla from the diary.

In one place, these observations had been written:

People have not had the education necessary to develop their mental and physical capabilities and have not learned to examine their emotions, but at the same time there is an attraction here that I don't

> know how to describe. The Bosphorus is one of the most beautiful places on earth, and perhaps because of Handan, I feel I never want to leave it. Bennett also likes it here very much. Perhaps they are a bit primitive. But they also have a strange bond to their country and a highly developed moral sense. Family ties are unbelievably strong. They are quiet, soft-headed, introverted people. The sultan is like a plaything in the hands of foreign ambassadors.

As she read the diary, Leyla was very curious about this young lieutenant, what kind of man he was, how he talked, walked and laughed... Indeed this curiosity was even strong enough for her to write a letter to the former intelligence officer Captain Bennett to ask him about her father. She had learned from Geoffrey that Bennett was still alive. More importantly, he had brought a book written by Bennett as a gift. In England the captain was an important philosopher. Leyla wrote asking whether her father had said anything in his last moments, during their last evening, in the car in which he was assassinated, but she didn't receive an answer. Either Bennett had not received the letter, or he did not want to relive this painful memory.

According to the diary Bennett spoke very good Turkish. The British army had taught him Turkish and instructed him in intelligence work. Consequently his friend Lieutenant Robert was able to enter higher Turkish social circles, which led to a brief meeting that was to change his life. Istanbul, which was occupied after World

War I and the Russian Revolution, was one of the most sensitive places in the world, and thousands of people passed through this center. They met some of the most important of these people, the mystic Gurdjieff and his friend Ouspenski, at the house of the liberal Prince Sabahattin, who was a member of the imperial family. Her father related the events of that evening with great excitement. Had he not been killed, he might have arranged his life according to this mystic's teachings and may even have become his disciple.

Captain Bennett mentioned this evening in his book:

> There are very few places where East and West are thoroughly blended, and no distinction can be made as to whether a person's or an environment's origins are Asian or European. I have never witnessed this fusion to the degree that it existed in the Kuruçeşme house of Prince Sabahattin, nephew of the last Ottoman sultan, and student of Christian and Islamic traditions.
>
> I met Gurdjieff there in the autumn of 1920, and no other place could have been more appropriate for this. Gurdjieff does not unite East and West, but eliminates their differences with a global view that does not take racial and religious differences into consideration. This was my first impression and remains one of the strongest.

Leyla hoped that she would find something about her father in this book, but she didn't. According to the biography in the book, after Captain Bennett returned to London in 1924 he served as a translator at the London Conference between Turkey and the Western Allies and that after this he abandoned this career and gave his life entirely to matters of the soul. Because after being shot in the car on the Maslak road and lying unconscious in the French hospital after a brain operation, he realized that the body and the soul belong to different dimensions. This experience changed his life. Now he was considered one of the world's leading mystics and had published countless books.

Leyla thought: This means that the cause of this change in his life was my uncle İzzet Kemal's bullet. How strange life is.

13

Among the jumble of apartment buildings, Leyla felt unhappy and helpless, but at the same time she was trying to get to know these strange young people she was meeting at this late stage of her life.

The unshakable principles of her solitary life didn't apply in this house because she was among people she didn't know.

She passed her first week in a tense atmosphere with these irritable young people. Actually there was no real problem with the young musicians, since they didn't live in that house, they just came in the evening to play music and to eat, but Roxy was very hard to take. Even if she wasn't quite as harsh as when they first met, it was as if Leyla represented every misfortune and injustice that had ever befallen her, and she constantly needled her, and let her know in every possible way that she wanted her to go and to leave this house.

The Great Lady tried to be patient, but like all her family before her, she was very stubborn, and she was also very proud, and she knew that she couldn't tolerate this situation much longer.

Meanwhile, it became evident that the young people were very hard up for money. The old refrigerator was completely empty. Sometimes there was nothing but half an onion, a dried-up little piece of cheese, and a wrinkled pepper. They ate pasta every night, and didn't have a very healthy diet. From the comments they made among themselves, Leyla realized that their financial situation was getting worse every day.

From what they said, she understood that Yusuf's salary at the newspaper was very low and that the group hadn't been able to find any work. Both the boys and the house were filthy. The toilet seat was missing, and the porcelain was stained brown. The pipes made an annoying, flute-like sound when you turned on the taps and continued to rattle all night.

In short, the Great Lady was living in poverty and filth and was treated like an enemy. She could see that Yusuf was very upset about this situation, and for his sake she wanted to leave as soon as possible.

In addition to all this unpleasantness, she also felt the lack of one of the most important elements in her life. For the first time in almost eighty years, she was not by the shore. She was accustomed to water in all its forms, and it was a natural part of life. Water, not just the currents of the Bosphorus that changed color from moment to moment. Sometimes a rain that lasted all night, sometimes the drops that accumulated on the magnolia leaves, sometimes drizzle in the morning; passing freighters that were turned into phantoms by the mist, a cloud the color of silver, it was dew, sometimes frost, somctimcs steam, or snow. And sometimes in that old mansion it was streaming tears.

Leyla loved how the currents of the Bosphorus turned aquamarine when it snowed, and she would watch for hours, wiping away the condensation from the window. Sometimes, seeing the extreme beauty of snow gathering on the fishing boats that had been pulled ashore made her feel restless. The strange light of the aquamarine sea on winter days, snow gathering on a pale red fishing boat, pine trees with their branches outlined in white looking like brides, the streams of thin, black smoke from the chimneys; all of this gave her a feeling of excitement, as if she'd entered an extraordinary landscape painting. Sometimes she would go out into the garden and stand up to her ankles in snow with her mouth open, and her heart would soar with delight as she tasted the cool freshness of snowflakes on her tongue. On days like that, the garden was like one of those little glass domes...

Now all these things were gone from her life. Here, among all these concrete buildings, she felt as if she was caught in a trap.

One evening she was sitting in her room trying to think of a way out of this situation, when an argument about money broke out in the living room.

As far as she could understand, they hadn't paid the rent in months, and the landlord was putting pressure on them to leave. They had no other recourse left. Roxy and

Other Animals had played at two festivals and had played a couple of gigs at an underground club, but recently they hadn't been able to find any work or earn any money. Roxy was saying that they were already having a difficult enough time getting by without having to be burdened by an old lady.

When the Great Lady heard this she began thinking deeply.

There were only two items left in the jewelry box that she had brought with her and that had once been full: a diamond broach and her grandmother's diamond ring. When these were gone, she would have no security whatsoever in life, and indeed wouldn't even have enough to pay for a shroud in which to wrap her body. In this situation, would it be right to give one of the pieces to the young people? Her conscience was not easy with this, and told her not to do this, but at the same time she felt bad about Yusuf's situation. In the end she decided she had to, so she got out the ring and brought it into the living room. She acted as if she had not heard their conversation.

"Yusuf," she said, "I have a favor to ask of you. Can you go to the Grand Bazaar tomorrow?"

Yusuf looked at her in surprise and said he could go. Everyone had fallen silent and was looking at the Great Lady.

"Good," she said. "Go to Mihran's son Varujan. Please give the ring to him. He'll pay you whatever it's worth."

She left something on the table and went back to her room. The young people went to the table to see what it was and were surprised to find a wonderful diamond ring.

Even though they knew nothing about jewelry, they could see that it was old and very valuable.

Mihran, to whom the family had sold jewelry for years, had died, but Leyla was certain the tradition would continue and that his son Varujan would do what he could to help her. As she was leaving her house, she had hidden the last two pieces in a little wooden box and put it in her suitcase. With this ring she could pay her debt to Yusuf and still have enough to move into a hotel and be comfortable. She knew that even the world's most uncomfortable hotel would be a thousand times more comfortable than this apartment.

The way the Great Lady had put the ring on the table and acted as if it was nothing reminded Yusuf of the old days. He remembered the way the Great Lady used to give him gifts of jasmine and fruit or spending money for the holidays, in such a way as not to offend his childish pride, as if she'd left a handkerchief on the table as she passed. Roxy watched in surprise.

The next day Yusuf went to the Grand Bazaar, found Varujan, conveyed the Great Lady's greetings to him, and returned home with a wad of money. In all his life he'd never seen or held so much money at one time. This woman was a miracle.

The results of this miracle were seen in the house that night. When Yusuf gave the Great Lady more than twenty billion, she asked him to put aside half of it. Yusuf put aside ten billion. The Great Lady gave him this money very delicately, as if she were passing him a plate of cherries.

"This should meet your expenses," she said.

"Yes, but...," Yusuf tried to object, but his heart wasn't in it. He needed the money desperately, or else he would be evicted. Leyla motioned for him to be quiet.

Roxy was more surprised by this than anyone. She never expected good things from life or from people. This old woman Yusuf had brought home had suddenly become a savior, and Roxy was amazed and perhaps a bit ashamed.

Roxy was so delighted by the ten billion that she wanted to go in and thank the Great Lady, but even though she tried to force herself she was unable to do this. She thought it would seem too self-seeking and hypocritical. She thought about the old woman all night. She wasn't at all like the old people in her own family. Her behavior, her erect posture, her voice, and the penetrating way she looked at people were very interesting. She realized that this woman was unlike anyone she had ever met. It was as if she had something that the Germans had. If she were to walk the streets of Duisburg no one would think she was Turkish, because her posture was erect like that of the Germans, and none of her clothes were wrinkled.

The next evening, something happened that surprised Roxy even more. They were sitting in the living room. They'd prepared a small meal with the money they'd received. At one point the conversation turned to music. Roxy was writing a new song, and she believed that it would be a hit. She hummed the melody. She was going to sing her song accompanied by a simple melody. Her friend was trying to get the chords of this melody right but got stuck. He got stuck on one chord, and after trying it four or five times said, "What should we put here, old man?" Somehow he just couldn't find the right chord. At this point a voice from within was heard to say, "C minor. And after that D major."

They were dumbstruck. The voice had come from the old woman's room. When the boy played C minor and then D major they saw that she was right.

They all fell silent. A little later Roxy began with the melody again. At this point the organist seemed to prefer to remain silent and wait. He didn't do anything. Roxy repeated it again, and then yet again. It was as if everyone was waiting for the Great Lady to give them more advice. A voice came from the room: "An octave too low."

The young people looked at each other. They didn't know this chord. Once again they heard a voice from the room: "Diminuendo."

The boy who was playing the keyboard said, "I don't know that chord!"

Then, as everyone watched in amazement, the old woman came out, sat on the stool, and played the chord. Later, she played the melody Roxy had been humming a little earlier, arranging the chords in order. Her fingers wandered across the keyboard with unbelievable authority, producing music that was both strong and as soft as velvet. In truth, it hadn't been at all easy for Leyla to reach this level of mastery. She could still hear Fräulein Annelise saying, "Touch, young lady. Do you understand? In piano touch is everything."

The young people were beside themselves with joy. They had never seen anything like this in their lives.

Yusuf was truly delighted and said, as if claiming his due, "You see, what did I tell you? The Great Lady knows a thing or two."

Roxy went up to the keyboard and said in an almost inaudible voice, "Thank you! You play the piano beautifully."

When Leyla retired to her room that evening, she was pleased with herself that everyone was beginning to show her deep respect. There had been a visible change, and the young people were almost ready to bow to her. In her eyes the money had less to do with it. There true respect came from her knowledge of music.

These young people did not seem to have had any musical education at all. They had neither knowledge nor culture and didn't know how to behave in society. They'd just grown up and gone off on their own. She was amazed by this.

She remembered the tutors who had come to teach her. Piano exercises, French grammar, the poems of Shelley, Blake, and Wordsworth, Goethe and Wilhelm Meister in German, all of these had been an inescapable part of her life.

If she had grown up with her father her native language would probably be English, but now she thought in German, and sometimes dreamed in French. Her father's language came after these.

14

One afternoon Roxy was sitting alone in the living room, watching a documentary about animal mating behavior on the National Geographic channel. Leyla was in her room. Roxy normally didn't watch nature channels because she was tired of watching how every gory detail of lions killing antelopes was filmed. But this documentary wasn't about hunting and death, it was about life, about mating.

First there was a long segment about how snakes mate. It was difficult for the male snake to get close to the female snake. Because the female snake could kill him if she didn't want to mate. Indeed it was dangerous even when the female snake accepted the male snake. After mating the male snake left the scene quickly out of fear of being killed. After watching for ten minutes, Roxy understood that for snakes, sex and death were very closely linked. It was difficult to approach females.

After that came a segment about the mating habits of lions. The biggest problem among lions was convincing the female to mate. Because if the female wasn't attracted to the male she would either chase him off or do something more dangerous to get rid of him.

As Roxy watched the documentary, she came to the conclusion that the human female was the easiest to mate with. Males didn't risk being stung, clawed, or ripped to pieces, and there was no problem about mating seasons.

Female animals were only able to mate at certain times every year, or perhaps even every two years, then only accepted a male with great difficulty, and after that didn't go near anyone.

Indeed the documentary related how the male lions would kill the cubs so that the female would have to mate again.

But it wasn't at all like that with people. Sex had all but lost its connection with childbirth. For this reason the human female simply lay down when approached by a male.

In Roxy's view, humans had lost their connection with nature in other areas besides sex. What animal would pay money to make love to another animal, or to see another animal naked. When money was involved, everything became messy, and people were left without the power of imagination. Pornographic films were so clinical that they left no part of the female anatomy to the imagination.

All of this seemed as absurd as Aşik Veysel's statement, when asked "What is passion?" that, "If you love, and can't be united with the one you love, it becomes passion."

If Young Werther from the Goethe novel she had read at school had had access to pornographic films, he would have just gone to the first sex club, and it would never have occurred to him to commit suicide. For men it was that simple. Because they were programmed to impregnate as many women as possible. The woman's duty was to limit this, and to give birth after finding the healthiest possible mate. From this point of view, men were behaving somewhat naturally. On the other hand, when women tried to be free in the way men were, they diminished their femininity and tried to change their nature.

She thought of how if a man rather than a woman said these things, the feminists would attack him. She smiled.

But this train of thought only added to the distress Roxy already felt. She thought of all the men she'd slept with since Mauritz, and of how meaningless it had all been. She regretted that she could not live in accordance with nature like animals did. She felt used and worn-out.

And the worst thing was that in all these years she had never fallen in love, and life had been empty. Lately it seemed as if the newspapers, television, novels, and books of poetry couldn't avoid mentioning love; love was selling books, and everyone was obsessed with love, but she'd never even had an inkling of this feeling.

To tell the truth, she found Yusuf better, cleaner, and more honorable than any of the men she'd taken to bed. And in a sense she did love this boy. There was a purity and goodwill about the way he looked at the world that attracted her, but was this love?

Perhaps everyone of her generation was like this. Nudity, free sex, and lack of privacy had put an end to love. Perhaps the family life she'd never experienced was a magical cure for all of this.

Suddenly she thought of Leyla who was sleeping in the other room. According to what Yusuf had told her, the woman had never married or fallen in love. Was it possible to live life completely alone?

What a strange woman she was. Despite her age, she insisted on being addressed simply as Leyla. People of her age and background generally wanted to be addressed more respectfully. But Leyla didn't want any of this and even treated children as if they were her equals. Her friends called her Leyla but still addressed her in the second person plural. "Leyla, can you show us this chord?," "Leyla, do you know how to make squash gratin?" The boys had become very fond of her and loved calling her Leyla.

It was as if there was nothing Leyla didn't know. After learning about her mastery of the piano, Roxy discovered something else about her that made her want to sink through the floor.

Because when Leyla first came to the house, she'd spoken to her friends in German, calling her an "old witch," and mocking her, thinking she couldn't understand. Until one day she found out that Leyla spoke perfect German.

Who could have known that this old woman knew such perfect German? She'd understood all the insulting things they'd said, but she hadn't let on. After this discovery Roxy became more wary of Leyla and began to look at her more carefully.

She'd never met anyone who knew so many things. Even her German teachers at school couldn't hold a candle to this Turkish woman.

It was strange to be thinking about her so much. Did she feel sorry for her, had she started to like her, did she feel respect? Later she said to herself, "Come on, what's this woman to you?"

But somehow she just couldn't get Leyla out of her mind. Her friends also seemed to have started to feel an odd sort of respect for her, and when she came into the room they moved awkwardly, as if they wanted to stand up to greet her.

Of course Yusuf was very pleased by all of this. To breach the wall of hatred Roxy felt for her family and for people in general, and because of her almost passionate bond with Leyla, she started secretly reading her memoirs one day about two weeks after the woman came to the house. The woman sat at a desk in the living room all day, writing something in a notebook, and then she would suddenly grow sleepy and retire to her room. A while later Roxy could tell from her breathing that she was in a deep sleep. She would go to the table and glance at the notebook. She found pages written in amazingly good German. She used the language so beautifully that even though Roxy was born and raised in Germany, there were words she didn't know, and she had difficulty understanding some of the sentences.

But one thing was very clear, that the old woman was suffering terribly. But there wasn't a trace of self-pity in what she wrote. She didn't use emotional words either. But the woman who had lost her house was afraid that she would lose her memories too, and it was clear that she felt terribly helpless. There were passages written to her grandfather, her grandmother, and her mother. She blamed herself for not protecting the house and asked for forgiveness.

When she read this, Roxy felt a deep shame for the first time in her life and began to feel a mixture of love and admiration for this old woman.

She opened the door quietly and watched the old woman sleeping for a while. In sleep, with her mouth half-open, Leyla's defensive walls had collapsed, and she'd turned into a pitiful, suffering woman. Roxy was surprised at how touched she was by this scene and wanted to put her arms around the woman's thin shoulders. She didn't do this but just straightened her blanket.

At the same time she was surprised by these "soft" feelings she was experiencing for the first time. She had been raised in a harsh world and felt it a sign of weakness to display emotion like this. Her harsh relationship with her family had taught her that the world was a battlefield. But for whatever reason, her feelings for the old woman were becoming clearer, and her behavior was becoming softer, and her heart was swelling with tenderness. Was the presence of a single old woman enough to bring about such a change? What was happening to her?

She was going to talk to Yusuf and say that she wanted to help the old woman get her house back. They had a number of close friends in Cihangir. They knew reporters, lawyers, and university professors. The first thing to do was to find and talk to the doctor who had filled out the false report. In Germany standing up for one's rights was a sacred thing, so why shouldn't it be so here?

Yusuf was surprised by this great change in Roxy. Where did this sudden interest come from? Was it because the woman had helped them financially and had brought some order into their lives, or did she really feel for her?

After talking about it they made a decision, and two days later they went to see the doctor who had written the phony report. The man was a university professor and was well-known. He also wrote some highly nationalistic articles for several newspapers.

At the university hospital, they made their way through corridors crowded with tired and intimidated patients, looking for the professor's office.

After waiting outside the door for a while, an orderly asked Yusuf and Roxy to come in. The professor with the glasses and bushy eyebrows, who they recognized from television, sat them down and asked them politely what they wanted.

They explained that Leyla had been evicted from her house on the strength of that report and asked how he could write a report like that without even having seen the woman. At first the man didn't know what to say, and then he asked, "Are you the woman's relatives?" Yusuf was about to say no, when he heard Roxy hurriedly saying yes. "She's my aunt."

The professor said, "Good God! They told me the woman was all alone." Then he pulled himself together: "The poor woman isn't sane."

"How can you say this if you've never even seen her?"

"I saw her, my girl, I saw her. How could I have written a report without seeing her?"

"First of all, I'm not your girl. Second, my aunt says that she never saw you, and that no one examined her."

The professor stared at the wall thoughtfully for a while. "Dementia!" he muttered to himself. "Dementia! What a powerful thing. How it wipes out the memory. I wouldn't wish it on anyone."

Then, pretending to pull himself together, he addressed the two young people. "Ah, the poor woman, she doesn't remember. Anyway, is there anything else you want?"

The professor stood, making it clear that the meeting was over. He smiled as he watched the two young people leave the room. It was an arrogant look that seemed to say, you're not powerful enough to do anything about this, and it would be better for you not to involve yourselves any further.

Just as she was going out the door, Roxy turned and said, "Actually, we came to see you for a different reason."

"We're reporters. My friend is writing an article about this."

When she said this, they saw a look of confusion spread across the man's face. Because he already had a bad reputation in this regard, he didn't want to be involved in a story concerning the seizure of property. Like all Turks in prominent positions, he was secure in his belief that no one could do anything to him, but he wanted to play his trump card against these two young and inexperienced reporters. He stopped the two young people as they were going out the door and asked in a low voice, "You know, don't you?"

They looked at him with curiosity.

"This woman," he said, "was born on the wrong side of the blanket."

Roxy didn't understand this old-fashioned phrase.

The professor continued: "She's the illegitimate daughter of a British officer in the occupation forces. That's why she's been excluded by Turkish society. And now the poor thing has gone mad."

These last words made Roxy so angry that she was furious with the man the whole way back. Roxy hated this kind of attitude. People who acted as if they knew everything, and looked down on you, and belittled you. Authority. When the man had addressed her as "my girl" and she'd said "I'm not your girl," it had made her feel a little better. These men didn't understand any other kind of language.

But no matter what she did, she was always treated the same way: being put down, belittled, an attitude that said you're not my equal. It happened exactly the same way in Germany. People would pretend not to see her in the streets. Especially well-dressed, middle-aged, wealthy, tall German women, who pretended not to see foreigners like herself. It was as if they saw right through and beyond you. Perhaps the only place it wasn't like this was the sex shop, where German men ogled her naked body.

She'd left Germany to escape those looks, but the way she was treated here was almost worse. Some belittled her for being *Almancı*, a Turk from Germany, some looked askance at her dyed hair, and some curled their lips at the music she made. They didn't understand this music here; the only thing they understood were the exhibitionist displays of singers who prettied themselves like show dogs. Sometimes she thought about this and felt sorry for herself because she would never be respected. She wondered where she'd gone wrong. The only thing she wanted was to be shown respect, that's all. This phony doctor was from the world of successful people that she hated so much. He was completely sure of himself. But the things he'd said at the last moment were enough to make him uncomfortable. The thing to do now was to find a lawyer to take on Leyla's case and start proceedings for her to get back her house.

Yusuf was very happy to see Roxy throw herself so wholeheartedly into the role of rescuer. He opened the hospital door and stepped aside to let Roxy pass through.

Once again, Roxy thought that everyone denied her respect, and that Yusuf was the only one who had ever spoiled her. The boy even loved the music she made. He submitted to all her whims and did his best to satisfy them.

To tell the truth, he was a strange boy. Someone so compliant, peaceful, and mature didn't fit any of her preconceptions of Turkish men. The German boys she knew were uninteresting and selfish, and Turkish men were rough and wild. Most of the girls she knew were beaten by their boyfriends.

Roxy tried to understand Yusuf's personality better and asked him questions: "Do you ever get into fights?"

"With whom?"

"I don't know, people who give you a hard time."

"Sometimes."

"OK, have you ever had a fistfight? Have you ever punched someone in the face?"

"No!"

"Why?"

"Why would I do that? Why would I need to punch someone in the face?"

"I don't know. All young men fight like that."

"I've never done that."

"OK, have you ever been in love?"

"..."

"Come on, tell me; there's no getting out of it, have you ever been in love?"

"Yes."

"With whom?"

"What's it to you?"

"What do you mean what's it to me? Tell me, have you ever been in love with a girl."

"Yes, I already told you."

"With whom?"

"You know."

"No, I'm not talking about me. Before me."

"No."

"You're lying. You're a liar."

"Then . . . I'll say perhaps."

"I knew it. Who was she?"

"I don't want to talk about it."

"You're going to tell me."

"Someone elegant and interesting."

"More elegant than me?"

"Yes."

"Did you love her more than you love me?"

"No!"

"How would I know?"

"Roxy, stop asking these questions. I want to sleep. It's almost morning."

"Tell me the girl's name and I'll leave you alone. Otherwise I'm not going to let you sleep."

"Come on Roxy."

"Tell me, just tell me her name."

"All right, I'll tell you. Leyla."

"What? Which Leyla?"

"The woman sleeping in the other room."

"You're terrible, you're lying."

"I swear I'm not lying. When I was a child I was in love with the woman. Everyone was."

"I wasn't talking about that kind of love."

"But that's all there is. Now you tell me. Have you ever been in love?"

As happened every night, their conspiratorial whispering had reached this unavoidable point. It happened like that every night, and Yusuf didn't stop until he brought up Roxy's former lovers and her previous sexual experience.

Roxy knew that a terrible jealousy gnawed at his pure heart, and she thought that in the end he wasn't all that different from other Turkish men.

She wanted to answer his question about whether she had been in love with a no, but unfortunately she knew it wouldn't stop there, and would continue until the end.

"No!"

"You say that with such certitude that people would think it was true. Didn't you have any boyfriends in Germany?"

"Yes I did!"

"So..."

"You asked if I'd been in love, and I said no. Boyfriends are another matter."

"So, did you sleep with them without being in love?"

"Yes."

"Why?"

"I don't know, everyone I knew was doing it."

"How many people have you been with?"

"Please stop this."

"How many men? Tell me. I want to know everything about you."

"All right, three. Are you happy now?"

"Why should I be happy, am I a pervert?"

"Then why do you insist on asking? These are things that belong to the past. I don't even remember."

"Did you do the same things with them that you do with me?"

"Yusuf, I don't want to talk about these things. Just shut up."

"Shh, don't raise your voice, but tell me. Did you satisfy them?"

At this point Roxy stifles an urge to cry and says whatever comes to her mind. "I said shut up, stop giving me a hard time. I don't want to talk about it."

"All right, fine. I've been an idiot again, please don't cry. I won't ask again."

When they had these crises they would hug each other, and he would say something like, "Stop being such an idiot, we're together now, what could be more important than that."

Then Roxy's sobbing would subside.

The worst night in a lifetime of being insulted occurred during the first week of her arrival in Istanbul. She was staying in a sleazy hotel in Sirkeci and was looking for work. Just when her money was running out she was hired to work in a place in Pera where they had music after midnight. And that night was a complete fiasco. It was a place frequented mostly by aficionados of hard rock, and they booed Roxy and Other Animals off the stage. The owner of the club threw them out.

Roxy was so destroyed, and felt she didn't need her friends to curse her, so she sent them back to the hotel and wandered the sinful streets of Pera by herself. She wandered into a couple of bars and started drinking hard drinks, and quickly became drunk, and cursed at the men who made comments to her.

Toward morning she found herself sitting on a curb near Taksim Square. She couldn't remember how she got there. She must have passed out for a little while.

When she turned her head she saw a little girl sitting nearby. A cold, unhappy little girl covered by the silence of night. Because the girl reminded her of herself, she sat next to her and tried to talk to her. The child looked around in panic and wouldn't answer her. Roxy lifted her chin and looked into her eyes. The little girl's eyes seemed expressionless, as if her soul had died. Roxy went back to where she'd been sitting.

Then a car pulled up next to them and two men got out. One of them was wearing a parka. They made the child stand up, then lifted up her skirt and looked, then pinched her and touched her breasts. One of the men was praising the child as if he were trying to sell her to a customer. Then they brought the girl into the car.

Roxy leapt to her feet and tried to stop them, shouting, "Police, help, they're kidnapping a child!"

The man in the parka punched Roxy in the face, and when she fell to the ground he kicked her in the stomach. As the car drove away, Roxy could feel that her eyes were full of blood. Her vision started to blur.

A little later some other children came and lifted her up. One boy said, "This is how it is. Don't interfere, or they'll hurt you very badly."

Roxy got up and managed to walk by holding on to the wall. Her head was spinning. She couldn't think of anything except how badly she wanted to get out of this disgusting city. There was no humanity left here; it was worse than Germany. But if she went back to Germany she would have to live with her father. Where could she go, where could she live? She had no money to start a life with.

She considered suicide. So many girls killed themselves in this country that it wouldn't attract much notice.

She walked and thought about these things until she found her way back to her hotel, and then she threw herself onto the bed and fell into a deep sleep.

The next day at the club she met Yusuf, a reporter who wanted to interview her. He liked the music, and he was polite and good natured.

At first Roxy thought: It can't be. There's something wrong here, and it will come out sooner or later. No one could be that straightforward.

But he was straightforward, more so than it would seem possible for a person to be.

He was compassionate, honest, and respectful.

Roxy began to think she'd encountered a miracle.

15

In this interesting apartment in Cihangir, Leyla met people who were different from anyone she'd ever seen in her life; she learned about a different facet of Turkey from each of them, and in the end she began to think that the life in the mansion garden that she'd enjoyed so much, this "withdrawal from the world and burying oneself in memories," was not such a wonderful thing after all. Was someone who was almost eighty capable of learning new things? If this person had Leyla's appetite for learning things she didn't know, everything was possible.

During these days of tribulation, Leyla's only consolation was being able to observe this new world. After so many years of sorrow and loneliness among the magnolia and jasmine, she was suddenly discovering Turkey's crazy energy, its careless, haphazard yet attractive side.

In recent years she had become aware of and thought deeply about an important point of view. People grew older, and there was no privilege in this, but some people matured as they grew older, and others died without ever becoming mature. The critical point was when a person stopped asking "How do I look?" and started asking "How do I see?"

The young people around her were engaged in a constant struggle to prove themselves to those around them. This was a necessary struggle. Because they could only discover what those qualities were that differentiated them from others by trying to prove themselves. Naturally the most important questions were for a person during this stage of development were "How am I perceived? Do they like me? Do they appreciate me? How do I appear to other people?"

But after a certain stage a person had to get over this struggle and, in order to mature, had to let go of the question "How do I look?"

At this point a person should be one of the judges rather than a participant in the race, to be seeking not gold but the identity of a dealer in gold, to pass from being appraised to being the one who appraises. This was what becoming mature meant. When Leyla saw those young people in the apartment in Cihangir squirming and struggling and trying to make themselves liked, she felt a deep compassion for them and wanted to share everything she knew with them. She herself was no longer an actor in this world.

There were some very interesting people among the friends who came in and out of the apartment. Among them was a theater director with a sandy, handlebar mustache that was reminiscent of Friedrich Nietzsche's, who, when talking about an interesting project, said, in his own words, that he wanted to use this old Ottoman Republican woman as a "consultant." Because he needed someone who knew the period of transition from empire to republic. They were putting on Refik Halit's *Crazy* in a little theater in Beyoğlu. Leyla didn't know this play, but when Leyla asked why, when there were so many new and talented writers they had chosen such an old writer, the boy from the theater told her something interesting.

The play *Crazy* told the story of a man who went into a coma during the last days of the Empire and then regained consciousness a few years later in the Republican period. The poor man had difficulty understanding all the tremendous changes he saw. The society in which he had lived was gone and had been replaced by a completely different society. The sultan was now gone, rule by decree had been abolished, and people were dressing like Europeans. Men were wearing hats like unbelievers, and women had forsaken the veil, and wandered about with naked chins and arms. The poor man didn't believe what he saw and thought he must have gone crazy. To find out what had happened, he asked for the *Tasvir-i Efkar* newspaper, and the boy said, "That newspaper doesn't exist anymore, now we get the *Republic* newspaper." When he heard this the man became very upset and said, "Please don't utter that word! If the sultan's spies hear it we could be in big trouble."

They struggled hopelessly to convince the man that they are now living in a republic, and when they brought him a copy of the *Republic* newspaper the man was in for another shock. Because the newspaper was printed in the Latin alphabet, and the poor man couldn't read it. In a single moment, he had become ignorant and illiterate.

Leyla laughed as she listened to this, and she liked the play, and the idea of it being staged. Since they needed help with the subject of the play, she was going to do everything she could to explain the profound changes that had turned the country upside down. She was just a child during that period, but she knew about what life was like when the new regime came to power after the Republican revolution. She'd heard many stories from those around her.

"How can I describe those times to you," she said to the young people. "From the moment Atatürk displayed his hat and said, 'Gentlemen, this is called a hat,' millions of men took the red fezzes or the turbans off their heads and rushed about trying to find one of these things that unbelievers wore on their heads. Because not wearing a hat marked you as an enemy of the new regime and of the revolution, and meant being a reactionary, and could result in your meeting a bad end. All over Anatolia, as in Istanbul, there was a hat panic.

"He would gather together all the prominent men and say, 'Gentlemen, you will get rid of your fezzes and turbans, and from now on you will wear hats.' This was an order, and an order that came from a high place. 'If you want to keep your heads on your shoulders, you had better start wearing a hat immediately.'

"Those who asked, 'Where are we going to find this invention called a hat?' did not receive an answer. Everyone had to take care of his own head. The gardeners, servants, and watchmen who lived at the mansion worried for some time about where they would find hats and then started wearing hastily sewn pieces of cloth on their heads. To the Albanian watchman who refused to give up his fez they said, 'I swear, they'll cut off your head. There's nothing we can do to help you.' Because failure to conform to the laws of the Republic was an insult. The stubborn watchman insisted that, 'This is all I know, so this is what I'm going to wear.'"

Leyla, who saw that the mustachioed boy from the theater listened attentively and constantly took notes, began to feel that she really was a theater consultant, and enjoyed herself a great deal.

"If I were you," she said, "I would put a hat-makers workshop or a symbolic hat factory in one corner of the stage. And above it I would write 'Borsalino.' Because at that time the major tradesmen of Istanbul put in orders for millions of Borsalino hats from Italy. The newspapers reported that the hat factories of Europe were working three shifts to send enough hats to Turkey but were still unable to meet the demand. It was impossible to find hats for millions of people all at once."

Sometimes Leyla wondered whether such a revolution could ever happen in Europe. For instance, would it be possible in France for everyone, within a single year, to be made to wear a turban, learn the Arabic alphabet, listen to oriental music, and practice Ottoman customs?

She didn't think such a thing would be possible, but it had happened in Turkey.

Leyla remembered something she'd heard or read about the breakup of the Empire. There were three ways to end an empire: The first was in the manner of the Roman Empire, to disappear slowly over time. The second was the British Empire. This was an example of planned transfer, where it was decided which country would be granted sovereignty when. The third was the Ottoman Empire. One night it went to bed as an empire and the next day, it woke up as a republic.

When she told this to the theater director, and everyone liked the idea, she regretted all the years she had spent alone.

And that night in bed, as she thought about this conversation, she felt somewhat regretful. She was trying to conform to the young people's lively mood and to say things appropriate to their mentality.

It was clear that these theater people didn't like Atatürk, and uttered the word "Kemalist" with a mocking smile, and made fun of the revolution. In her youth it would have been impossible to think such a thing. Because then the name Kemal was a symbol of the war of independence and the struggle for survival. All the peoples who made up the Empire had rebelled one by one and had embraced their freedom. Istanbul and Anatolia were occupied. The prime minister of England had talked of "driving the Turks back into Central Asia." In this situation, the Muslim Turks had no choice but to engage in a war of liberation, and the name of Mustafa Kemal, the leader of this movement, had always been greatly respected in her family.

Kemal Pasha had encountered the civilizations of both East and West, and there was nothing strange in his choosing the civilization of the West. Because he was born and raised in Salonika, and when he compared the European part of the Empire with those of Asia, North Africa, and the Middle East, the general came to the conclusion that the East was falling apart and that it was finished. Development was in the West. Like many revolutionary leaders in the world, the general was a child of the French Revolution.

In the end, like Leyla's family, the intelligence, heart, civilization, and leaders of the Ottoman Empire were in Europe, that is, in the Balkans.

When she thought about these things, it saddened her that she hadn't enlightened the young people. It had been a mistake for her to share their jokes. From now on she would have to tell them what was what. Yes, during the revolution there were some tragicomic incidents, but these were for the purpose of saving the country from the grip of religion and reactionary tendencies.

Tomorrow night she would tell them that Atatürk's revolution was not the first time in history that the Turks had changed their culture and civilization. Having adapted the civilization of their neighbors the Chinese, they converted to Islam during their migration to Anatolia and came under Arab Iranian influence. And the past two hundred and fifty years had been a time of Europeanization. Both China and the Balkans were part of their culture. It contained both the Middle East and the Caucasus. It contained the traditions of North Africa, the Greeks, the Armenians, and the Kurds. Leyla didn't think there was an example of this much variety anywhere in the world.

The next evening she was going to tell this to the young people: about the journey from China to Europe, the end point of this migratory culture.

Leyla remembered the aged nanny in the neighboring mansion. When she met her the woman was already very old, and she would wander around in her slippers muttering, "He did it, he really did it." When Leyla wanted to learn what this meant, the children who lived in the mansion told her the reason. When Mustafa Kemal was a cadet at the Harbiye Military School, he came to the mansion to study with his friend. She would bring coffee to the two cadets when they were studying in the garden. Mustafa Kemal pointed to the sultan's palace across the water and told her, "Look, I'm going to turn that place into a museum!" The woman said, "You're talking nonsense," and scolded this blond youth who spoke so disrespectfully about the great palace. This was why, in her last days, the woman wandered around muttering, "He did it, he really did it!"

When Leyla remembered this story, she was once again amazed at how the unthinkable had been accomplished.

She was going to tell this story to the young people too. She was also going to say that the War of Independence was really defensive and how Anatolia became a sacred shelter for Muslims fleeing three continents.

That night she felt the need to read Lieutenant Robert Whitaker's morocco-bound diary once again.

This was what her father wrote:

> The moment I left school I found myself in a sea of blood, amid the screams of people killing one another, of children left without mothers or fathers. For people from a place like England, cut off as it is from the rest of the world, it was difficult to understand this violence, and this mixture of races, cultures, languages, and religions. But Bennett says we have to see this as a war about property and the division of spoils. And he's right.
>
> Many people have their eyes on the lands of the Ottoman State, through which the trade routes of the world pass. This is why the Turks were driven out of the Balkans and the Middle East with terrible massacres, and later the Turks who were afraid of losing their country did the same thing in Anatolia. In the end millions of people lost their homes, and other people came to live in these houses. Now we Europeans have occupied Istanbul and Anatolia. We have to see these disasters that have befallen us, the death of millions of people, the hunger, the misery as a struggle over land.

Leyla sees herself in this passage and wants to translate it for the young people. At first glance it seemed such a simple explanation, but after thinking about it she understood that her father was right. There were small fights over small properties and large fights over large properties. Her father didn't live to see the collapse of the Ottoman State and the population exchanges between Greece and Turkey, but he felt it coming. In the end, people who had lived in the same place for hundreds of years were uprooted. Serbs, Bulgars, Montenegrins, Greeks, and Arabs threw the Turks out of their lands after hundreds of years of occupation, and the Turks, fearing for their survival, secretly organized the oppression of the non-Muslims in Anatolia, the last remaining piece of their homeland, and later the newly founded Republic expelled a million Greeks. Everyone moved into each other's houses, and the property of millions of people was under occupation. These things had happened to simple people. This was the inalterable fate of these lands.

During her long life, Leyla had heard about the suffering of people who had lost their houses, their countries, their lands, and their native languages. These were the heart-rending stories such as the one about her great uncle sucking milk from the bloody breast of his dead mother at Nevrokop. For years the story that Kurdish Memo the firewood man told about the fiddle-playing Armenian haunted her dreams.

When the Armenian civilians were expelled from Harput, to be brought to Syria, they were attacked by Kurdish bandits about an hour outside of the city. The bandits brought the Armenians to a place that was later known as Bloody Stream, and, after taking their gold and their valuables, started killing them. A little later the stream was red with blood. Then a strange thing happened, and the silence was broken by the unlikely sound of a fiddle. An old Armenian had taken out his fiddle and was playing a sad tune. The chief of the bandits was very annoyed by this, and he went to the old man to tell him to stop. The old man looked into the bandit's eyes and continued playing. Everyone had stopped and was watching the scene. The sound of the fiddle continued until the bandit stabbed the old man. The man's fingers slid down the strings, and no one could tell whether the sound they heard was the man screaming or the last screech of the fiddle.

No one knows who is living in these Armenians' houses now, who is tilling their fields, who is doing business in their shops.

All this blood was shed for the sake of property. It was a process that didn't distinguish between Turks, Bulgars, Serbs, Greeks, Armenians, Kurds, Jews, or Circassians. Some were taken out of their homes, and some were put into other people's homes. This was the drama of millions of families.

Leyla had also been moved by a story Geoffrey had told her. It was a story about a professor of Armenian descent named Adamyan who lived in America. When the professor suffered a stroke, he found himself in the hospital, surrounded by his wife, Mary, his son, John, and his daughter, Eileen. Mary took his hand and asked him how he was. But the professor didn't understand, and he was speaking a language they had never heard. The woman and her children looked at each other in bewilderment. They didn't understand what the professor was saying because he wasn't speaking English. In panic, the daughter said, "Father, say something." The professor said, "What are you saying? I don't understand you." He spoke these words in Armenian. The following week the doctor told them the truth. The professor, who had migrated from

Anatolia to America in his youth, had lost his ability to speak English because of the stroke. He only spoke Armenian, which he had spoken with his mother and father, who were killed by bandits during a forced migration. Because his American wife and his children didn't know this language, they were unable to talk to him properly for the rest of his life.

Leyla had heard about the suffering of millions of people who had lost their homes, without knowing that one day she would share the same fate.

One winter day at home she had been reading Dostoyevsky's diary. Some sentences about Istanbul caught her attention, and she thought: so even great writers see things this way.

Dostoyevsky wrote the following:

> Yes, the Golden Horn and Constantinople, all of this will be ours. To begin with, this will come to pass of its own accord, precisely because the time has come. Not only because it is a famous port because of the Bosphorus Straits and because it is the "center of the world." Not only from the standpoint of the long-understood need for the tremendous giant that is Russia to emerge at last from his locked room, in which he has already grown up to the ceiling, into the open spaces, where he may breathe the free air of the seas and the oceans…

The great writer from St. Petersburg listed the reasons for taking Istanbul and was lyrical about saving the city from the Turkish yoke, but after this Leyla was not so interested. Dostoevsky's words praised a certain view. Because, as he said, Russia could only reach the warm seas by passing in front of her house. From her own private shore, she would watch them sail past on the dark blue waters, so close she could almost reach out and touch them. But it was not as if this pride did not cause her to feel sadness. Because if even a voice of human conscience such as Dostoevsky could covet the property of others, how could she condemn the things ordinary people had done? Perhaps he wanted to say that the Turks were not from here, that they came from Central Asia to take Istanbul, but if history was to send everyone back where they belonged, Manhattan should be given to the Native Americans, and several countries in Europe should be given to the Etruscans. There was no way out of this.

Dostoevsky was not the only one who wanted to take the Bosphorus. Whenever she read a foreign book, there was always something about capturing Istanbul and the Bosphorus. What an interesting desire this was. But at the same time it was very strange for Leyla. Because people were fighting over a place that was her whole world, the place where she'd spent her childhood, and caught fish, and watched the ships sailing past from her own private shore.

Before falling asleep she thought: The problem of shelter. Damn this problem. This is the cause of all our suffering.

16

The young people came home one evening to find Leyla in a frenzy of activity. She was sitting at the table with the purple tablecloth, and there were papers in front of her, and she was writing.

When asked what she was doing, she replied, “I’m writing letters to everyone and explaining the situation.”

It was clear which situation she was talking about.

“Who are these letters going to?” they asked.

Leyla showed them the envelopes one by one: “This one is to the president, this one is to the prime minister, this one is to the minister of justice. These are to newspaper owners.”

It was as if Leyla was experiencing a burst of energy after days of sadness and weakness. She was making a big effort to write the letters and put them in their envelopes.

“I want everyone to hear about the injustice that has been done,” she said. “The men who seized my house may be powerful, but there are people more powerful than them in this country, and among them there must be men of conscience."

When she said this, Yusuf swallowed but still didn't say anything. Because he was sure the letters would never reach the people they were addressed to and would be read by people low in the ranks of the bureaucracy. Who would listen to an old woman's cries for help? He'd seen with his own eyes how these things work at the newspapers. Who knew how many letters the owner's secretary threw into the trash every day. Hundreds of letters came every day, asking for help for everything from scholarships to money for surgery. Not one of them was read. But he still wanted to take part in Leyla's game and preferred to see her in an enthusiastic frame of mind.

"Mail these first thing in the morning Yusuf," said Leyla.

"Of course, Leyla," Yusuf answered politely.

Leyla was the kind of person who cannot countenance defeat. The moment she felt defeated she became ill. For this reason, what she was doing was as much to preserve her psychological health as to get her house back.

With the letters, she was undertaking another effort, to go to the big Catholic, Protestant, and Orthodox churches and the synagogues to light candles and pray. Like many people from Istanbul, she knew that one could pray to God in any house, and that there wasn't really much difference when it came down to it.

In Istanbul, people had been praying to one another's saints for hundreds of years.

The next day Leyla hired a taxi and went to pray at the Süleymaniye Mosque, the Neve Shalom Synagogue, and St. Anthony's Church.

In the afternoon she went to perform devotions to the sacred talismans that were believed to have protected Istanbul.

In truth she trusted these talismans more than she did the places of worship. These talismans were so powerful that they could offer protection from earthquakes as well as from scorpions and snakes. For instance, the column in the Hippodrome was made from three hundred thousand stones, and a strong magnet had been placed at the top. This column was believed to have prevented earthquakes. Despite the many earthquakes that had occurred since it was built, this column had not been damaged at all. Though because of all the earthquakes that had occurred since then, it could be considered to have lost its power.

In Sultanahmet there was also the bronze column composed of three intertwined serpents. After a Janissary cut off two of the heads the city was invaded by scorpions.

For Leyla the most wonderful of these talismans was the rooster talisman. When there was a famine the rooster would crow, calling all the birds of the world to Istanbul. When these birds arrived, they fell dead out of the sky, and the people of Istanbul gathered them up and ate them hungrily. From another point of view this is a story of a treacherous crow, but it was acting for the sacred aim of saving Istanbul.

When it came to work, health, fate, sickness, and death, the people of Istanbul did not practice religious discrimination, but hoped for help from one another's sacred practices. Many times Leyla had seen Christians and Muslims visiting the holy wells side by side. Istanbul has a great wealth of holy wells and springs. There were fountains and springs everywhere. Muslims would fill their jugs at the Orthodox holy wells and use the water to ward off trouble of all kinds. One of the holy pools contained fish that were yellow on one side and brown on the other. Muslims who came to get water there pretended not to know the story of these fish. The story goes as follows. A Byzantine monk was frying fish when news came that Mehmet the Conqueror had breached the walls of the city. On hearing that the city had fallen to the Turks, the fish jumped from the frying pan back into the pool. They remained cooked on one side and raw on the other. If Istanbul were ever to become Byzantine again, the fish would once again be a single color.

Leyla didn't look for these fish, but she did visit all the Byzantine talismans she could find, as well as lighting candles in churches. According to the traditions of the local Christians, a prayer had to be repeated for seven successive Tuesdays to be accepted. Leyla was not sure but thought this might be because the city had been conquered on a Tuesday.

If Leyla got her house back, she was going to have to make small offerings of thanks to all the religious institutions and talismans of Istanbul.

17

Ali Yekta came from a family that upheld the traditions and customs of the society in which they lived, and indeed believed that doing so was of the utmost importance. They always felt this responsibility deeply and feared making a social faux pas like the plague.

The thing that had been troubling him so much lately also had its source in a matter of good manners. Seeing that the renovation of the mansion his son had bought was proceeding so quickly, he would soon be leaving the Kadizade Mansion where he was born and had served and move to his own mansion on the other side of the Bosphorus. But how was he going to explain this to his master, Rıza. He felt in his bones that it was impolite of him to leave in this way, but he wanted to explain the situation as soon as possible so that they could look for someone to replace him. But somehow he couldn't gather the courage to face Rıza and tell him that after all these years he was leaving to move into his own house.

This wasn't an easy thing after so many years of serving first the master's father and then the master himself. Night after night he thought about how he was going to do this, and every night he made up his mind to talk to the master the following day, but somehow, in the course of his daily duties, he somehow couldn't gather his courage to explain the situation.

On one hand, he had a feeling he wouldn't be as happy in his new home as he was here. There was no chance of finding any peace in the same house as that ill-mannered Necla. Who knew what fights, tensions, and wars of nerves he would live through. But he also believed that his son's deep respect for his father would come before everything. In the end. Necla would understand that she was just a handmaiden, and the day she understood that she couldn't come between this father and son, she would understand who the true master of the mansion was.

The problem was this girl's lack of manners.

Even though Ali Yekta had been raised according to Ottoman traditions and had been schooled in this subject by his father, he changed suddenly with the establishment of the Republic and was proud of the fact that he had been clever enough to adapt to the mores of this new culture.

Indeed the lifestyle in the mansions had been looking to Europe for the past century and had become practically European. Foreign governesses, piano teachers, and literary afternoons had become as enduring a part of the landscape as the sea.

But while the revolution was raining down like a cloudburst, Ali Yekta saw that people were confused and had no idea what to do in this race to change the culture. Commands were coming down from on high, from Ankara, and to disobey them was unthinkable, but in an Islamic country where men were allowed to have four wives and countless concubines, and women were veiled and kept behind screens, it was painful to suddenly have to adapt to modern European cultural norms.

Books on the new etiquette were published to help people learn what to do and how to live. Those who learned the Latin alphabet read these books and tried to learn the new rules. Though after the Arabic script was banned and replaced by the Latin alphabet there weren't many people left who could read. There was a nationwide campaign to get people to learn the Latin alphabet, and classes were started everywhere. Men and women of all ages went to these classes to learn these strange-looking Latin letters.

With the help of the family for whom he worked, Ali Yekta was among the first to learn the Latin letters, and he read all the new etiquette books he could get hold of, and took notes, and shared what he learned with those around him.

Because without these books, people had no way of knowing what to do. A nation was learning how to live all over again from books.

For instance, he memorized these rules from a thin, illustrated book that was published in those times:

> On the boat, train, tram, and all other modes of public transportation, do not stare at the woman across from you as if she were edible. She is not a fashion model there to display her clothes.
>
> It is inappropriate to walk the avenues of the city with one's head uncovered. No matter how well you are dressed, how politely you behave, and how handsome your face is, you will definitely be regarded by many as unrefined if you do not have a hat on your head.

Another rule stated:

> When we have been out walking in the summer heat, and then board a ferry or a train, do we take off and air the shoes that have been confining our feet and inflaming our corns? We prefer to suffer rather than behave in such an uncouth manner.

There was also advice for women who had started wearing modern clothes and who felt naked when they went out without being covered by a veil:

> For instance, on public transportation, do not sit with your knees squeezed together and your stockings rolled down below your knees. This is

> both laughable and uncouth. Use either garters or elastic to keep your stockings up.

Or this rule:

> If you are worried that your corset or garters might fall, do not find an excuse to stand in front of a shop window and pull your clothes this way and that. You will have many watchers, and such incautious movements may attract unwanted attention.

The pencil drawings that illustrated these books helped to etch these rules on Ali Yekta's mind. In these illustrations, stylish women wearing hats stood in front of shop windows, and the well-dressed gentlemen seemed very proud of the fedora hats that they either wore on their heads or carried in their hands.

There were also rules concerning the telephone, which was now becoming more common:

> When speaking on the telephone one must always be brief and to the point, and it is considered uncouth to be longwinded or to speak in a loud voice. It is not considered proper to telephone a workplace simply to ask after someone's health.

Ali Yekta enthusiastically defended these rules that he read in books published at the beginning of the 1930s, and especially now, when everyone had a cell phone stuck to their ear, he thought these books should be republished.

The changes gave rise to incidents that challenged belief. For instance, when the first female jurist was appointed in 1924, people were so astounded they thought they were dreaming. After local elections in 1930, when women were given the right to vote and to run for office, women were elected as mayors, and in later years were elected as representatives to parliament, it was difficult for people to get used to the idea.

Because the Kadizade Mansion where Ali Yekta was raised supported Atatürk's revolution wholeheartedly, it was only natural that he and his father embraced it with enthusiasm. Throughout his life, he never had any doubts on this subject and remained loyal to the "Great Man" who had once visited the Kadizade Mansion.

To leave this mansion where he had worked for years and of which he had become a part meant breaking much older rules of behavior, rules particular to the East that governed the complex world of human relationships and that had been created over a period of hundreds of years.

After agonizing over the matter, Ali Yekta decided to inform his master of the situation by letter first and then talk to him later.

One evening he sat down to write this letter in the elegant penmanship he had been taught in the schools of the Republic.

"Esteemed Sir," he found it suitable to begin. But somehow, no matter how he tried, he couldn't manage the rest of the letter or think of how to explain his reasons for wanting to leave.

Because even though he wanted to leave, he also felt as if he belonged to this mansion. His feet knew the creaking stairs, his hands knew the carved banisters and the porcelain doorknobs, and he didn't need to use his eyes to turn on any of the light switches.

After attempting a few more drafts, he realized that writing a letter was too impersonal a way to do what he had to do.

Whatever happened, tomorrow he was going to brace himself and go up to Rıza's room and explain the situation. He was going to begin by saying that since his father had started working for Rıza's esteemed parents, they had never been treated badly, never been looked askance at, had felt for years as if it was their own home, and had never had a single complaint.

But he hoped that the gentleman would understand that he wanted to spend his last years in his son's house, with his grandchildren. And he was aware that he had reached a mature age, and he could no longer find the strength to go up and down the mansion stairs and would no longer be of us much use to the gentleman. He hoped that the gentleman would take all of this into account, understand that his working life in that house had come to an end, and give him leave to go.

After making this decision, Ali Yekta felt he could drift into a comfortable sleep. His anxiety concerning this mansion had begun to ease, but another anxiety, concerning the arguments he was likely to have with Necla, remained.

He didn't really think his son would allow such a thing to happen, but still, after talking to his master the next day he was going to go to his son's mansion and solve the problem once and for all.

Who knew, perhaps after he had moved, his old master would come visit him and see that he was living a better and more affluent life than he had before. Ali Yekta knew that even when he was his old master's equal, he would still treat him with the same faultless respect and would still love him as his benefactor. Because, no matter what else could be said of him, he came from a family that knew the rules of proper behavior.

18

Roxy and Yusuf's moans were audible from the next room. Leyla could hear their heavy breathing. Leyla had spent her life completely alone and had never been touched by a man, and although in her youth she had passed nights of frustration, all of that was past now.

Only the sound of the piano from the neighboring mansion still echoed in her ears. And only once in a while. It seemed so long ago that it was as if someone else had lived it.

She remembered the days when she had been in love with the mysterious pianist who she had never set eyes on, and about whom she knew nothing except that his name was Nejat, and that he was sick and melancholic and never went outside.

After listening for a time, she would go to the piano herself and begin playing, and when she heard the piano next door stop, she knew that Nejat was listening to her.

Nejat played in the Turkish style. And Leyla played in the European style. While one played classical Eastern melodies, the other answered with Chopin and Brahms. It was as if they were expressing the split in the personalitics of the Bosphorus mansions that were both Turkish and European. For a time, they made love by means of the piano.

On summer nights, Leyla would feel as if her body was on fire. But in the bright light of summer afternoons she was seized by a strange melancholy. There was nothing for her to be upset about, but she felt a boundless sadness within her. These were the moments when she yearned to live.

In that summer light she saw the world with a clarity that left no room for dreams, emotions, or fairy tales. It was a rawness that saddened her, that made her feel cool toward life, and that she had difficulty explaining even to herself. She didn't like this openness, this clarity. She preferred the Bosphorus in winter, with its fogs and mists and winds, the way the water turned a milky white mixed with green when snow fell into it, the sound of unseen motorboats passing to and fro, and the cries of the seagulls. At those moments the Bosphorus had an element of adventure, as if the currents were flowing more quickly. And of course the winds were fiercer.

But as she grew older and her physical urges lessened, she was also free from the depression caused by the bright light of summer. She'd learned to make the most out of every hour of the day. Since childhood she'd been in the habit of spending summer days lying in a hammock reading, looking at the magnolia flowers above her, and, toward evening, watching the birds and the clouds beginning to turn pink.

When she remembered these happy moments, she felt increasingly bitter about being torn from her house, as well as increasingly helpless.

The pain that during the first days had burned like a bullet wound had become deeper and bowed her down so much that it took an effort to stand up straight.

But she was clever enough to see that she was depressed and that this attitude would slowly wear her down. She yearned for her house and her own shore. She wanted to be on the shore where, as a child, she would sail paper boats, and fish, and watch the huge ships sail past, dreaming of the faraway places they were going. In this season the smell of wild violets was everywhere, and the nights were heavy with the smell of jasmine.

Among the crowded concrete buildings of Cihangir, the summer heat was so unbearable that she felt she was going to suffocate. She was used to living by the seashore, and her body needed water; it missed moisture, dew, clouds, and fog.

But what wounded her more than this yearning was the sense of being defeated and helpless. She had no choice but to bow her head to the injustice being done to her and her family. The way they had cut her off from her memories amounted to a betrayal of her family.

Yusuf and Roxy didn't fail to notice how she had withdrawn, how she seldom emerged from her room, how she wrote for hours in her diary, and how day by day she grew thinner and more drawn. It was clear she'd reached the limits of her strength.

Leyla was surprised that it was only at such a late age that she understood the importancc of having a home. This meant that you only knew the value of something when it was taken away from you.

One evening she said to Yusuf, "Tomorrow I'm going to see the house. Hire a taxi for me."

She said this in such an authoritative and decisive manner that Yusuf had no choice but to agree.

The next morning he woke to find Leyla dressed and wearing a hat and beige gloves and waiting for him.

He tried to insist on going with Leyla, but she wouldn't hear of it. She was going to go alone. She had to see with her own eyes what they'd done to the house.

And that's what happened. The taxi brought her to the ferry station in Eminönü. Leyla boarded a ferry, sat up in the front, ordered a tea from the waiter, and quietly sat and watched the Bosphorus.

Once again she was surprised by the water traffic at the mouth of the Bosphorus. When she was a child there weren't this many ships passing through. Now, according to what she had read, fifty thousand ships a year came through.

As the ferry approached Vaniköy her excitement increased, and her heart began to beat faster. As the ferry stopped at stations on both sides, it passed close by the waterfront mansions, and Leyla's emotions were in turmoil as her mind filled with old memories.

She breathed in the cool Bosphorus breeze, felt the spray from the prow of the boat, watched the birds that skimmed the surface of the water, as well as the castles, palaces, churches, and mosques that they passed. She was pleased by the view and felt a childlike joy that she had difficulty containing.

She realized how much she had missed the birds that darted like lightning from one end of the sparkling waters of the Bosphorus to the other, so swiftly across the water. When she was a child her grandmother told her that these birds were the souls of people who had lived on the Bosphorus. They flew constantly over the waters because they couldn't bear to leave. Leyla had watched these birds all her life and had thought of them as departed members of her own family. Her grandfather, her grandmother, her mother, and her uncle flew among these little flocks. The strange birds who flew alone reminded her of an unlucky Englishman in his twenties. With their boundless energy, the birds were trying to return home, and this is why they constantly sped like lightning along the Bosphorus from the Black Sea to the Sea of Marmara.

She couldn't stop her tears when the ferry passed Bosnalı Abdullah Avni Pasha's mansion. Her grandfather's house looked like a bride standing before the dark blue water. The waves of passing ships slapped against the quay and splashed up onto the house itself. There didn't seem to have been many changes made to the house. She felt that if she looked carefully enough, she could see her grandparents drinking tea on the quay.

Leyla got off at the station, leaping off the ferry before the ropes had been tied to the bollard, though with slightly less than her former agility, and, passing through a cobbled square shaded by a huge plan tree, started walking toward the mansion. Those who were sitting drinking coffee in the square, as well as the waiters setting tables for lunch at the fish restaurant, watched her curiously. Most of them knew the old lady.

As she walked toward the house, Leyla didn't even know what she'd come there to do. She wondered if she would be able to get in, if she would manage to talk to the new owners. She probably wouldn't be able to, but she reached the house feeling as if she wouldn't be able to live if she didn't go there. She stopped in front of the green garden gate, in the shade of the plane tree. No one came to her; either they hadn't noticed her yet or they were pretending not to notice.

After watching the house for a while, she saw a well-dressed, elderly gentleman get off a red city bus and start walking toward her. He was dressed like a gentleman of the old style, in a beige suit with a patterned tie. When he reached her he looked at her with curiosity and asked politely, "Are you looking for someone, madam?" He had a full voice, of the type that was called plumy in her time.

"I'm looking," said the old woman, "I'm looking at the mansion."

"I understand," said the man. "It's a beautiful mansion, isn't it? It belongs to my son. I haven't had the pleasure of meeting you, are you from the neighborhood?"

When he said this, the woman felt that this must be a lucky day. It was as if her instincts had drawn her here simply to have this encounter.

"Sir," she said, "you are a godsend. I've been standing here wondering what to do."

"If there's any way I can be of assistance? . . ."

"Yes there is," said Leyla. "There is indeed. You were sent by God."

Ali Yekta was very impressed by this well-dressed and elegant woman whose accent and tone of voice reminded him of the old days. It was clear that she wasn't just anyone.

"I'm at your service, madam," he said.

"Please," said Leyla. Then she added, "I am Leyla Bosnalı. I am the granddaughter of Bosnalı Abdullah Avni Pasha, who built this mansion."

Now it's happened, thought Ali Yekta. He was a good judge of people, and he could tell an aristocrat at a glance. And he'd felt something like that about this woman. Perhaps she'd been living in the mansion garden and had sold the place.

Gesturing to the door he said, "Welcome, madam. No matter how often this mansion changes ownership, it will still be considered yours."

Leyla hesitated, and said, "I don't know . . ."

Ali Yekta insisted. "Actually the work is still in progress, but no doubt we'll find a place to sit in the garden. Please, you go first."

And so, almost two months after she'd been thrown out, Leyla entered her garden once again. She looked around with curiosity. Because it was forbidden to alter the facades of historical buildings, everything looked the same as it had. It just looked as if it was in better condition, the wood had been painted white, and it looked clean and bright. Sounds of hammering and sawing could be heard from within.

But there was still a great change, an unfamiliar emptiness.

When the servants saw Leyla enter the garden with Ali Yekta they were very surprised. The old woman who they'd dragged out of there was now a guest. By coincidence neither Ömer nor Necla were around. They could only be alerted by telephone. This is what they did.

Meanwhile, Ali Yekta had invited Leyla to sit in one of the wicker chairs in the garden and then sat across from her. He told the servants to bring tea.

Ali Yekta was very impressed by Leyla's aristocratic manner, and in his excitement he became nostalgic for the old days. You didn't meet people like this very often anymore. The way Istanbul has been overrun by Anatolian villagers, he thought, Balkan aristocrats have become like relics of the past.

And now the most elegant of these relics was sitting across from him. With extreme politeness he asked, "Would you be offended if I were so bold as to ask the reason for your visit?"

Leyla said, "How very kind of you," and then was silent for a time.

She wasn't sure if she should tell the whole story. How much did this man know about it? She'd never seen him before. Did he not know about how unjustly she'd been treated?

When she looked hopelessly around the garden, and at the little house at the foot of the wall, she felt as if she'd been slapped, and she gave a little cry and covered her mouth with her hand.

"What happened, madam?"

"The tree, the magnolia tree!"

"Excuse me?"

"It's nothing, it's passed."

From the moment she saw that the magnolia tree had been cut down she'd been shaken by the desire to cry. But she held herself together and decided to tell the gentleman everything.

"If you want to know the truth, I don't know what I came here to do, sir," she said, "but I needed to see my house. I'm desperate."

Then she told him how her house had been seized, how no one had listened to her when she said she had a separate deed, how she'd been physically dragged out, how after waiting helplessly in front of the gate for two days she'd taken shelter in the gardener's grandson Yusuf's apartment in Cihangir, and how a doctor had declared her incompetent without even having seen her.

As she spoke, Ali Yekta's eyes opened wide in amazement, and his face turned bright red.

When Leyla had finished speaking, he asked, "Was it my son who did all of this to you? I don't want there to be any mistake, it was Ömer Cevheroğlu who evicted you from your house?"

"Unfortunately yes!" said Leyla. "I have to tell the truth even at the price of hurting your feelings. I was thrown out of my family home by your son and his wife."

"My daughter-in-law," the man hissed. "I'm certain that she's behind everything. My son wouldn't have done something so unconscionable on his own."

Later, Ali Yekta made it clear to Leyla that he was very sorry about her situation, that he would do everything in his power to put things right, and that he would talk to his son about this matter right away.

After taking the telephone number of the house in Cihangir, he walked her respectfully to the gate.

Leyla was making her way back to the ferry station when she saw Yusuf walking toward her, and, with feigned harshness, she asked him what he was doing there when he should be at work. Her talk with Ali Yekta had given her hope, and despite the magnolia tree, she was in good spirits.

Yusuf sensed this, and, with the familiarity of someone who had been living in the same house as her for some time, he tried to turn it into a joke. "I can't live without you," he said. "Wherever you go, I'll be there."

Leyla laughed and, wagging her finger, said, "Don't confuse me with Roxy, Yusuf."

On the way back she told him about her promising talk with Ali Yekta, and said, "Let's see what happens."

19

His master Rıza put him at ease, and he felt a sense of relief after days of struggling with his conscience. When he finally went to see him, Rıza didn't give him a chance to say much, and as soon as he began talking said, "I know, Ali Yekta. Don't worry, I'm aware of everything. I know that the renovations to the mansion are almost finished and that you want to move there." Then he said, "I give you your due. You've done so much for our family . . ."

At these words Ali Yekta felt his eyes begin to water.

Once again, he asked himself the question that had been bothering him: Was he going to be this loved where he was going? As soon as he thought this he became upset; even though he was ashamed of his anxiety about his son's house, he couldn't help but feel it.

Will I be loved and respected in my new home as much as I am here? Even though he was a servant here, and would be master there, he couldn't get this poisonous question out of his mind.

Recently he'd become aware that he never saw his daughter-in-law Necla. Every time he went to the mansion the woman found an excuse not to be present.

In the end he decided to solve the problem once and for all and to go to the mansion and put a few personal belongings in the big room. It was on the morning he went to the mansion to carry out this decision that he unexpectedly met Leyla. He was shaken by what the woman told him. Ömer could never have behaved so cruelly to an old woman; Necla must have been the one who did it, and without his son knowing about it. Yes, yes, he hadn't known; he was sure of this; his son couldn't have had anything to do with this. Was it worth throwing an old woman out of her family home just to have a little guesthouse in the garden?

As he thought these things, Ali Yekta went into the mansion, climbed to the top floor, and headed for the big room. The work in this room seemed just about finished. The walls had been painted a pale violet, the ceiling decorations had been renewed, and the joinery had been painted white. The huge ships on the Bosphorus seemed to be in the room itself. At just that moment he saw a bright red ship passing. It was an exciting thing to see. He could have watched it lying in bed.

He hung the amber prayer beads he'd brought on the handle of the window, and put his Quran, in its case, on the windowsill. Now the room seemed a little more his own.

Just as he was descending the stairs feeling pleased with himself, he saw that his son had arrived. The watchman must have sent word to him.

Ömer said, “Father, so you’re here.”

“Yes, Ömer, I was just leaving my Quran, the one your grandfather left me, in my room. Move out the bed that’s in there. I’m going to bring my own bed.”

He noticed that his son had fallen quiet and wasn’t saying anything. Then Ömer suggested they have lunch together, so they went to the fish restaurant in the square by the ferry station. They sat at a table under the noble plane tree that had been standing there since Ottoman times. Ali Yekta thought that there was nothing as pleasingly cool in the summer heat as the shade of a plane tree. As if this shade had provided centuries of peace.

The father and son felt strange throughout the meal. As if there was more left unsaid than said, and an invisible curtain had been drawn between them.

For instance, they didn’t talk about the room. Every time Ali Yekta brought the subject up, Ömer managed to evade it. This deepened the father’s suspicions and brought to mind possibilities he didn’t want to believe. Was Necla’s influence over his son stronger than he’d thought? Had he lost his son? He tried to chase these poisonous questions out of his mind.

Finally he mentioned Leyla. He told him about their meeting this morning.

He saw that Ömer was uneasy about this subject. He was answering in a guilty manner. They didn’t think it right for the woman to live with them in their garden. She wasn't quite sane anyway.

Ali Yekta said he had a long conversation with Leyla, and he was certain she was quite sane.

Wasn't it disgraceful of him to have thrown this aristocratic lady out of her house at her age? This kind of thing brought bad luck and didn't bring anyone any peace. Don't they say that if you harm the innocent, in time it will come back to haunt you? Why did they need that little house in the garden when they had the whole mansion? They should have let the poor woman stay in her little house.

Ömer saw that there was no way out of this and tried to shift the blame off himself a little by saying, "Necla wanted to turn it into a guesthouse."

The moment he said this, he saw the look of anger cross his father's face, he regretted having said this, but it was too late.

He saw that Ali Yekta's face had turned bright red.

"Necla, Necla, Necla!" he shouted. The people at the other tables turned to look. "This woman is behind everything. Since when has this woman made decisions about our lives? Who does this woman think she is? What kind of person is she? There's a proper way to do things. Is this any way for a daughter-in-law to behave? She should be respectful of her elders and abide by their decisions instead of being such an upstart. I'm tired of hearing about what this Necla says."

When all the hatred that had built up in him came bursting out like this, Ali Yekta suddenly fell quiet. He wondered if perhaps he'd gone too far. Ömer's face was expressionless, and he didn't say anything.

For a while they remained silent and gave their attention to the red mullet on their plates. They listened to the cries of the seagulls. Sometime later Ali Yekta said in a low voice, "Do you think there's any way out of this situation?"

He looked into his son's hazel eyes in an almost pleading way. They both knew exactly what he was talking about, but for whatever reason, Ömer pretended not to understand.

"What situation, father?" he asked.

For a time Ali Yekta felt too sad to look up, and then, fearing the answer he might get, changed the subject.

"You should give that old woman back her house," he said.

"Father," said Ömer, "that business is over and done with. The old woman has lost her house."

"But, my son, this is a bad deed . . . in our religion there's such a thing as being cursed for cruelty. No good can come out of doing wrong to someone like that. Believe me, something bad will happen because of this."

"Father," said Ömer, "there's no chance that Necla would accept a solution like that. She's going to turn it into a guesthouse. Necla has made up her mind."

Then Ali Yekta felt something snap within him. Twice now he'd seen the power this Necla woman had over his son, and he was terrified. The father and son ate the rest of the meal in silence, without looking at each other, as if they were strangers.

That evening when Ali Yekta went back to his room in the mansion where he worked, he came down with a fever, and for two days he couldn't get out of bed and vomited everything he ate.

20

Because Cihangir was built on a steep slope leading up from the sea, some of the streets were stepped. Drivers who didn't know the area could suddenly find themselves at the top or bottom of a long flight of steps and would panic when they realized they didn't know if they could back out through the narrow streets.

Because Yusuf's building was on a relatively level street, Leyla was able to get out of the taxi at the front door. Otherwise, this old woman with her weak heart would have had to climb these stairs. The stairs in the building were difficult enough for her to manage. She had to rest and catch her breath at each landing.

This time, as she stopped to catch her breath on the third floor, the door opened, and she was confronted by an elderly man with tangled hair and beard, and his shirt open at the front. He was seeing off a boy who was carrying a guitar case. He said, "You must be the famous

Ottoman woman. Everyone in the neighborhood is talking about you."

Then he noticed how tired and worn out the woman looked.

"Are you all right? There's nothing wrong? Let me bring you a glass of water." He ran to get a glass of water, then looked at Leyla leaning against the wall, and then ran back to get a chair for her to sit on, and said, "Please come in. Catch your breath and then you can continue on your way."

Leyla hesitated and said, "I don't want to put you out," but then she went inside.

It looked like a place where an old family had lived for a long time. The furniture, the paintings on the walls, the piano, and the musical instruments gave the impression of a home that had seen better days.

The man introduced himself. When the man says that he was Constantine Palaeologus, she held back a laugh. She looked at the man suspiciously, hoping she hadn't wandered into the home of a madman. Is this man who's claiming to be the Byzantine Emperor a bit soft in the head?

The man said, "I understand your confusion, and I don't blame you. I'm not crazy, I'll show you my identity card if you like."

Then he added, "I going to tell you something that will surprise you even more, I really am a descendant of the Palaeologus dynasty. That is, my ancestors were the emperors of this city."

Leyla said, "It's possible, it's possible," but it was clear from her attitude that she didn't believe it.

Constantine Palaeologus said, "Just as you still have families descended from the Ottoman dynasty, we still have families descended from the Byzantine dynasties."

Leyla suddenly felt that she had to believe the man because he was talking in a serious and coherent manner.

"This building was ours," he said. "My grandfather had it built, but unfortunately we had to sell one apartment after another. Let me make you some lemonade."

"No," said Leyla, "don't go to the trouble. Are you a musician?"

"Yes, I'm a music teacher. I give classical guitar lessons."

Leyla found all of this very interesting. She was delighted to finally find someone she could talk to, and she started asking questions.

"What method do you teach? What do you have your students play?"

"The Carcassi method. I have them play the Tárrega etudes. As the students progress I have them play Villalobos, Barrios. The boy you just saw leaving is working on Bach. Don't pay attention to his appearance, he comes from a very poor Roma family, but he plays very well.

"That's very interesting. Where did you study?"

"I had a teacher. There was a famous Armenian guitar teacher, perhaps you've heard of him: Raffi Kaplanyan, I'm his student."

"I haven't heard of him," said Leyla, "but how interesting: the Armenian teacher's student is a Palaeologus, and his student is Roma."

"That's the magic of this city," said Constantine. "For centuries this was the only cosmopolitan city in the world.

It was much more colorful than the New York, Paris, or London of today, but unfortunately all of that has been lost."

"Why?"

"Being a pasha's granddaughter, you know the answer to that better than I do."

"I don't understand. Please explain."

Hesitantly, and in a low voice, the man said, "Nationalism, Turkification, the expulsion of non-Muslims. You see how Pera is. There are only a handful of non-Muslims like me. But we're the ones who built all these buildings."

Leyla didn't know what to say in response to this blame. She could only say, "You're exaggerating. It's not that bad. Are there only Turks living in Pera now?"

"You're right," said the man, "it's not just Turks living in Pera. After they expelled the non-Muslims, Kurds started moving in too. In the name of the Republic, you replaced Byzantine culture with Mesopotamian culture."

Leyla was astounded by what the man said. He was speaking calmly, and he wasn't being rude, but there was a deep resentment beneath his words.

"Why are you saying such harsh things, sir?" she asked. "Every nation has the right to defend itself. During the occupation of Istanbul and the Aegean region, Greeks allied themselves with our enemies, and isn't this treason against the nation?"

"Which nation, madam? These are occupied lands. Wasn't this once Byzantium? Who betrayed whom?"

When he said this Leyla began to suspect once again that he was mad. Here was a man who was still reacting to the conquest of the city five hundred years ago.

“Sir,” she said, “they taught me to see history from a contemporary point of view. Among those defending the city against the Turks was Mehmet the Conqueror’s relative Prince Orhan. They also called the Turkish soldiers who had converted to Christianity ‘*Turkopouli*.’ ”

Palaeologus said, “That doesn’t mean anything. There were also Greek soldiers fighting in the Turkish army.”

“Fine. This is what I’m saying. We can’t solve this with a nineteenth-century nationalistic mentality.”

“What you say is true, but this doesn’t prevent me from being saddened by the fall of Byzantium or from mourning the emperor whose body was identified by his red boots. And if you’re not responsible, why are you defending those who were? You are an Ottoman. Do you know what Ernest Renan says? A nation can only develop by struggling with its past. This is what the Republic did.”

After he said this, Leyla decided that the best thing for her to do was to keep quiet and not answer him. Because if things continued this way, there was going to be an argument. She’d had a chance to rest, anyway, and was feeling a little better.

She rose to her feet and politely asked to be excused. Her heart wasn’t beating wildly anymore.

At the door, Constantine apologized. “Please excuse me. I didn’t want to be rude. I’m not really that kind of person, it’s just that my nerves have been on edge lately.”

Leyla asked him what the matter was. Was he ill?

“No,” said the man. “I have to move out of here by the first of the month. I’m being evicted from the building my grandfather built.”

Then Leyla felt almost dizzy. She couldn't believe this coincidence. "Who's evicting you?" she asked. "Why? By what right?"

"They forged some documents to seize my house against debts. Then somehow this house ended up belonging to the mafia."

"Didn't you try to stand up for your rights?"

"I tried, but how could I get anywhere with a name like Constantine Palaeologus?"

Leyla said, "My name is Leyla Bosnalı, but this name wasn't enough to keep me from being evicted from a house to which I had the deed."

"I'm not at all surprised, madam," said Constantine. "This is the fate of this city. Every newcomer takes over the property of the people who were here before."

As she was making her way to the stairs, she saw two tears form in the man's eyes.

"A family has a beautiful house, and the next year you look and see that the house has slipped out of their hands." She suddenly remembered the words of the banker Zarifi. "Nowhere do fortunes change hands as quickly as they do in Istanbul," wrote the banker who used to lend money to the sultan.

It was true that the mansions of the Bosphorus never remained in the hands of their original owners; with every change of power and with every new age they changed hands.

So I'm not the only one in this situation, thought Leyla. This is the custom in this country. But in spite of everything, it was meaningless to go back five hundred years to the conquest.

21

Nothing can be kept secret in the neighborhoods of Istanbul, even a passing fly is noticed, but sometimes people pretend not to see.

Leyla's visit to the mansion was one of those things people pretended not to see.

Of course they saw her from afar, and they watched her encounter with Ali Yekta and their conversation in the garden, but they pretended not to have noticed.

They preferred not to do or say anything until they knew which way the wind was blowing.

Cemile, who had taken the lion's share of the Great Lady's furniture, took the same attitude, and pretended not to notice the English officer's illegitimate daughter.

In any event, the religious teacher in Beykoz was always telling them of the terrible things nonbelievers did to Muslims.

Cemile was now going to the teacher with her friends three times a week. On their advice she'd exchanged the old headscarf she used to tie under her chin for more eye-catching headwear composed of two different cloths. First she wrapped a black cloth around her head, then she added a colorful scarf that reached down to her shoulders. This new look was very nice; it made her feel more fashionable and different from those older women in the neighborhood who wore dull brown headscarves. With her new look and her new curiosity about religion, Cemile cut quite a figure in the neighborhood.

Before she started going to the religious teacher her life was empty and meaningless; she used to be a simple woman, but now she was learning all kinds of things.

After she became a religious woman, she started going from door to door to collect money for the neighborhood's third mosque. Every week she gave the money she'd collected to the teacher's assistant.

The teacher taught them about every aspect of life, from the most private matters to how to behave according to the rules of Islam.

For instance, Cemile learned that it was permissible for a husband and wife to look at each other's reproductive organs. Before, she would have thought this was forbidden. Now, she could look at Hasan's organ, and he could look at hers. This is what the great teacher said. But he could not help but add the following: "To look at a woman's reproductive organ for a long time brings about forgetfulness. This is written in books. The man who does this will start to forget everything. If he looks too much he'll forget even his own name. Beware."

The teacher was always reminding them of the following rule: "If a woman wants to learn about a religious matter and her husband happens not to know about it, it is religiously permissible for the woman to go ask someone who is knowledgeable."

This put Cemile at ease, and going to the teacher's three times a week and asking a man about private matters seemed to conform to religious norms.

For instance, the books said the following: "If a woman cuts off her husband's reproductive organ and his testicles at their base she has to pay full blood money."

At this a woman asked, "What is full blood money?"

"The full blood money for a free man is a hundred camels or the equivalent amount of money."

Even if they didn't quite understand the meaning of the phrases "free man," "full blood money," and "equivalent amount," they memorized these rules every week and repeated them the next time they came.

"If a man should cut off his wife's nose and ear at their base, he has to pay the full blood money for a woman for the nose and half of this for the ear."

"If a man slaps a woman and she dies from the blows after rolling down the stairs, the husband must pay blood money."

"If a man has sexual relations with a little girl who is not sexually mature and damages her internal organs to the extent that she becomes incontinent…"

At this point Cemile thought that the man would be put in prison, but the teacher said, "The man must pay the blood money for a woman." And then added, "If the man and the little girl are related by marriage it is not necessary."

Some of the women found these rules unnecessary. In any event these rules were made in Arabia in the time of the Prophet, but some of them did seem to apply to their own lives. The Prophet himself said: "If I can find a man who can control the organs between his jaws and between his legs, I will take him to heaven with me."

The teacher continued: "If a pregnant woman takes medicine to bring about a miscarriage without her husband's permission, the woman must pay *gurre*."

The woman asked, "What is that?"

The teacher answers from his font of deep knowledge: "*Gurre* is five hundred silver dirhams or its equivalent."

One day Cemile gathered up all her courage and asked the teacher this question: "Is it a sin to use an unbeliever's property?"

The teacher thought about this for a while and then said, "No it's not, my child. Wasn't the city of Istanbul once the property of Byzantine unbelievers? Mehmet the Conqueror took the unbelievers' property and used it well."

This answer eased Cemile's conscience. Her pangs of conscience and sense of guilt at having gone into the Great Lady's house and taken her things was completely erased. Since it was all right for a Muslim to take an unbeliever's property, then taking valuables from the Great

Lady's house, even if it had been done secretly, was in fact a good dead. The mountain people had taken the things piled in the garden without thought, but they'd acted secretly when they took things from the Great Lady's house and hid what they'd stolen. This was a shared secret that everyone knew but no one spoke of.

"Oh my beautiful Allah," she said to herself, "never let our religion and our piety be parted from us."

The teacher not only taught the women about religious rules, he also opened their eyes.

Seventy-five years ago a devil had come to the Ottoman lands where Muslims had been living for centuries, and, deposing the caliph, had established godlessness in the country. Ever since then, the faithful had suffered. Mosques were closed, Muslims who tried to worship were thrown in prison, people were forced to wear the hat of the unbelievers in place of the fez and the turban, and men and women mixed together in an immoral way, embracing each other to do the dances of the unbelievers. Those who didn't conform were brought to the Republican courts and sentenced to death. When he spoke of these things the teacher became excited, and after a while could no longer hold back his tears. Tears like pearls would fall from the holy man's black eyes, roll down his cheeks, and wet his beard. When the women saw this they started crying too. Now, if great Allah willed it, it was time to end this godless regime and replace it with the rule of Islam. The blessed day was at hand when Muslims would live according to sharia law. Because the community of the faithful was waking up and distancing itself from the unbelievers who forced them to accept Kemalism.

As she listened, Cemile thought of the Great Lady and was amazed that for all these years she didn't notice she was an unbeliever. This was what the teacher meant when he said, "Satan tricks those who are not vigilant."

That week, Cemile had more important things to do than look at her husband's reproductive organ, the first of which was to take down the Turkish flag that the municipality had distributed for Republic Day, and which she herself had hung above the sideboard, and to tear up and throw away the official card bearing a picture of that blond devil.

Perhaps this picture was bringing bad luck to the house.

The thing that upset her most was that her children's minds were poisoned every day at school by the words of the Republic and of Atatürk, but her duty as a Muslim mother was to enlighten them and to prevent them from following the path of that devil.

22

That evening Leyla had such a bad experience that it seemed as if her whole life had been turned upside down. If anyone had ever told her that she would be in a situation like this she would have looked at them as if they were crazy. The crazy incident caused her, when she went to bed at the end of that night, to remember the refrain, "I've become lively, I've become quick. Come son, look, I've become a conjurer," from a folk tale her grandmother had told her developed like this.

When she returned to the apartment in Cihangir feeling as if her body and her senses had been buffeted after that tiring day, Roxy was beside herself, jumping about, and it seemed as if she was dancing rather than walking. Her friends had been infected by this delight as well, and they were all enthusiastic, as if they'd been freed from their sluggish, heavy state and had become lively, and even their skin seemed to glow.

When Leyla entered the house, Roxy asked her, "Do you know what happened?" At the same time she was hopping and jumping around the old woman.

The old woman, who was worn out from being outside all day and wanted nothing more than to throw herself onto the sofa, asked, "I hope there's nothing wrong. What happened?"

The girl started telling her breathlessly. Leyla thought that Roxy looked more beautiful when she was excited and let herself go. At moments like that she had an enthusiastic expression on her face, and her cheeks reddened. These were some of the moments when the poison within her wasn't reflected on her face.

Someone had called from one of the famous underground night clubs of Beyoğlu. Because the soloist of the group that was going to appear on stage that night had been in a car accident, they weren't going to be able to come to the concert. They had to make a last-minute change. Was there any chance they wanted to appear on stage?

Roxy was so surprised and delighted by this news that she said yes before even asking how much money they would be paid. "Yes, yes, we want to very much. What time should we come? How long will we be on stage?"

Now she'd spread the contents of her closet all over the house, and as she talked to the boys about their repertoire she struggled to decide what she should wear on stage.

After Leyla had congratulated them and told them how genuinely pleased she was, she went to her room and lay down on the bed. But there was no chance of sleeping!

The boys were yelling out songs and playing some things on the piano.

In spite of this, she got used to the noise from the living room after a while and drifted off. She didn't know how long she slept; when she opened her eyes she saw Roxy and Yusuf bending over her and looking at her. Right away she tried to sit up.

Yusuf said, "We have a request to make of you. I'm sure you won't disappoint us."

"Anything I can do . . . ," murmured Leyla.

Roxy said, "We want you to come and see us perform at the night club." Then she added, "We want this very much."

This was a very strange thing for Leyla; she had no idea how to behave or what to do in that kind of club. Or rather she didn't have a clue what "that kind of club" might be like.

But the young people insisted so much, and put so much pressure on her, that she realized it was going to be impossible for her to say no.

In fact she was going to understand that whether her age was appropriate for the night club was not important when they went to the club in the middle of the night, and she would relax. The club was so dark that people couldn't see each other. In a big hanger-like hall that shadows struck the eye, and a deafening sound of drums came from the stage. She became excited, and her heart started to pound. She started thinking about what kind of pleasure people got from coming here, and why young people would gather in a place like this. The high frequency of the drums made her heart jump and made her tremble all over.

A little while later Roxy and Other Animals were announced, and Roxy and her friends rushed onto the stage.

With the same loud drums, the keyboard, and an electric bass that made everything tremble, Roxy started doing some things as if she was talking and rolling. Even though Leyla couldn't see Yusuf next to her she could feel his excitement.

After finishing the first piece Roxy said, "I'm calling someone onto the stage," and her secret aim in bring Leyla to the club was revealed.

"A great pianist, Leyla Bosnalıııı!"

The boys shouted "Whoa!" Leyla felt a hot flash, and didn't know what to do, but she felt herself being dragged through the darkness and being taken by the arms and brought up the steps. A light shining straight into her eyes made her blind and prevented her from seeing anything. She heard applause and shouting. Somone sat her at the keyboard. Her head was spinning, and she felt nauseous. She felt as if she was going to collapse right there. She was very angry at Roxy and couldn't understand why she had put her in this position. The clapping and shouting became increasingly louder. It seemed to excite them to see someone of her years on the stage. Leyla suppressed her nausea and ran her fingers lightly along the keyboard. Even the slightest touch was greatly magnified, and it startled her to hear the sound echo through the dark hall. Was it she who was making so much noise?

Slowly the noise of the crowd died down, and the hall fell silent. Leyla had an unpleasant feeling. She couldn't believe that she was in front of all these people, in a place that was noisier than anything she was used to, with lights shining on her, and she was very angry at those who had done this to her. But there was nothing she could do about it now. She didn't know what to do. If she got up to leave she couldn't manage it on her own and wouldn't even be able to see the stairs. She felt as if her grandfather the pasha and her grandmother were staring at her. "What are you doing there?" they asked her. "Is this appropriate for your age, and how do you think it reflects on our family honor? They announced our family name without feeling any shame." The artery in her neck had begun to throb, and she felt hot all over. As always she began to defend herself, saying, "It's not my fault. You saw how they brought me here so suddenly. Was I the one who wanted to come here? Did I want to be thrown out of my house and end up in Cihangir? Unexpected things can happen to people."

"Fine, but you should think about where your first step is going to take you, and you should behave accordingly. Isn't that what we taught you? In life, every tragedy starts with a small and innocent step."

"In that case I'll get down," she whispered. "In that case I'll get down and get out of here. I have no business being here." Two teardrops rolled out of her eyes.

At the moment she was about to stand up, Leyla felt two hands pressing down on her shoulders. Roxy was saying, "Please play something," in her ear. "I'm begging you to touch the keys. Like you did at home. There's nothing to be ashamed of. Isn't music *music* wherever you are? Please don't disappoint me."

When she heard these words Leyla pulled herself together, took a deep breath, and started playing Beethoven's "Moonlight Sonata." How loud the keyboard was. As if it filled the whole world. With years of mastery and ease she touched the keys softly, and the sound seemed to echo throughout the universe. Fräulein Anneliese was standing over her controlling her hands. She had never liked what she played and had never heard her say "bravo!" in satisfaction. When she finished the piece there was silence at first. Leyla remained seated without raising her head or looking anywhere. Then a deafening applause broke out. The audience was beside themselves, screaming, "Bravo, bravo!" She was surprised, delighted, and excited, and felt as if she was going to fall off her stool. Then she realized she was sitting in the spotlights like a rabbit caught in the headlights. But then she pulled herself together, gave a small nod of her head, and began smiling. She was perspiring. It would never have crossed her mind that in her solitary life she would end up in a situation like this. The audience was clapping and shouting, "Encore, encore!" She looked around helplessly for Roxy but couldn't see her. There was a sour smell in the air. Suddenly the drum and the bass began playing with an earthshattering clamor. They were playing the piece for which they'd asked her help with the chords at home. This noise is far too much for my ears, she thought to herself. She felt a sudden sense of heat in her ears. She turned her head: She saw Roxy, she was saying something to her, but no matter how much she shouted it was impossible for Leyla to hear. Then Roxy signaled for her to start playing the keyboard. She wanted her to play that noisy song too. Leyla looked at her helplessly; with her heart pounding she began playing the chords she'd taught the boys. Then she started improvising to the bass. The audience practically went wild and were clapping hard enough to hurt their hands. Perhaps for the first and last time in the world, an elderly, white-haired lady was accompanying a crazy hip-hop piece. In truth it was a sight to be talked about for years.

Roxy left Leyla's side and began singing. She was shouting something in a harsh, staccato manner. As Leyla played, she found she was losing her sense of alienation, and that she was even beginning to get a strange kind of pleasure out of this. She got into the rhythm and started improvising, with her fingers flying over the keyboard. She didn't know what she was playing, but her fingers did, and with her ingrained sense of rhythm and harmony, she was making sounds to drive the audience wild. So when the piece was over and the crowd jumped to their feet and started applauding, she started smiling even though she was drenched in sweat. When Roxy came over, took her hand, and helped her to her feet, shadows were playing before her eyes. The young people were clapping, whistling, and shouting enough to bring the place down. Leyla was never going to forget this night as long as she lived.

The boys took her arms and helped down the stairs and practically dragged her outside. She felt completely exhausted. She would have collapsed right there if they hadn't been holding her up. She wanted nothing except to get home as soon as possible.

When she finally lay her head on her pillow, she had a feeling of shame, of having done something wrong.

The next day the owner of the club asked Roxy if she would work there regularly. But only under one condition: That elderly woman had to appear on the stage with them. The club owner thought it would make for a world-class show, and that together they would all go down in hip-hop history.

But of course this idea was never realized, and it took Leyla a long time to shake off the feeling of weariness and shame at having done something like this.

The refrain from the Balkan folk tale her grandmother had told her echoed through her mind until morning.

In the tale, an evil-hearted bride locked up her mother-in-law in a chicken coop. The troubled mother called to her son with these words: "I've become lively, I've become quick. Come son, look, I've become a conjurer."

Leyla thought to herself: This is just the situation I ended up in. At my age I became a conjurer. The only difference between me and the woman in the tale is that I have no son.

23

Hüseyin clinked his *rakı* glass against Yusuf's and said, "Welcome. This is a nice surprise. I'm very pleased. I heard you'd become a journalist. Is that why you've come? Are you going to interview me?"

"Not now, cousin," said Yusuf. "But hopefully later on I'll do my first interview with you."

Then he told a joke from the book he'd read on the bus.

"I thought of it because you mentioned my being a journalist," he said. "Do you know what a foreign writer said? He said it was a shame for scientists to perform experiments on guinea pigs; they should perform them on politicians and journalists."

He was a little put out that his cousin didn't appreciate his joke. He laughed to himself and then fell quiet. Hüseyin was a serious politician now; he didn't smile, and he walked with tensed shoulders, and always had a serious face. He didn't appreciate jokes.

Yusuf didn't know Ankara very well, and like most people from Istanbul he preferred not to go there. But this time he'd had to go. He needed to ask his cousin's help with Leyla's situation.

This is why he felt at ease that evening sitting across from Hüseyin at a famous kebab restaurant in Ankara. He also genuinely liked and missed his crafty relative Hüseyin.

As dishes came and went, he understood how his cousin had gained so much weight. Everything was delicious. Hot bread, cheese, various Anatolian appetizers, and then Adana kebab made with the tail fat of the flat-tailed sheep. And as if all this wasn't enough, Hüseyin insisted that they eat desert too. Yusuf ate so much that he felt he didn't want to eat again for the rest of his life.

Most of the people in the restaurant were men in dark suits and ties. Ankara was a city of men. Here only a few men and women went out together the way they did in Istanbul, and it was mostly men who ate out together. Politicians like his cousin met every night and talked politics, either because their homes were in different districts, or simply to fit in with that community.

Yusuf was always surprised that two cities in the same country could be so different. The capital, steeped in politics, didn't resemble Istanbul at all.

Ankara always complained about the media in Istanbul, and Istanbul always complained about the politicians in Ankara. But in Yusuf's brief experience, these two realms resembled each other a great deal. They both had the same fundamental rule, to consider the present day important and to survive, and the headlines were important both for the journalists who prepared them and for the politicians who would read them the next day.

Hüseyin was already of short stature, but his belly and the weight he'd gained made him seem even shorter. The sleeves of his white shirt seemed too long and extended out of the sleeves of his jacket, covering half of his small hands. Yusuf knew him as a loyal friend who could be counted on in the most difficult times. He hadn't forgotten his friends and relatives once he became an "important man" in Ankara.

When Yusuf needed to borrow money, he sent it at once without question. When he'd arrived in Ankara in the evening and called him, he insisted on picking Yusuf up at the bus station and taking him right to the famous kebab restaurant. He had a car with a driver and official red license plates. He was insisting that Yusuf come with him to parliament tomorrow. Because he was the head of the budget committee and he was in a position of power. He wanted to show off when he received rare visits from relatives.

When every avenue he followed to try to help Leyla ended up being blocked, and he realized that Ömer Cevheroğlu's lawyers were powerful enough to take on even the army, Yusuf began to feel hopeless. This was now the most important subject when he whispered with Roxy at night. They didn't know what to do or where to go, and they struggled to control their growing sense of anger.

One night Roxy asked, "Isn't your cousin a member of parliament for the ruling party? Perhaps he can do something."

Yusuf was surprised at himself for not having thought of this earlier. It was true, perhaps Hüseyin could help Leyla. Two days later he took leave from the newspaper and took the bus to Ankara.

Now he was telling Hüseyin about what had happened to Leyla. Like everyone else, Hüseyin thought a great deal of Leyla. He couldn't believe that the poor woman had been thrown out of her house at her age. Because Leyla and her house had seemed like the only constants in a changing neighborhood.

"What times we live in!" he said. "Come to parliament tomorrow, and we'll see what we can do."

After the meal he brought him home. His wife, Gülsen, welcomed them to a well-furnished apartment in one of Ankara's new high-rise buildings.

At night they could see the whole city from their apartment. And this dirty, gray city could be said to look beautiful at night. Again Yusuf felt the strange arrogance all people from Istanbul feel when confronted with Ankara and thought: I could never live here. They themselves were of rural origin, but it was as if Ankara was the first stop in the transition from rural life. When Yusuf was a child his grandfather used to spend the summer months in his village. Despite living on the Bosphorus, he would miss the run-down, mud-brick houses of his Anatolian village and take Yusuf there with him. These were fun days for Yusuf. He loved the village and would follow the flocks with the shepherds, catch fish in the pristine water of the stream, and would drive the threshing sled even though he knew he would itch all night. After his grandfather died he stopped going to the village. From time to time Yusuf remembered those days and missed the times he'd spent in the village as a child. But rural manners in the city were not as nice as they were in the village.

When Hüseyin took off his shoes before going into the apartment, Yusuf felt he had to do the same. Men's, women's, and children's shoes were lined up side by side at the door. As soon as they went inside, Hüseyin's wife handed them slippers as she said, "Welcome!" Like all mountain people, Yusuf's family did the same. No one he knew in Cihangir did this. Whether or not you took your shoes off at the door made a big difference, thought Yusuf.

This house was not the only example in Ankara of rural manners in the city, and the next day at parliament he was to see many more. Hüseyin brought him there in a black Renault with red license plates. For this reason the police at the entrance to parliament didn't stop them. Yusuf guessed that if he had come on his own, he would have had a very difficult time getting in. But it's not at all difficult when your cousin is a representative. Despite all this security, the front of the parliament was always crowded with voters and visitors. They didn't mind waiting for hours and going through police controls, and they'd come to tell their troubles to their representatives. Most of them were villagers, and most of them had no concept of wasting time. The women had their heads covered, and the men were dressed in a manner that identified them from yards away as villagers, and they had a different manner of walking. Yusuf had read somewhere that on the one day a week when visitors were allowed, eighteen thousand visitors came. An ordinary person couldn't get through the crowds, and the dim corridors outside the representatives' offices were packed with people.

These were the poor, troubled people that the press and television of modern Turkey tried to hide and pretend didn't exist. They should have seen these exhausted and hopeless petitioners waiting in the corridors or the crippled children huddled in the corners of hospitals.

When Yusuf went to Hüseyin's office he wasn't there, but they sent word to him, and he arrived half an hour later. He looked as if he was anxious. Because that day an extraordinary meeting had been called by the opposition.

As they were drinking their coffee, Hüseyin said to Yusuf, "A little while ago I spoke to the interior minister. He's going to look into the matter and let me know."

As Yusuf watched Hüseyin's dictatorial manner, and the respect with which the people around him treated him, he thought about how different the political class was. This meant that rising from the masses to the ruling class could change everything. Would it have been possible for him to achieve so much power, and to be able to talk to the interior minister? Every day he entered the newspaper's huge glass building feeling as if he didn't belong, a humble reporter who no one respected. This meant that Hüseyin had chosen the right path. He was respected, and his salary afforded him a comfortable life. He had an official car, a driver, a secretary, and an adviser.

Hüseyin hadn't struggled any more than he himself had to become successful. It was just that he chose the right path. To rise as quickly as he had, it had been enough to sense that a party was on the rise, become a member, and run for office. Yusuf thought that Hüseyin was likely to become a minister soon. But he was still a good guy. His cousin always behaved humbly toward him and never put on airs.

At lunchtime they passed once again through the crowded corridors to the restaurant in the main building. They entered a large room where hundreds of people were eating. There was a crowd of men in dark suits and ties, and most of them had mustaches. Yusuf thought that here, too, rural attitudes were prevalent. Because it was while eating that rural manners became most evident. The way they wouldn't pull their plates in front of them, the way they held their forks and spoons, the way they leaned over their plates to scoop food into their mouths, the way they spoke with their mouths full; he'd seen his father do the same things and hadn't liked it at all.

When Yusuf saw a representative take the pin out of his lapel and use it as a toothpick, he could no longer eat the food in front of him. And he started thinking: Yes, this was the parliament of the people. The people chose their representatives, and they chose people like themselves. Yes, it was democratic, but was this the right way to do things? It was only natural for the representative of an uneducated people who had been kept in darkness for centuries and whose heads were full of superstition to be like this. Mustafa Kemal, who looked down sadly from a large picture on the wall, had chosen the opposite approach, and had opted for "educating the people." But recently his approach has been condemned as Jacobinism.

Which of these approaches was the right one: to pander to the religious and nationalistic feelings of the people, or to educate them? Yusuf became confused, and didn't have an answer at that point.

As they came out of the restaurant they met the interior minister. He'd come to eat lunch with a group of voters and representatives from his region. The minister kissed Hüseyin on both cheeks, and in a strong Anatolian accent said, "Hüseyin, I've looked into the matter you talked to me about. But the new owners of the mansion have a doctor's report. The poor woman has gone mad; she's lost her marbles. The court appointed a guardian. They did everything according to the law and left no loopholes. I'm sorry."

When Yusuf heard this, something snapped within him. It seemed Leyla was never going to see her house again, he thought. If even the interior minister said this, then there was no hope left.

On the bus back to Istanbul he stared out the window and thought about what was going to happen. Where was Leyla going to live? How was she going to get by?

No matter how much he thought about it, he couldn't find any solution except for Leyla to continue living with them. But Roxy wasn't going to agree to this. He had no idea how he was going to convince her.

Suddenly, all these thoughts left Yusuf's mind. The bus was passing the shores of Lake Sapanca, and he was absorbed in contemplation of the way the water reflected the red of the evening sun. Perhaps for the first time, he understood deeply what Roxy meant to him.

This was why, toward morning, in a strange bed, he had muttered "Roxy" in his sleep. In the darkness he didn't know where he was, but he was seized by panic to discover that Roxy wasn't next to him. Perhaps he had woken from a dream about Roxy, but he couldn't remember. The only thing he knew was that he missed her deeply. He'd panicked when he hadn't found the girl next to him. What a strange thing that was. Roxy wasn't the girl he'd been most attracted to in his life. There were several prettier, more likable, and more congenial girls at the newspaper. These were girls whose decency and good nature showed on their faces. When he compared Roxy to them she seemed contrary, harsh, and querulous. It was impossible to find peace with her. He always had to be on his toes, because something another person might not even notice was enough to set her off.

All this might have been true, but he still saw Roxy as completing him both personally and physically. He couldn't compare her to anyone else. Was she more beautiful, or uglier, or more irascible? These questions made no sense. It was like comparing yourself to another person.

No matter what you do, you are what you are, and you have to live with yourself. There was no arguing about that. Roxy was Yusuf, and Yusuf was Roxy.

He was returning unsuccessful from his trip to Ankara, but he was also returning with the knowledge that he could not live without Roxy's skin, smell, and voice.

24

Toward noon the *lodos* wind started to blow from the south. As always, this hot south wind, which the Greeks called *notos*, caused headaches and frayed nerves among the people of Istanbul.

So when Roxy saw how pale and weak Leyla was, she put it down to the effect of the *lodos*. In fact, Leyla had just received a telephone call from Ali Yekta that had dashed all her hopes and dreams and had left her feeling desperate.

In a low and feeble voice, Ali Yekta had said, "There's nothing I can do, madam. If there was, be sure that I would do it. May Allah help them change their ways."

Leyla thanked the man for his trouble and then went to her room and thought for a long time. Until today she'd kept herself going with dreams, and with the hope that she would find a solution, but now she saw that there was no way out. There was no way she could defeat this rich, spoiled, and powerful family.

Yusuf and Roxy had come back empty handed from the doctor's, and they had learned that the doctor's report was false. This subterfuge worked so well that elderly people from the old families of Istanbul were losing their property one by one.

All day, Leyla thought about how she was up against a power that she could not defeat. What was she going to do? She couldn't go home, so where was she going to live? Where was she going to move? For a while she buried herself under the blanket and fell asleep.

During that short afternoon sleep, Leyla had a terrible nightmare. She was standing as a little girl on the shore, watching in terror as the two sides of the Bosphorus moved toward each other. The shore she was standing on was in motion, swallowing the sea as it moved toward the other side. The European shore was moving toward her in the same manner. Leyla wanted to scream and warn her grandmother, but she wasn't able to make a sound. The two shores moved toward each other so quickly that they had joined within a minute or two. Asia and Europe were now joined. What had been the sea in front of her was now an asphalt road. The houses that had been across the way were now right in front of her. Concrete had swallowed the sea, and the continents had been joined. Even after she woke, Leyla couldn't shake off the dream. Her head ached, there was a bitter taste in her mouth, and she felt deep within her that her dream was true.

One day, she'd stood on the same shore, watching the huge ships slide through the wonderful whiteness of a heavy fog. It was as if they were sailing through the air as their foghorns sounded. Several fishing boats that looked as if they were suspended in the air were trying to return to the shore. Then the far shore disappeared, and it was as if the two shores had joined. The cries of seagulls could be heard. Leyla had suddenly felt frightened and had run to her grandmother. Her grandmother was surrounded by fog in the back garden. It was as if she had been caught up in a cloud. She threw her arms around her legs and began to cry. Her grandmother stroked her hair and said, “Don’t be frightened, my little one, my beautiful girl.”

Leyla remembered that she’d thought about death for the first time that day. All the deaths in her family had accustomed her to the concept, and like rural people she came to see death as a natural thing. She thought about death not from her own point of view but from the point of view of the people she had lost. But that day in the fog on the shore, she’d suddenly felt lost, and felt a deep loneliness and fear of death. This was the first time she realized how fleeting a person’s time on earth was. It was something she had thought about often later. If it didn’t matter whether you died a little earlier or a little later, what was the point of being alive? What was the point of building sandcastles that would just be washed away? People involved in a great struggle didn’t think these things but devoted themselves to succeeding in life. But this was a basic human emotion. Fear of the world, temerity about life, the heartache of impermanence. That is, emptiness, a great emptiness.

At moments like that, she would feel a deep sorrow about the two of them living alone in that huge mansion.

There was no one; the rooms and halls were empty. The servants and gardeners had all left one by one. Only a single faithful retainer lived on the ground floor with the daughter he had brought from his village. And also Fräulein Annelise, who had given Leyla's mother piano and German lessons, and who was being charitable and giving the little girl lessons without asking for money. There was still a pension from her grandfather, who was listed on her identity papers as her father. This was paid to her grandmother, but it didn't amount to much. In the end, even selling off the jewelry didn't bring them enough money to meet the expenses of that huge house, and the mansion was sold, and new people came. The grandmother and granddaughter sought shelter in the little white house.

In the evenings she would sit in front of the house, looking at the magnolia tree and drinking the tea her grandmother had made. Her grandmother was teaching her how to sew. At the same time she was weeping about her family's ill fate. She was still in mourning for her husband, her son, and her daughter. "Ah," she would say sometimes, "it was all because of that pale-eyed English unbeliever. In the end it's just the two of us, all alone, because of him."

Leyla was covered in sweat. Just then Roxy came to her door. She was looking at her in a strange way. She wondered what the girl wanted from her. Presumably, as the situation was hopeless, she wanted her to move out. She was right too. She had to find a solution as soon as possible.

Roxy said, "I heard you moaning. Are you all right? Is anything wrong?"

"There's nothing wrong!" said Leyla. "I just dozed off a little. I must have been dreaming."

"It must have been a very scary dream. Your face is as white as a shcct."

"Yes, it was, to tell the truth."

"Do you want to tell me about it?"

Leyla was not in the habit of sharing her troubles or her dreams, but the closeness she'd begun to feel to this girl overcame her defenses and made her a different person.

She told her dream, about the two shores of the Bosphorus coming together, and the disappearance of the sea, and how real it had seemed.

This dream didn't seem terribly frightening to Roxy, but Roxy saw it had affected Leyla a great deal; she was still shaken by it.

She brought her some tea and sat next to her.

"Do you think this dream has anything to do with losing hope of getting your house back?" she asked. "Is this why you're so shaken?"

"I don't know," said Leyla. "I suppose there's no hope left. There's nothing more I can do. Perhaps I'll never see that house again as long as I live. The other day when I was in the garden, I could have gone into the house, I could have looked, but I didn't want to, or rather I was afraid of what I might see."

They fell silent for a while, and Leyla drank her tea while Roxy looked at her nails. There was nothing left to say.

Leyla thought the same thing once again: Since she's come to the room, Roxy probably wants me to find a solution now. The girl is right, I can't stay here. I'll be a burden. If I had a place to go, I'd leave today, but where can I go, what can I do?

Just then Roxy said, "As a matter of fact, there's something I want to talk to you about."

So, she was bringing up the subject. Before the girl said anything, perhaps she should say she was moving out in a few days and that she was looking for a place to rent. Might it be possible to find a little place in her old neighborhood? Would the mountain people help her? She hadn't seen any sign of them on her last visit, but at least they were old acquaintances.

Roxy said, "I want to tell you a secret."

"What kind of secret?"

"Everyone will hear about it soon enough, but I wanted to tell you first."

Leyla looked at the girl with curiosity.

"I'm going to have a baby," she whispered. She was smiling.

"What?" shouted Leyla. She hadn't been expecting anything like this.

"I'm pregnant! It's unbelievable, isn't it? Me… Roxy… pregnant… a mother. It just doesn't seem possible."

Then Leyla stood up and embraced her.

"Congratulations, congratulations."

Because Roxy had irregular periods, she hadn't been very concerned when she was late, but when she started getting nauseous she decided to take a pregnancy test.

No one else knew yet, not even Yusuf. Leyla was the only one who knew.

Now Roxy understood the source of the feelings of softness and tenderness she had been feeling. That meant her hormones were at work. In spite of the nausea she was very pleased to be pregnant; she just didn't understand her fierce craving for bratwurst with German mustard. But she really didn't think about that much. She shared this with Leyla too. Sausages were sausages wherever you went. There were plenty of them at the food stands in Taksim. When Roxy made this joke, something interesting came to Leyla's mind.

Yusuf's going to Ankara and leaving Leyla and Roxy alone together in the house had brought about the special warmth of people sharing life's basic needs. Sharing shelter and food and providing for the next generation had made them partners. Even though they'd met only recently, sharing life's basic needs made them almost like relatives.

Leyla, greatly excited by the news about the baby, offered to cook for Roxy. That day she was going to cook, and Roxy was not to interfere. She was going to make a magnificent meal, and it was going to be a perfect display of Balkan cuisine. In any event, a baby was on the way, and Roxy had to "eat for two."

Roxy had to admit that she was pleased because she didn't like to cook and couldn't manage to prepare even the simplest of meals. That's why she cooked pasta, eggs, and sausage every day.

When Roxy had done the shopping and brought back the ingredients, Leyla went into the kitchen. To prepare her first meal, which was going to be a dish from the

Danube culture, she began slicing a leg of lamb. After the meat had been boiled, she covered it with a mixture of yoghurt and eggs beaten together and put it in the oven. Then she beat eggs and sugar together and added milk and prepared a Balkan dessert that resembled crème brûlée. She prepared all this with an air of mastery, and Roxy was amazed to see how quickly her old hands moved.

For her Bosnian family, the preparation of meals like this meant much more than filling the stomach, because these recipes were seen as a spiritual inheritance from the beautiful lands they had lost in the Balkans. Spinach pastries, peppers with cheese...these meals were a way of reliving the past. The passing of these recipes from generation to generation was seen as a sacred trust.

As the warm and appetizing smells filled the apartment, what until then had been simply a house became a home. That evening, as Leyla, Roxy, Yusuf, and the three young musicians ate this extraordinary meal with great joy, they thanked Leyla over and over again. The meat melted in their mouths. The dessert was also wonderful. These young people were all of Anatolian origin and didn't know these dishes. Only Yusuf remembered having tasted such things at Leyla's house.

That evening, after the young people had washed the dishes, they all sat in the living room drinking coffee, and for the first time felt as if they were a family.

25

As soon as he stepped into the house, he was very surprised to notice the expression of happiness and peace on the girl's face, and this sense of surprise lasted all evening. Throughout the meal, as he talked about Ankara, parliament, politicians, the kebab restaurants in Ankara where men ate with men, rakı-drinking parliamentarians, and the minister, he watched Roxy out of the corner of his eye, and couldn't understand her peaceful expression and the warmth she showed Leyla.

But it was something very nice. As if Roxy's face was glowing with a light that came from within.

The girl was quiet this evening and said little except to shower Leyla with praises. When Leyla started to get up after the meal she said, "No! Don't get up. After such a wonderful meal it's only right that we do the dishes. I'll make you some coffee."

Yusuf didn't believe his eyes. This evening he was being given the gift of a new Roxy. He began to feel a sense of trust that the girl to whom he was bound by passion would not upset the comfort of his life. What a terrific thing this was.

Throughout the meal, they didn't talk about the answer Hüseyin had given Yusuf. This showed that everyone was aware of the situation. Leyla didn't ask either. It was clear that if the news had been good, Yusuf would have told them. His avoidance of the subject made the situation clear.

That night in bed, Yusuf said to Roxy, "You're different tonight!"

Roxy changed the subject, saying, "I suppose you didn't get anywhere with Hüseyin."

"He was very hospitable to me. He picked me up at the bus station in an official car and brought me to a restaurant, but somehow I didn't feel that comfortable."

"Why?"

"I don't know, but it seems as if my cousin belongs to a different world now. I don't know whether these politicians want to be treated extremely respectfully, or if it just seems that way to us because they behave like that to each other."

"But things aren't the way they used to be between the two of you."

"No, they aren't. It seems as if there's something artificial in our relationship, as if something is missing. Then there was the interior minister…"

"What happened, did he behave badly?"

"No, just the opposite. Hüseyin introduced me as an up-and-coming journalist from Istanbul. The man was very interested."

"Yes?"

"But there was still something about Hüseyin's attitude that made me very uncomfortable. As if he was embarrassed to be taking up space in this world and wanted to efface himself in the presence of this man."

"I don't see anything surprising about that. Politics is just like life. You're oppressed by those more powerful than you, and you oppress those less powerful than you. Don't worry, Hüseyin didn't let on, but there are a lot of people he has power over."

"Perhaps," said Yusuf. "But enough about that. I'm tired of Ankara. Tell me why you seem so different. Why are you so happy? Because I went away to Ankara?"

Roxy laughed delightedly. Then she sat up in bed, and made Yusuf sit up too.

The boy was confused.

"Get up!" she said.

"What's going on?"

"Get up. I have a proposal to make."

Yusuf got up, wondering what this proposal was, and stood where Roxy told him to stand; then he saw the girl kneel down before him.

He was used to her strange and often crazy behavior, but this time he was very confused. He was very uncomfortable that she had knelt before him with this mischievous expression on her face.

Then Roxy said, "I have a proposal to make to you."

"Stop joking around."

"No, I'm very serious, and I'm making a very serious proposal."

"What is it?" asked Yusuf.

Roxy took his right hand, held it in a ceremonial manner, looked into his eyes, and asked, "Will you marry me?"

Yusuf was surprised and didn't know what to say, because he didn't know if she was serious or if she was joking.

Not paying any attention to his surprise, Roxy said, "Does it always have to be the man who proposes? That's such a silly rule. Now I'm asking you seriously, Yusuf Yılmaz, will you marry me?"

Yusuf said. "Of course! Of course I'll marry you. But why did this come up so suddenly?"

"It's because of your naughtiness," said Roxy, laughing.

"What do you mean, what naughtiness?"

"What you do in bed at night, for instance."

She touched him on the belly suddenly, and he doubled over.

"I swear, Roxy, I have no idea what's going on."

Then Roxy took his right hand and put it on her belly. In a calm and mysterious manner she asked, "Now do you understand?" Yusuf suddenly felt as if his heart would stop, and he embraced Roxy. He kissed the belly where his child was growing. He applauded her boldness in proposing marriage to him. He thought that he worshiped this girl's hidden places, her warmth, the taste of her mouth, and the tension in her belly that would begin to grow in a few months.

He no longer minded that Roxy's former lovers had known her body and given her pleasure. Because she hadn't been as close to another man as to become his wife and carry his child.

That night, their lovemaking was a more tender, more intense, and deeper exchange.

26

Something happened to spoil those days when they were starting to find a little bit of peace.

Leyla was sitting at home alone, feeling bored and closed in, and trying to kill time that strange, still afternoon, when she heard the doorbell and went to answer it. People she didn't know were standing outside the door.

There was a short, fat man with a black mustache in front of her. Next to him was a woman who was clearly a foreigner, and two children.

"Can I help you?" asked Leyla.

"This is Rukiye's house, isn't it," said the man in a thick Anatolian accent.

"Yes," said Leyla, "but she's not home at the moment."

"That's all right," he said. Then turned to the woman and said in broken German, "We found her at last."

Leyla noticed that they had suitcases when they picked them up and started to enter the house.

"Excuse me sir, I told you Rukiye wasn't home. If you would come back in the evening…"

"What do you mean 'come back in the evening'?" asked the man. "I'm her father. That means this is my home too. Who are you?"

At this, Leyla had to retreat into the corner. She said something like, "I'm a guest here."

As soon as the family entered, the children even started running around tugging at this and that. Rukiye's father went around looking at the rooms and deciding which one they would move into.

A while later he showed his wife the room where Leyla was staying and told his wife in German, "This one looks like the best one for us. Come on, open the suitcases."

Leyla was in a strange situation. The way the newcomers had taken over the house left her standing there bewildered and not knowing what to do. She knew that Roxy didn't have a good relationship with her father, but this knowledge wasn't of any help to her. She had no rights in this house. She couldn't tell people not to come in. She'd have to wait until Rukiye and Yusuf came home and make a decision after she saw what happened. So she didn't say anything about them moving into her temporary room. She even made tea for them and began waiting anxiously for evening.

When darkness fell, Yusuf was the first one home, and, as soon as he saw people in the house, he was terribly surprised. He was even more surprised when he learned that these people were Roxy's family, and in fact you could say he was terrified. He knew how much Roxy hated this man, and that when she came home all hell was going to break loose.

Meanwhile the children were playing with the keyboard and filling the house with a strange sound as they banged on it with their hands. The plump, middle-aged, pale, blond woman he assumed was Ute was looking around disdainfully at the furniture and wasn't saying much.

After Leyla whispered in his ear and told him who they were he said, "Welcome. Rukiye hasn't arrived yet."

The man asked, "Who are you?"

Yusuf said, "I'm Rukiye's friend."

"Do you live here too?"

"Yes, in fact…"

"You mean you live together?"

"In a sense…"

"There's no in a sense, or are you married?"

Yusuf didn't know how to answer this and turned and went into his room. The situation was very confused now.

But this was nothing compared to what was going to happen when Rukiye got home.

Because when this quick-tempered and fiery girl got home and quickly got over her surprise at seeing these unexpected guests, she asked, "What business do you have here?"

Leyla didn't miss that her face had paled and that her lips were trembling. She had to be deeply shaken.

Her father said that they were driving to their village, and were very tired, and they'd decided to stop over in Istanbul, and had decided they wanted to see her. He was a coarse man and looked like he didn't give a damn about anything, but even so he seemed wary of Rukiye. He'd got her address from her friend Hatice in Duisburg. All this talk made it clear that the family was going to stay the night, and there was an unspoken agreement that they would all have to put up with each other until the following day. Rukiye softened a bit and gave some attention to her siblings. Yusuf whispered an apology to Leyla, and said they would have to manage somehow for tonight. Leyla had already long since got used to the idea that she was going to spend the night on the old velvet sofa in the living room.

After Yusuf had disappeared outside for half an hour and come back with pizza boxes, the children were fighting among themselves in German. The house was incredibly noisy.

There was a tense atmosphere as they sat at the table. Roxy was breathing quickly; it was clear she was under a lot of pressure, and in fact she was like a time bomb that was about to explode. Yusuf was trying to say whatever he could to lighten the situation, and once again Leyla realized what a good-natured boy he was. This boy loved harmony; he longed for harmony in a country full of fights. He dreamt of a world where people treated each other well.

It seemed as if the meal was going to end this way, but her father couldn't keep his mouth shut, and he repeated that question: "Are you two married?"

Yusuf murmured something, but Roxy banged her fork on the table, looked her father in the eye, and said, "No, father. We're not married."

"Then how can you live in this house together?" He was clearly itching for a fight.

"A little earlier we saw a room. Do you two share this bedroom."

"What's it to you?" said Roxy.

"What do you mean 'what's it to me'? I'm your father. Are you living as someone's mistress. Is this woman the boy's mother? Is she closing her eyes to this disgrace?"

Roxy moaned as if she was in pain and said, "Shut up, father. Shut up already."

Leyla was not a part of the situation, and to prevent this family drama she said, "Sir, please calm down."

But the man started shouting at the top of his voice, as if he got agitated by the sound of his own voice.

"Why should I shut up?" he shouted. "We, too, have our family honor. What are we going to tell people. Are we supposed to say that Rukiye is living in sin in Istanbul. Are we going to say she became a kept woman? *Kapatma olmuş diye mi anlatacağız?*"

Leyla saw tears of anger form in Roxy's eyes. God, shut this man up, she prayed to herself. But the man was really carried away and had no intention of shutting up. He seemed to derive pleasure from having caught his runaway daughter, and was raining insults on her, and then, as if he was talking to himself, he muttered "slut" between his teeth. "It's my fault, she became a slut because I didn't break her bones when she was little."

Roxy suddenly jumped up, went over to her father, and, looking straight into his eyes, shouted, "Yes, I became a slut. Do you have anything to say about it?"

At that moment something unbelievable happened, and Leyla turned her head to see Roxy get a slap to the face.

The situation was out of hand. Yusuf was frozen in surprise and panic.

Roxy was shouting and sobbing. She seemed on the point of having a crisis. "Yes, I became a slut. Yes, do you have anything to say about your daughter becoming a slut? I'll sleep with anyone. I screw men in the street. Do you have anything to say about it? Go out and shout that your daughter is a slut and ask if anyone wants to screw her. I'm sure all your friends will stand in line. Maybe your brothers will too."

The violence of Roxy's anger surprised and startled even her father; everyone had fallen into a bitter silence now, but it was as if Roxy had gone mad.

She wailed and ran out onto the balcony; just as she was about to throw herself off the balcony Yusuf caught her by the waist. The girl was really struggling to jump. Yusuf had to hold her tightly for some time. Her thin body trembled in his arms, sweat was pouring from the roots of her hair, and her heart was pounding as if it was about to jump out of her chest. In his sweetest and most soothing voice, he whispered, "Take it easy, darling, calm down, shhhh."

A while later the poor girl let herself go like a lifeless doll, and he brought her through the living room and into the bedroom. He lay her down and covered her and stood over her as she started crying violently again. Her body trembled wildly as she wept, and all the while

Yusuf stroked her hair, and hugged her, and tried to soothe her.

Quite some time had passed, and in the tense living room, Leyla tried not to meet anyone's eyes, when Yusuf said, "Get out of my house or I'll kill you."

The man muttered something about this being "his daughter's house." Yusuf said, "No, it's not your daughter's house, it's my house. And I'm telling you to pack up your things and get the hell out of here right now. Or else I'm going to call the police."

At this point the German woman went up to her husband and said something about "*polizei*." The children were watching all of this in silence. Yusuf went into Leyla's room, took the suitcases and the things they'd unpacked, and threw them out onto the stairs.

Pointing to the stairs he said, "If you don't get out of here right now I'll kill you, you bastard."

And for the first time Leyla saw how decisive Yusuf was, and how terribly frightened Roxy's father was.

It was as if the man understood that Yusuf was serious and was ready to follow up on his words. He took his children by the hand and rushed out, and the woman followed him.

Leyla and Yusuf listened to their footsteps on the stairs, the man swearing at and threatening Yusuf and Rukiye.

After everything was over, there was silence in the apartment. As Yusuf calmed down he apologized to Leyla with a shy smile. It was the first time he'd sworn in her presence. Leyla stroked his cheek and then went into the room to check on Roxy.

The girl had rolled herself into a ball, and, sleeping deeply in a fetal position, she moaned deeply and occasionally shook with sobs.

Leyla covered her, and for the first time in her life felt a deep compassion for another person.

27

Today the people of Istanbul have headaches.

The sea is choppy, the ferries have been canceled, and the *lodos* wind that makes even the fish feel drunk is blowing toward the shore and laying low twelve million people. On both shores, people walking along the avenues, and eating in restaurants, and studying in school are all suffering from strange headaches and dizziness.

There was only one group of people who benefited from the *lodos*. They put on waist-high rubber boots and examined the flotsam that washed up along the shore, gleefully picking up anything valuable they saw. Once, one of them even found the world's biggest diamond. The rest of them all have the same hope. They don't mind the dizziness and, after, are a different kind of drunk.

In his bed on the ground floor of the large mansion on the European shore, Ali Yekta, under the influence of the *lodos*, was burning with fever and seeing visions. His son Ömer played a leading role in these visions. When the servants came in to try to bring down his fever with cloths soaked in vinegar, he called out, "Is that you Ömer?" Even when Rıza came to visit him, he thought it was Ömer. Though he quickly realized his mistake and tried to sit up in bed. He only calmed down when Rıza took him by the shoulder and forced him to lie back own. Later the servants try to get him to take the medicine prescribed by the doctor who came to see him.

Ali Yekta's mind had become woolly. Most of the time his mind wandered, and he had difficulty remembering where he was. Later he came to his senses, wondered how he got into this situation, and felt sorry for himself. Until that day, even in spite of Necla, he'd had no doubts about moving to his son's mansion and had even told Rıza that he was leaving. But the new attitude Ömer had displayed on their last meeting showed him that things weren't going to be quite as he'd thought. What was he going to do, and where was he going to live? Was he going to go back to Rıza and tell him that his son and his daughter-in-law didn't want him? He could never say this. Sometimes he overcame his pessimism and repeated to himself that his Ömer, his only son, would never do this to him. After all, he'd sacrificed everything for Ömer.

Hadn't his wife left him because of his passion about Ömer, his ambitions for Ömer, his inability to see anyone else? One day when Ömer was ten she went to stay with her relatives in Germany. About a month later she informed him that she wasn't coming back, that she was staying there and starting a new life, and that she wanted to have custody of the children. In her letter she wrote, "They'll have a better education here, and at least they'll have grown up in Europe." Ali Yekta was willing enough to send the two girls, but he wouldn't give up Ömer. Even though so many years had passed, the husband and wife never saw each other again. He knew that Ömer saw her sometimes when he went to Germany on business, but he didn't mind. Because no one could be more important to Ömer than his father, and no woman, not even his mother, could be closer to him than his father.

At this point, when he thought of Necla, he felt as if a sharp knife had been plunged into his heart. It seemed that the unimaginable had happened and that this skinny, dried-up girl, this ugly, monstrous, conniving, and poor girl had managed to gain control over his son.

Ali Yekta couldn't bring himself to believe this and told himself that there must be some mistake, but at the same time he knew that it was true. The servants changed his sweat-soaked sheets every day. He was well taken care of, but his spirit was broken.

Because of his lifelong habit of taking responsibility, he didn't forget his promise to the old woman even in his worst moments. From the telephone on the bedside table, he dialed the number the woman had given him and in a hoarse voice told her that he was not going to be able to help her, and that she shouldn't hold any hopes. Even if this news were to destroy the old woman, he had to tell the truth and prevent her from clinging to false hopes. Because he'd seen how helpless the poor woman was, and how much hope she had attached to him. When he'd caught her glancing at that little house he'd realized how deeply she was wounded. He couldn't allow her to continue hoping in him. He would have liked to have said, "My son and his wife have become monsters; don't expect any human kindness from them," but of course he couldn't.

A servant had come to change his sweat-soaked pillowcase. He put a dry towel under his back. Then, saying, "This came for you," he left a package wrapped in yellow paper on the bed. Ali Yekta opened the package with trembling fingers and saw the Quran and the prayer beads he'd left at the mansion!

At the newspaper office, Yusuf held his head between his hands and thought. Ever since he was a child, the *lodos* had made him dizzy and caused a buzzing in his ears. It was the same now, there was a buzzing in his ears. He felt as if he were under water. He felt tied up and weighed down by helplessness. He felt bad that he hadn't been able to do anything for Leyla.

Ömer was so powerful, and his influence so extensive, that they didn't let him write anything for the newspaper, and they didn't even pay him a decent wage. Now he was getting married, and he was going to have a child, and didn't know how they were going to get by on such little money. How was he going to raise his child? Perhaps he should go somewhere else. But where? Who was going to give him a job in a country with so much unemployment? Here at least there was a chance he might get a raise after a while. But what was going to happen to Leyla? In Cihangir Leyla was wilting before his eyes from sadness like a flower that had not been watered. Roxy had been more careful and indeed more tender with her lately, but who knew how things would work out in the long term.

Necla was lying in the large room in her new house with a violent headache. When she'd gone into the room, what had she found on the windowsill but a Quran and some amber prayer beads. They must have been put there by that inauspicious old man. If it hadn't been the Holy Quran she would have thrown it into the sea, but she had no intention of committing a sin because of that servant. She gave them to the butler, saying Ali Yekta must have forgotten them, and ordered him to have them sent to him. And immediately! At once! When the man got these he'd realize that he shouldn't entertain false hopes, and, if he was smart, wouldn't have the courage to approach them again.

Necla thought that her head hurt this much partly because of yesterday's visit. This visit had brought the migraine back. When she got up yesterday, she decided that after such a long time she was going to go to her parents' house and bring them a couple of presents.

Then, unable to resist her mother's insistence, she stayed to have dinner with them. If Ömer hadn't had a business dinner he'd had to go to this wouldn't have been possible, but in the end she was pleased by the coincidencc. Bccause even though the house where she'd grown up depressed her, it brought back memories, and it also made her incredible social ascent all the more enjoyable. No matter how much care she took with her appearance and behavior, her parents didn't seem to consider it important, even though the neighbors saw her as a superstar because of the BMW and the chauffeur waiting outside. They treated her as if she was still the girl who'd lived there in the past. She wasn't "Ms. Necla." It irritated her that they kept asking if she was comfortable, and if her husband was treating her well. When her mother went into the kitchen, her father even asked her if she needed anything. So that she wouldn't have to feel dependent on her husband's money, and so that she knew her family was always behind her, and that if she fell on hard times she could rely on her father's savings.

At first Necla was horrified by these words, but then she felt a kind of pity. "How much money have you managed to save, father?" she asked.

With pride he said he had "exactly two billion" in the bank.

Necla thought: I wonder if my father knows that this is the price of a meal in one of Istanbul's better restaurants? At first the difference in their incomes horrified her, but then she threw her arms around her father's puny shoulders and started crying. "Thank you, father, thank you!"

When her mother came in from the kitchen and saw her embracing her father, she didn't make anything of it. She just thought Necla missed her childhood home.

On the way home Necla thought: What poor, well-intentioned people. Their hearts were clean, but they were unsuccessful. Perhaps that's why they were unsuccessful. No weakness, she told herself. If you let yourself go you'll even start feeling sorry for Ali Yekta. You'll even feel sorry for that old woman. Be strong, no weakness!

There was something touching about an unsuccessful man who had lived his life on a limited income wanting to give his meager savings to his daughter; true, but that was all there was to it.

She had no intention of returning to the life of poverty that Ömer had rescued her from. There were two types of people in this world: oppressors and the oppressed. She herself was never again going to be among the oppressed. When she was going to school she'd had to wait for the bus for hours in Istanbul's dirty, gray rain, and she'd seen the contentment of the people in the cars that splashed mud on her as they passed. Everything was possible with money, and Ömer worshipped her. Her husband, Ömer, everything! She wasn't going to let that man, that servant, take it all away from her! Tomorrow she was going to move her things into that room and finish furnishing it. She was going to lock the door of the "sin room" where she and her husband were going to make love night and day. In any event, the restoration work was just about finished.

In her dim room, Leyla had pulled her blanket up to her chin in spite of the heat. The darkness of the room made her dark thoughts even darker. From outside came the incessant sounds of Cihangir: the sirens, the music, car horns, men and women shouting. The pipes groaned, and doors banged. She just didn't belong here. Even if she lived here for years she could never get used to it. Though she didn't need to get used to it. But what was she supposed to do? Should she go out into the streets, should she try to get into the home for the destitute? Was the daughter of a Balkan hero of no consequence in this country? Was there no one left who remembered her martyred uncle? Tears were about to flow, and she made an effort to hold them back. When the *lodos* touched her heart she felt sadder and more broken than ever. The only good thing was the news that Roxy was going to have a baby. She was truly pleased, and the way she had embraced Roxy had nothing artificial about it and indeed had been heartfelt. In fact it was the kind of display she'd fled from all her life, but the girl had looked at her so strangely, and she'd felt so close to her, that she'd embraced her thin shoulders tenderly. But at the same time she knows that the news of the baby will make her stay in this house even shorter. There was no longer room for her here. As she thought about this, Yusuf came to her mind. He didn't even know about the baby yet, didn't know he was going to be a father. But Yusuf and Roxy weren't married, were they? So what was going to happen now? How would the baby be registered? Leyla thought of her own strange identity papers. She'd been registered as her grandfather's daughter. Because there was no father around. But she didn't even want to think about the lifelong torment of not having a father. She remembered the stain that had walled her in, that had kept her from mixing with society, that had prevented her from starting a family like other people, and that had imprisoned her alone for life in the little house in the mansion garden. The English occupation officer's bastard: Who would want to approach a girl like that? What family would want their son to marry this girl? No one, of course. If she'd had a normal father, perhaps she could have had a baby like Roxy. She was going to tell Yusuf and Roxy to marry right away so that their child wouldn't have to suffer the torment she'd suffered. There was no other way. They had to do this for the baby.

Ömer was driving across the Bosphorus bridge; he and Necla had arranged to meet at the mansion tonight. It was just growing dark. The ferries had stopped running because of the *lodos*. The traffic was impossible. His skillful driver tried to change lanes, but it was impossible.

He rubbed his head and thought: Ah, father. Why are you doing this? Why are you trying to ruin my life? It's as if you're trying to destroy the person you created and taking back everything you gave him. He thought that his father disliked Necla from the start. Or was Necla right? Did his father not want to share him with anyone else? Would he have behaved this way with any other woman besides Necla? Ah father, he thought, why do you insist on living with us? Don't you know that things are not the way they used to be, that we live in smaller family units now? We're interested in different things, we enjoy different things, we live in different worlds; why are you making things difficult for me?

For the past several days he hadn't called his father to ask how he was. His father hadn't called him either. For perhaps the first time in their lives they were being stubborn with each other. Let's see, who was going to call first? Even though he thought his father was wrong, the situation was tearing Ömer apart. He didn't want to be disrespectful to his father, he loved him to the point of worship and wanted to do what he said and to make his old age comfortable, but this time Necla was right. No one lived with their parents anymore. Perhaps he could talk to Necla a bit and soften her stance. Perhaps he could give the old man another room besides the large room. Indeed—at that moment he was excited by an idea that occurred to him—we could give my father that little house in the garden; was that such a strange idea, couldn't it work? His father could live there the same way the old woman had lived there. At the same time part of the house but outside of it. He seized on the idea. If he could get Necla to accept the idea, his father could furnish the little house however he liked. He could do whatever he wanted. If only he could make this work.

Roxy was lying on her bed daydreaming. She didn't feel the effects of the *lodos* because she was already nauseous. Because she hated the concept of family she'd never thought of herself as a mother, but now she was trying to imagine what it would be like. She would be like earth into which a seed had fallen, and would germinate, and grow, and finally send out a shoot. This is how she thought about her pregnancy, as an exciting natural event. Perhaps for the first time in her life she was filled with happiness and peace. She remembered how surprised Yusuf was at the news, and at her proposal of marriage. Though he always had a sort of surprised expression. You could tell he was a little naive the first time you saw him. Roxy still loved him more than anyone else she knew.

The man who had made Roxy happy when he said he would come to the club to do an interview. Because no one had ever suggested anything like this to Roxy before, no one had taken her seriously as an artist. When they'd played here and there no one had really even listened. Despite their dreams, they hadn't been able to make a name for themselves in the bars of Istanbul. No one had heard of the group called Roxy and Other Animals. Of course that's why they'd remained so desperately poor. Now they didn't have any money at all left and were getting by on the money Leyla had given them, but soon Yusuf would be promoted and would be a real journalist.

Roxy was never going to show her baby to her father and that plucked chicken Ute, she wasn't even going to tell them about it. Neither them nor her other relatives. Maybe Leyla would give their child lessons, teaching it the languages she knew, and piano, and help give the child a cultural foundation. The woman was very learned. Later she laughs at this thought. Who knew what would happen to Leyla over the years. Then she thought about what she had said. She was right! There was no way she could live with them for years. Especially after the baby. Roxy felt a warm happiness to think that thcrc were at least a few people she loved. She loved Leyla, and she loved Yusuf, and of course she loved the baby most of all. Was it going to be a boy or a girl? It would be some months before she found out. She started thinking of nice boys' and girls' names.

28

That evening Ali Yekta felt too weak and tired to get on the bus. After two days of fever and vomiting he had no strength left in his body. So that evening he broke his habit and had one of the servants call him a taxi. The people in the house were against the idea of him going out, but he didn't listen to anyone and, worrying everyone with his wheezing and staggering, left the house.

As Ali Yekta crossed the Bosphorus bridge, he watched the lights along the shore. He thought of the lives of the people in those magnificent houses. His head was leaning against the window, his eyes were bloodshot, his skin was pale, and his hair was uncombed. Ali Yekta was no longer the well-dressed, self-assured man he used to be. That man had gone and been replaced by this elderly invalid.

He'd received the Quran and the prayer beads that had been returned to him yesterday, and ever since he'd been beside himself. This handwritten Quran that had been passed from his grandfather to his father and then to him, and which his father had kissed three times before passing it on to him, was supposed to have passed to his son after him. But his son had returned it to him. And why? For the sake of a room.

All night he talked to Ömer in his sleep, and at one point in his feverish state Ömer was kissing his hands and crying and asking forgiveness, but toward morning, in another nightmare, Ömer was slapping him; him, that is, his father.

When Ali Yekta woke in the morning he found himself in tears. What a strange thing this was. He'd never woken up crying before. Just before he woke he imagined his wife entering the room. As the first light of day streamed in through the shutters the woman said to him, "Look, have you seen what you've done? Was all this worth it, Ali Yekta?"

When he woke there was no one there. Another strange thing was that he kept thinking about Leyla. He couldn't forget her frightened glance at the little house as she was leaving the garden. The way she had been mistreated broke his heart, and it was incomprehensible to him that it was his son who had done this. As if Leyla had been the key that had opened a room full of secrets that had suddenly altered the relationship between father and son. He didn't believe it. His polite, well-educated and well-behaved son. He'd seen this boy as an extension of himself and had been both mother and father to him. When he'd been ill he'd sat up with him praying until morning. Wasn't this the same child, wasn't this the same person? When Ali Yekta thought about this in his feverish state he sighed so loudly that a servant came running to see if anything was wrong. On the second day they rubbed ointment on his back, but it didn't help. The man was burning up.

Ali Yekta didn't know anything about his son's working life. He knew only that he was known as a well-educated, refined, and successful businessman, and he was proud of this. He had no knowledge of how he had swindled the first company he'd worked for when he returned from America, or of how he had gone from bank to bank with faked company portfolios. He didn't know about these kinds of things anyway.

It was dark by the time the taxi left him at the mansion gate. There was no one around. The watchmen greeted Ali Yekta as respectfully as always, but they'd never seen him in such a state and looked at him in surprise.

When Ali Yekta entered the mansion he heard his son and his daughter-in-law talking on the top floor. They were speaking in loud voices and seemed to be arguing about something. Ali Yekta climbed the stairs silently, went to the top floor, and waited outside the door of the large room before entering. Because he heard that they were talking about him. His ears were buzzing. He heard Necla refer to him as a butler. She shouldn't have called Ömer a butler's son; the past should be forgotten. Moving to the mansion was a chance to break with this cursed past. And they were going to give parties there. All of Istanbul would come. Did this man always have to be with them to remind them of the past?

He heard his son answer Necla's shouting in a soft and convincing voice.

His son said that he understood her. She was right, but these things can't happen all at once.

"All right," said Ömer, "you're right. Let's not take my father into the house, let's not give him the large room, but at least let us give him the little house in the garden. Let him live there. He'll live separately from us, but we won't have hurt his feelings."

"What difference does it make whether he lives here of there?" asked Necla. "What is the difference? What you have to do is cut off your relations with him. If you have to see him, go see him secretly. Don't advertise the fact that you're a butler's son. You created yourself, you changed your family's fate, and you don't owe them anything."

When he heard this, Ali Yekta suddenly felt perfectly calm. A family of butlers, he thought. He pictured his father and his grandfather. He remembered Halepli Cevher Ağa. His heartbeat slowed, and the fever in his brain died down. Once again he felt the strength of those who have made up their minds. Knowing full well what he was going to do, he took out his revolver and entered the room. His son and his wife were talking in front of the window. When his son saw him he shouted, "Father!"

Ali Yekta shot Necla in the head with the revolver his father had given him. Necla fell to the floor with the right side of her forehead gone. Blood sprayed onto Ömer, who'd been standing right next to her. There was a crazed expression on his bloodstained face. Blood also sprayed onto the newly painted wall. The watchmen came running when they heard the gunshot.

Ali Yekta sat calmly on the bed. He didn't even hear his son screaming. The gun was still in his hand. They saw that he had no strength left. He sat there staring at the floor until the police came, oblivious to his son's screams, the watchmen's shouting, and the policemen's questions. As if he was no longer alive. One of the policemen thought: It's as if there are two dead people in the room, not one.

The residents of the Bosphorus talked about the murder at the Bosnalı Mansion for years, and various stories were invented, and it became a subject the mountain people never stopped talking about. Because Ali Yekta didn't speak throughout his trial, and wouldn't give a statement, and refused even to talk to the court-appointed lawyer, people gave free rein to their imaginations.

One of the more attractive and creative things that were said had to do with the curse on the Bosnalı Mansion. The mansion hadn't been of any use to the new owners either. The women nodded their heads and said, "What good is all of their money going to do them now?" They were thankful that even though they had less money, they were in a better situation. The mansion had become cursed the day the English officer soiled a Muslim girl in the garden. It wasn't enough that Bosnalı Abdullah Avni Pasha's family was destroyed, Salih the merchant who bought the mansion had died at a young age, and the next owners, the Cevheroğlu family, suffered the worst disaster of all.

Some maintained that Ali Yekta went mad and committed the murder for no reason; some, like the court-appointed lawyer, maintained that the gun went off when it was being cleaned and that Necla was killed by accident, and still others maintained that Ali Yekta had planned the murder for years and that the killing was premeditated.

The witnesses were important because Ali Yekta refused to open his mouth.

Of course the watchmen were the main witnesses. Mehmet the watchman said that Ali Yekta was behaving strangely when he arrived at the mansion that night. Indeed he'd mentioned this to his colleague, and they'd argued about whether he might be sick. But of course they hadn't thought of stopping him. Because he was Ömer's father. Later, when they heard the gunshot and ran inside, this is what they saw: Necla was lying in blood on the floor, and Ali Yekta was sitting silently on the bed. He either hadn't noticed them enter the room or he didn't care. He hadn't even looked at them when they took the gun from his hand. Ömer was beside himself, and shouted, "An ambulance, I beg you, call an ambulance!" before running to the phone to call an ambulance. Meanwhile the whole neighborhood had gathered in front of the gate and was trying to find out what had happened. The ambulance came about half an hour later and took Necla away, but by then the woman was long dead. Ömer seemed half-dead and got into the ambulance and went with her.

A Year Later

That morning, the baby Leyla woke with a big smile that showed her dimples. Rukiye loved the way this child woke with a smile every morning. She was a good-natured, peaceful baby who didn't cry much at night. Rukiye didn't understand how someone as rebellious as her had given birth to such a calm child. She must take after her father, the good-natured Yusuf. On the day the baby was born, Roxy named her Leyla, and then changed her own name back to Rukiye. She believed that this was a more suitable name for a mother. Roxy was a name that belonged to her rebellious period.

Leyla, who Rukiye thought was the most beautiful baby in the world, had large dimples, and Rukiye loved to touch them. The child laughed beautifully when she felt her mother's fingers on her face. Every time she sees this smile Rukiye swells with happiness and feels a needless urge to cry.

She didn't believe in luck, but the way this baby had changed everything showed that there must be something like this in the world. As soon as she became pregnant with this baby, it seemed as if everything that was wrong in their lives began to go right.

The impossible problem of the mansion had been solved in such an unexpected manner that it seemed like a small miracle. Even Leyla, who was very surprised by this miracle, believed that her prayers at Istanbul's talismans and places of worship had been answered. But she was very sad that Ali Yekta had been hurt in order to bring about this solution. Who would have thought that the poor man would kill his daughter-in-law and be put in prison, and that Ömer would go mad with grief and shout, "I never want to set eyes on this mansion again!" And then, miraculously, add, "Give that little house back to the old woman."

Or, like everyone else, did he believe that the mansion was unlucky? Did he think that throwing the old woman out of her house had brought about this disaster?

Because at that time the phrase on everyone's lips was: "If you harm the innocent, in time it will come back to haunt you."

Even the mountain people said this now. After the murder they turned away from Ömer's family and once again supported Leyla.

"Leyla is an aristocrat," they said. "She's not an upstart like Ömer. At least aristocrats don't go wild like that."

The Great Lady's return to her house became almost a festival in the neighborhood. However it was that they heard about it, men women and children gathered in front of the mansion gate until it resembled a fairground. When Leyla's taxi approached they'd opened the gate and then lined up to kiss her hand. There were even some who shed tears.

After Leyla had thanked them, she waited a few minutes outside the door of the house. It could almost be said that she was even afraid to go inside.

They saw her go pale as her trembling hands tried to open the door.

Later, when she was telling the story to Rukiye, she said, "Believe me, it was even harder to go back into the house than it was to leave."

We will never know whether she was afraid of what she would see in the house, if she was afraid to witness how her privacy had been so rudely invaded, or if she thought she was entering the house as a stranger.

The first thing she noticed was that the smell of the house had changed. The old familiar smell she knew had been replaced by another, somewhat sour smell. Apart from this, nothing else had been changed. Perhaps they hadn't got around to it yet. She knew that the watchmen had stayed there while the mansion was being rebuilt. Poor men, she thought. They didn't do anything wrong.

When she opened the drawers of the commode she experienced a deep disappointment. Because all her souvenirs were gone. Neither the shawl from Hijaz embroidered with prayers, nor her mother's hat, nor her notes, nor the embroidered shawls, nor the sultan's signatures, nor the calligraphy, nor the photographs. At that moment Leyla felt like a complete stranger in this house. Even the oil paintings on the wall had been taken. That's why it didn't seem like her house. At least that's how she felt, and she went back outside with a sense of deep weariness.

As she entered and left, she didn't look at the place where the magnolia tree had been. Her heart couldn't bear it. She didn't think she would have had the courage to do this while there were so many people around.

The crowd was waiting silently. When Yusuf gave her a questioning look she was amazed to hear herself say, "Let's go home Yusuf." Because she now thought of Cihangir rather than this house as home.

Silently, the people of the neighborhood watched Yusuf and Leyla get into the taxi and drive away. Then, timidly, they went into the house. They were curious about what the Great Lady had seen there. They noticed the dirty covers on the beds, the dirty teacups on the table, the silver saucers full of cigarette butts, the brown stains in the toilet, and the film of grime on the windows. And of course the emptiness, the absence of anything that belonged to the Great Lady. The emptiness of the house seemed like a betrayal and mockery of the past.

That evening there was a great deal of activity in the neighborhood. Dozens of women came and scrubbed every inch of the house clean. They scrubbed the floorboards with soft soap, made the windows shine, poured nitric acid into the toilets, and washed the dishes until they were squeaky clean. Before midnight the house was sparkling clean and smelled of soap. The women filled a vase with flowers from the garden, and the smell of lilacs filled the house. Then everyone went home.

No one had decided on anything like this. Everything happened at once, of its own accord.

Toward morning some shadows were seen in front of the house. People were silently entering and leaving the house, but none of them saw each other, or rather they pretended not to, and waited for those in the house to leave before they went in. Most of these people were women.

In any event, the Great Lady was going to gather her strength and return.

Meanwhile, in Cihangir, the greatest change was that Yusuf had been promoted and given a raise. This happened right after Ali Yekta shot his daughter-in-law, when the editor called Yusuf in and asked him to cover the story. Istanbul had been shaken up by this murder. The disaster that had befallen the Cevheroğlu family had turned the press against them, and for days there were headlines about details of the murder. The editor wanted Yusuf to write the story of Leyla and her family before the other newspapers got wind of it. The next day Leyla's picture would be on the front page and there would be a story about how the Cevheroğlu family had thrown her out of her ancestral home and treated her unjustly. They'd thrown the granddaughter of an Ottoman pasha out onto the street, but fate had punished them for it. The public was going to be thrilled by this. Because Yusuf knew the story better than anyone it was a wonderful opportunity for the newspaper. The editor said, "This is going to be great, Yusuf. Write about the woman's past, her grandfather the pasha, how she was evicted, how miserable she was. Bring any old photographs you can find. We can stretch this out for four or five days."

This incident taught Yusuf that journalism was a harsh profession that did not allow for sentimentality. Just like being a doctor. Dealing with death every day and cutting up people's organs during surgery, a doctor can't survive if he's sentimental. It was necessary to put distance between one's work and one's feelings. Because no one can stand that much death and pain.

When he realized that journalists must live in a harsh and completely professional environment, Yusuf started to question for the first time whether he was suited for the profession of journalism.

Reporters had been camping outside the house in Cihangir for days, hoping to get Leyla's picture or some comments, but she wasn't seeing anyone.

Ali Yekta, whose picture had been on the front page of all the newspapers, stared fixedly at the bottom of the upper bunk for hours.

Whether it was fate or coincidence, it was interesting that Ali Yekta had been sent to the Toptaşı Prison. Because this historical prison was right next to the palace where his grandfather Halepli Cevher Ağa had worked as a butler. Indeed the judicial building was part of the palace.

Ali Yekta was imprisoned in this stone building built by the architect Sinan in the sixteenth century. He knew that before him famous writers and poets were imprisoned there, and indeed from time to time he found things they'd written on the walls.

This was the extent of his relationship with the prison. He didn't speak to the other prisoners, he didn't answer any questions, and he lay on his bunk with his eyes closed from morning to night.

The prisoners who were curious about this dignified man and who wanted to learn the story of why he killed his daughter-in-law were soon daunted by his stubbornness and left him alone. Because the newspapers had been full of the story for days, everyone knew what had happened. And since he was the father of a famous bank owner, news of him had reached the prison before he did. For this reason, a few prisoners who thought they might make money from him tried to be of service to him, bringing him tea and so forth, but he didn't acknowledge these efforts.

The man refused to see his son when he came to visit.

On visiting day the prisoners saw Ömer get out of a black Mercedes accompanied by bodyguards and wait with his head bowed, but the old man didn't come out, didn't leave his cell, and remained lying on his bunk with his eyes closed.

In the face of such stubbornness everyone slowly abandoned the man and left him to the loneliness he wanted.

No one bothered him anymore.

Ali Yekta had also erected barriers in his mind. Ömer was not present among the thoughts that passed through his mind and couldn't get in. It was as if all memory of him had been erased. The old man had cut himself off from the world and didn't think about Ömer once. He didn't remember him.

Instead, he often thought about Ece and Melike. What were they doing now? What kind of people had they become? He'd never before felt such warmth for his daughters. As he thought about them he realized that he'd forgotten them. He hadn't thought of them in years.

Later he thought about his wife; he pictured the first years of their marriage and the birth of their children. He remembered Ece's and Melike's births, but not Ömer's.

Once, the warden called Ali Yekta to his office. He couldn't refuse to go. Two guards brought him down narrow, vaulted corridors to the warden's office. The warden sat Ali Yekta across from him, ordered coffee without asking, opened his cigarette case, and offered him a cigarette. He asked after his health.

Ali Yekta answered these questions with noises and gestures. He was heard to say, "I'm fine, thank you." His coffee arrived, and he started to drink it. The warden was asking him questions, trying to start a conversation, but Ali Yekta wasn't interested, and just looked out the window at the garden and the flowers. For a while he watched a fly crawling on the window. When the warden noticed he wasn't listening he said, "You're being impolite, Ali

Yekta. I invited you here out of respect for your age, but I find you won't even answer my questions."

Ali Yekta said, "Excuse me, sir."

The warden was the highest authority in the building, but he felt he had no power over this poor prisoner, and this annoyed him. The man was nothing but a butler, but how haughtily he was behaving. As if he wasn't a prisoner but a justice minister who'd come to inspect the prison.

For his part, after a life of obedience to authority, Ali Yekta was free for the first time and felt now that he was living without a master.

His prison cell had brought him freedom. There was nothing more he wanted from life, and he didn't have to ask anyone for anything. For this reason he was free and able to hold his head high. It wasn't a mansion but prison that had freed him from the fate of being a butler.

Ali Yekta knew that a person's own desires can be a worse form of captivity than a prison cell.

The warden was very annoyed and was trying to control himself. "You have a visitor behind this door Ali Yekta," he said. "Now I'm going to ask him in, and I'm going to go, and you can have a father to son talk."

Ali Yekta was startled, and bowed his head, and fixed his eyes on the corner of the coffee table.

He heard the door squeak, and then footsteps, and then later he heard Ömer's voice.

"Father," said the voice. "Father!"

Without looking at his face, he got up and walked toward the door. Ömer tried to hold him back and wanted to embrace him.

"Father, why did you do this incomprehensible thing? Do you know that you've destroyed my life?" he said with tears in his eyes. "The son you raised and cared for is nothing more than a living corpse. You took everything from him, you took away his reason for living. How could you do such a monstrous thing?"

Then he started crying loudly again. "In spite of everything, you're still my father, but know that you've killed me. You killed your own son when you killed Necla."

Ali Yekta didn't look at Ömer and didn't answer him. As soon as his son let go of him he went through the door and stood next to the guard. He could hear Ömer crying inside.

When he went back to his cell and lay on his bunk, he forgot all about this incident. He tried to picture Ece and Melike. He wondered how they'd grown up, and whether they'd become beautiful women.

But that night, in his uneasy sleep, Ali Yekta didn't dream about his daughters. Instead, terrified and covered in sweat, he had another dream. He saw the old mansion just as it had been. He was standing in attendance with his father and grandfather, serving their master as he sat at the table. His grandfather Halepli Cevher Ağa was pouring him water from a crystal pitcher, his father was serving food, and he himself was waiting his turn with a glass of cognac and a cigar. His master's face wasn't visible. There was a deep silence, and when he approached the table after his father and respectfully presented the cognacs and the cigar, he saw his master's face. A ten-year-old child was sitting there. The child, dressed in a suit and tie, with his hair slicked back, looked at him with malice. The child insisted on drinking the cognac and smoking the cigar. Ali Yekta slapped the child. With a malicious expression on his face, the child got up and lunged at him. When Ali Yekta saw this he wanted to retreat, but the child suddenly pushed his chest and knocked him over, then took a knife out of his pocket and started stabbing him. As Ali tried to ward off these blows, he also tried to warn his father and grandfather to stay away from this child. "Run," he said. "This isn't who you think he is. He's going to kill us all." But unfortunately his father and grandfather had their backs turned and didn't hear him. Even though he shouted at the top of his lungs, he wasn't able to warn them. He was able to get away from the child and started fleeing toward the stairs. It was strange that even though his wounds were bleeding he felt no pain. Meanwhile he saw the child approach his father and grandfather and start stabbing them. He started screaming at the top of his lungs, and this scream woke him. The other prisoners gathered around him and looked at him in pity. One of them brought water and, holding his head as if he were a baby, made him drink sip by sip.

After that, the relationship between Ali Yekta and the other prisoners improved. He looked at them tenderly, and when they brought him tea he accepted it with a slight nod of his head, but he still didn't open his mouth or say a word. The other prisoners came to understand that the best thing was to leave him alone.

Ali Yekta maintained the same attitude in court. He didn't talk to anyone, and he didn't answer any questions.

The court-appointed lawyer came to visit him several times. He wanted to learn if there were any mitigating circumstances that might lighten his sentence. But Ali Yekta wouldn't say a word.

He was to remain in prison until he died of emphysema, and he wouldn't even answer the doctor in the infirmary who asked him what was wrong. This is how the great Ali Yekta left the world.

Leyla couldn't stay in the house in Cihangir anymore. Even if it was difficult and frightening and felt strange, she had to go back to the mansion. Two days later she said goodbye to Rukiye, whose pregnancy was not yet apparent, and, with Yusuf carrying her heavy brown suitcase, set off for the mansion.

It was autumn, and the woods of the Bosphorus had started to turn reddish brown. The whole way Leyla looked at the woods and at the currents of the Bosphorus. She didn't talk at all.

This time she went into the house with Yusuf. As she stepped into the house she felt a warmth rising to her head, as if she was about to faint, and she held on to the door for support. The house was almost in a better state than it had been before, it was sparkling clean, but this is not what excited Leyla. Her family had returned. Her grandfather the pasha was back in his place on the wall, and so were her grandmother and her uncle. Even the panel that had once hung in the mansion, and that read *This too shall pass*, was there.

Her old shawls had been placed carefully in the drawers of the commode. Leyla thought that this was yet another miracle. Istanbul's talismans and places of worship must have been very powerful indeed.

Meanwhile, the neighborhood was watching in careful silence, and without coming too close. Throughout the night, the women had put back everything they had taken from the Great Lady's house. Even Cemile did this because she was no longer so sure that the Great Lady was an unbeliever, or even that it was right to take the property of unbelievers. And anyway, she had been the Great Lady for years and was the famous pasha's granddaughter. The story about the English officer had probably been invented by her enemies to discredit her. And wasn't her name Leyla? Wasn't Leyla a Muslim name? Ah, our people, she thought, our two-faced people. It seemed someone had tricked them. Perhaps it was that flashy, upstart Cevheroğlu family who had done this.

From then on, the Great Lady's days seemed to be just as they'd been before; she sat in the garden the way she used to, did her embroidery, read her newspapers and watched television, gave jasmine, figs, and pomegranates to the neighborhood children, but somehow she had a feeling deep within her that in fact nothing was as it had been before. Even if the house was the same, she herself had changed. The dew that gathered on the leaves in the morning, the cries of the seagulls, the familiar and heavy sound of the propellers of the enormous ships that passed in the night, the calls of the nightingales and the finches, the footsteps of the albatross on the roof that sounded almost human, all of it seemed the same, yet it was different. She became aware that she was bored of being alone in the house, and this was a very strange discovery for her.

The armor of loneliness that she'd woven around herself had been breached, and something had seeped in. She wasn't quite sure what this "something" was, but she was aware that her own company wasn't enough for her anymore. There was a world outside of herself, and now Leyla had come to know this world. It could never again be the way it had been when she hadn't known it.

It was only on the second evening after she had moved back in that she could gather the courage to look at the felled trunk of the magnolia tree, and then she went and sat next to it. The thick and healthy trunk had been cut right at its base, and already moss had begun to grow over the place where it had been cut. It lay there like a human corpse. Who knew how deep beneath the ground the roots extended, but only a short little stump now remained above ground. She ran her hand along the felled trunk. "Even though most of what's left of you is underground, I know that you can hear me," she said. "Just like my family. Your death is my death. This means that my time to leave the world has come too."

That day the baby was going to come to her house for the first time. So she got up early in the morning, decorated the house with flowers, arranged a place for the baby to sleep on the sofa, and then thought that the baby might sleep in its carriage. If the weather was warm enough, they could even swing her in the hammock in the garden. Of course she wouldn't want the baby she loved most in the world to get sick. When Leyla went to visit them from time to time, she lived through Rukiye the experience of raising a child, and when she smelled the smell of milk that wafted from them she was filled with happiness. She admired the baby for hours and began to think of her as her own granddaughter. For the first time after years of loneliness, she felt the warmth of family. Yusuf and Rukiye had become like her own children. And if this was so, the baby that bore her name was her granddaughter.

The series of articles that Yusuf wrote aroused great interest, and it became an issue that was talked about all over Turkey and then, of course, forgotten after a few weeks. But Leyla was very happy that this series of articles had brought Yusuf a regular job and salary. At least her situation had brought some good to this kindhearted boy.

The best time was had at Yusuf and Rukiye's wedding at the Beyoğlu marriage bureau, followed by a celebration at a restaurant in Beyoğlu. Rukiye didn't have a wedding dress but looked very natural and attractive in a white dress and with her hair restored to its original black. Even though they weren't happy about the bride he'd chosen without consulting them, Yusuf's family attended the ceremony. Cemile put a bracelet on the bride's wrist.

Leyla was one of the official witnesses. The other witness was the boy from the theater with the mustache like Nietzsche's. Before they left the house that day, when

Leyla pinned on Rukiye the brooch that was the last remaining piece of the jewelry she had inherited from her family, the girl's eyes became swollen from crying, and they had to force her to calm down so as not to ruin the ceremony.

When the judge asked her name, she said with pride that it was Rukiye, and then threw Leyla a glance. As if she wanted to say that she had made peace with this name. I'm becoming a mother now, I'm not crazy anymore, and I'm at peace with my name. Leyla nodded her head tenderly.

Rukiye thought that she was too happy, and didn't believe what was happening to her, and kept wondering what she had done to deserve this. The belief she'd arrived at in childhood, that people are bad, had begun to change; she still thought the world was an evil and merciless place, but even so you could find a few good people here and there.

On the day little Leyla first honored Leyla's house and garden with her presence she wanted it to be like a holiday, but it didn't work out that way. She put the baby in her childhood hammock that was slung between two trees and watched her face for a long, long time.

The young people experienced a mixture of delight and surprise. After so much distress and sorrow and the fear of being homeless, here they all were in the mansion garden. As Rukiye sat in this peaceful, quiet garden and sensed the deep tenderness Leyla felt for the baby, she made an appraisal of how this house had influenced and changed the lives of everyone who had lived in it.

Rukiye had never met poor Ali Yekta; she felt sad about the poor man's fate, but in a single moment his action saved all of them. Somehow she wasn't upset that this had been brought about by a murder, and even though she felt a little guilty, she was trying to put herself at ease by thinking about the gossip she'd heard that Necla had deserved it. Indeed a lot of people put themselves at ease this way.

"Did they make a lot of changes to the mansion?" Rukiye asked Leyla.

Without taking her eyes off the baby Leyla said, "I don't know; I haven't been inside."

"You weren't curious enough to take a look?"

"No. What good would looking do? It's not my house anyway. That old world is finished and gone and used up. It's better to remember the house as it is in my dreams."

Yusuf said, "I looked. It's not bad; they didn't make a lot of changes."

"So what," said Leyla. "It's still not our house. Tomorrow or the next day some other rich person will appear and buy the mansion. It doesn't make any difference whether I see it or not."

She's right, Yusuf thought to himself. There's not a single one of these waterfront mansions that still belongs to its original owners. They've all changed hands.

Lately, Leyla had been looking sad. Everyone had expected her to be delighted at getting her house back, but instead she withdrew into herself more and more, and seemed not to be at all happy about what had happened. What could the reason for this be?

Had the old woman been so hurt by what had been done to her that she just couldn't get over it? Or was she upset that a murder had been committed in that house?

That day Yusuf gathered up all his courage and asked Leyla about this as politely as possible. He wanted to know why she was upset. Leyla pointed to a tree and said, "Look Yusuf, look at how much the plum tree has grown. You must remember the day it was planted. What a puny little sapling it was. Look at it now, look how much it's grown."

When she said this, Yusuf fell silent, and didn't bring the subject up again.

The doors and shutters of the mansion were closed. The roof had been repaired, the wooden siding had been renewed, and the windows had been replaced, but it still had the air of desolation of a place that had been deserted for years.

The meal they had to celebrate little Leyla's visit to the house turned into a complete fiasco. Actually, the conditions were perfect for a nice celebration: a warm and bright late summer sun, the intoxicating fragrance of laurel and jasmine, the buzzing bees and the decorative butterflies, a baby sleeping peacefully in the open air.

But for whatever reason, Leyla's melancholy state gave this meal an air more of mourning than of celebration.

Yusuf and Rukiye didn't attach much meaning to her mood and kept a respectful silence. Indeed, ever since

Leyla had moved back to her house, it was as if something had come between them. There was nothing left of the closeness that had been created by the extraordinary situation in Cihangir. Rukiye couldn't bring herself to address her informally the way she used to, despite Leyla's insistence. Sometimes she blushed when she remembered how arrogantly she'd behaved during those first days. Although Leyla had done nothing to influence her, her presence and her personality had changed Rukiye and turned her into a completely different person. Now she felt herself caught by Leyla's power of attraction, and without realizing it had begun imitating her manner and turn of phrase.

In that bright light Leyla was experiencing one of those moments of deep despair that overcame her from time to time.

She couldn't even feel happy about returning to the beloved house she had missed so much and dreamed about for so long. It was as if she was stuffed with straw.

Why was this?

Was it the sense of emptiness people feel when they achieve an important goal? Was it the confusion brought on by aging?

Perhaps it wasn't any of these things.

Leyla was overcome by the same sense of disquiet that extreme beauty had brought her when she was young. The blue Bosphorus sparkling under the September sun, the cries of the birds, the trees, the baby sleeping in the hammock were all so beautiful that perhaps they formed the most distinct contrast to death, and as always this thought gave Leyla a deep sense of emptiness and sadness.

The meaninglessness of life, the fleeting nature of existence, the feeling of terror she felt in the presence of extreme beauty.

Because of these thoughts, the meal was joyless despite the young couple's efforts to celebrate and be merry, and as they ran out of things to say, there were long silences.

After the young people left, Leyla immersed herself in loneliness again. Once again, she began thinking about her grandfather, her grandmother, her mother, the father she had never known, and her uncle.

She felt that every moment she didn't think of them was a betrayal, but burying herself in the past was also like a salve that eased the pain of the present. It didn't matter that this alone was no longer sufficient. The balance of life had been upset. Or more truthfully, she herself didn't quite know what had happened.

The next day the people of the neighborhood saw that Leyla had called a taxi and had left her house. Her behavior during the past days had perplexed everyone. The woman was acting as if she had urgent business to finish.

She wasn't seen in the area all day. When she returned in the evening as it was growing dark, she was in a worn-out, miserable, and breathless state. When a neighbor saw her climb out of the taxi with difficulty and place her hand on her chest, he ran to help, but she insisted she didn't need any. She smiled and said, "I'm just catching my breath. I'll be all right in a moment."

In the evening, the worried men sent their wives to help her. Each of the women brought a plate of food. She thanked them and said she was going straight to bed. She was very tired, and she wasn't going to eat. They wanted to gather the white sheets that were hanging on the line in the garden. She didn't let them and said she would do it herself tomorrow. There was no harm in letting them hang there one more night. The women knew better than to argue with Leyla and went back home. But they didn't miss how strange this business of the sheets was. The sheets had been hanging there for almost a week. Leyla would never have done this knowingly. Why was she doing this?

That night an impenetrable fog descended once again on the Bosphorus, and everything turned milky white. All night, the passing ships sounded fog horns heart-breakingly reminiscent of the cries of wounded animals. The supporting towers of the suspension bridge rose up toward the sky like giant guillotines.

The next morning the fog had not dissipated and indeed had grown thicker. The trees in the garden looked like ghosts. The fog was so thick that it was as if the clouds in the sky had descended to the garden. Leyla felt as if she was not walking on the ground but rather on top of the clouds.

She walked toward the white sheets hanging on the line. As she expected, they were wet, because even if they'd been dry the previous afternoon, they'd absorbed the moisture. Every day they dried, and every night they got wet again. But she wasn't waiting for the sheets to dry, she wanted to be swathed in those white sheets as her mother and grandmother had been, and then to go away.

She remembered her visit to the prison the previous day. How much poor Ali Yekta had sunk into himself.

In the dimness of the prison visiting room, his eyes were deeply sunken, and he seemed withdrawn and ill, and at first wouldn't speak to her. This didn't seem at all strange considering that he hadn't given any statement at the hearings, he never opened his mouth, and he refused to meet the court-appointed lawyer. But in response to Leyla's insistent questions he opened his mouth just once, and when she asked, "Why, Ali Yekta?" he said in a hoarse voice, "It was a family matter." Leyla understood this answer to mean, "Don't ask me about this again!" In order not to distress this poor, honorable man any further she left the gifts she'd brought with the guard and said, "May Allah keep you, Ali Yekta!"

This visit reminded her once again of the bitter fate of Prince Cihangir. The fate of the apple of Suleiman the Magnificent's eye, the son for whose succession to the throne his mother had struggled so much.

The newspapers had reported how Ali Yekta had refused visits from his son, Ömer. As well as the fact that he had not once looked at his son during the hearings and seemed not to see him.

The Great Lady swayed on her feet when she felt a sharp pain in her chest and clutched at the sheets. The pain in her arm and her jaw that she experienced from time to time, and more frequently in the past months, had been at its worst during her visit to the prison the day before.

She tried to fill her lungs with air. She swayed for a moment, and then, just like her grandmother, she fell to the ground wrapped in the sheets. Her hands slid along the cool sheets. The fog covered her like a cloud. She could feel the fresh moisture of the earth and the autumn leaves.

She made one last effort, pulled herself toward the hammock by its edge, and lay down. She hadn't let go of the damp sheet, and now she pulled it over her. Death could come for her now and take her in her childhood hammock. It gave her infinite peace to lie in the hammock where she had dreamed, and read books, and watched the clouds and the leaves of the trees, and all her fears were gone.

She closed her eyes; the last sound she heard was the savage cry of a seagull diving into the garden from the roof.

Leyla's lifeless body lay in that hammock wrapped in a sheet all day and all night. Because the people of the neighborhood, knowing how the Great Lady liked to be alone, did not want to disturb her.

The next day when the man from the electric company came to read the meter and saw Leyla lying in the hammock without moving or making a sound, he informed the neighborhood of the suspicious circumstances.

After the Great Lady's funeral the next day at the neighborhood mosque, she was brought to the family mausoleum and buried next to her grandfather, her grandmother, her uncle, and her unlucky mother. They raised their hands and recited the prayer for the dead. At the funeral, the women of the neighborhood wept a great deal, and remembered her good deeds, and repeated to each other that there was no pasha's granddaughter like her. Cemile cried the most; she cried her lungs out until evening.

For Yusuf, the most surprising thing that happened on that difficult and bitter day was finding an envelope addressed to his daughter on the table in Leyla's house.

Yusuf felt strange when he saw the name Leyla Yılmaz written on the envelope. He was seeing his daughter's name written on an envelope for the first time. He understood that the Great Lady had left a letter for his daughter before she died. At first he hesitated to open the letter, and didn't know if it was the right thing to do. Perhaps he should put the letter away and give it to his daughter when she grew up. But the Great Lady had left no such instructions, and besides, there was no chance she would have expected them to wait so long. He opened the envelope with trembling hands.

"My dear daughter Leyla," the letter began. Yusuf read the letter to the end with tears flowing from his eyes, and tears even fell onto the letter…

My dear daughter Leyla,
Your parents will open this letter first and will read it to you when you have grown up.

Because it will be difficult for you to imagine events from the past, you may not fully understand what I want to say. Because if this nation had not lived through such upheaval, and if the foundations had not collapsed, perhaps my family and I would not have lived a tragedy of such dimensions.

They were well-intentioned people who lived in this garden, this mansion, this little house. They all loved one another very much, but the undefeatable love between my mother and father went too far and was the beginning of the disasters that befell my family. In spite of this, I cannot bring myself to blame this young girl and this young officer. There is something touching about them being so in love as to accept the risk of death. I don't know if the word love will still mean the same thing in your time, but I think we have to respect them for this emotion.

My dear daughter, I loved you very much. When I held you in my arms and breathed in the smell of your skin, I felt as if those who had once lived in this mansion would live again through you. I kept the hope that the Bosnalı family would not disappear into history with my death.

For this reason I have left this little house to you in my will. I want you to live here, and be happy, and to remember us.

My last words: Leyla's house is for Leyla.

Your grandmother,

Leyla Bosnalı

About the Author

Zülfü Livaneli is Turkey's bestselling author and a political activist. Widely considered one of the most important Turkish cultural figures of our time, he is known for his novels that interweave diverse social and historical backgrounds, figures, and incidents, including the critically acclaimed *Bliss* (winner of the Barnes & Noble Discover Great New Writers Award), *Serenade for Nadia* (Other Press, 2020), *Disquiet* (Other Press, 2021), *The Last Island* (Other Press, 2022), *The Fisherman and His Son* (Other Press, 2023), *On the Back of the Tiger* (Other Press, 2024), and *My Brother's Story*, which have been translated into thirty-seven languages, won numerous international literary prizes, and been turned into movies, stage plays, and operas.

About the Translators

Brendan Freely was born in Princeton in 1959 and studied psychology at Yale University. His translations include *Two Girls* by Perihan Mağden, *The Gaze* by Elif Shafak, and, with Yelda Türedi, *Like a Sword Wound* by Ahmet Altan.

Yelda Türedi was born in Mersin, Turkey, in 1970 and studied chemical engineering at Boğaziçi University. Türedi has translated, with Brendan Freely, Ahmet Altan's *Like a Sword Wound* and *Love in the Days of Rebellion*.